# On Deadly Ground

## Books by Michael Norman

*The Commission*
*Silent Witness*
*On Deadly Ground*

# On Deadly Ground

## Michael Norman

Poisoned Pen Press

Poisoned Pen Press
6962 E. First Ave., Ste. 103
Scottsdale, AZ 85251
www.poisonedpenpress.com
info@poisonedpenpress.com

Printed in the United States of America

*For Steve Norman, brother and friend*

# Acknowledgments

Many people had a hand in the creation of this book. I would like to thank several friends for patiently reading drafts of the manuscript and offering suggestions for improvement. To Eileen Land who has critiqued each of my books, my heartfelt thanks. Your words of encouragement have always boosted my confidence, and your insightful observations have always improved the books. Thanks also to my friend Mike Andrews of Park City, Utah, for reading a draft of the book and offering your candid impressions of what worked and what didn't. You have a keen eye. To my brother-in-law, Liam O'Brien. Thanks for your detailed critique of the book. Your careful analysis identified some of the book's strengths and many of its weaknesses. You could easily be a book editor. And finally, my thanks to Sara Dant, Professor of History at Weber State University, for her counsel on questions of public land use policy.

I'd like to offer a special word of thanks to the dedicated men and women who serve as Law Enforcement Rangers for the Bureau of Land Management (BLM). In particular, I would like to thank Jeff Long who became the first BLM Ranger assigned to patrol the vast, nearly two million acre Grand Staircase Escalante National Monument. Jeff was kind enough to invite his granola-eating former college professor (that would be me), to ride with him on patrol. For three days, Jeff led me around by the hand and patiently answered my endless and inane questions on everything from using maps and GPS units to get around, to questions about plant and wildlife species common to the area. I couldn't have written the book without his help.

Thanks to everyone at the Poisoned Pen Press including Publisher Robert Rosenwald, Executive Editor Barbara Peters, Associate Publisher Jessica Tribble, Marilyn Pizzo, Nan Beams, and Annette Rogers.

And finally, to Diane Brewster-Norman—my wife and best friend—you are a terrific teacher of writing. I couldn't do it without your love, encouragement, and support.

These red rock canyons in southern Utah are an acquired taste. They are short on water and, as a result, short on green…It's tough country to visit. It's even tougher country to live in. So powerful is the sun in summer, one adopts a perpetual squint. Summer can bring biblical periods of forty days of heat well over one hundred degrees, reducing you to a lizard state of mind, no thought and very little action. You sleep more and you dream. It is a landscape of extremes. You learn sooner or later to find an equilibrium within yourself; otherwise, you move.

Terry Tempest Williams
*Red: Passion and Patience in the Desert*

# Author's Note

This book is a work of fiction. Names, characters, places, and incidents are either the product of the author's imagination or are used fictitiously.

The above disclaimer aside, many of the environmental issues raised in the story are very real and extremely contentious throughout the West. Perhaps a few statistics are in order. The federal government owns more than 650 million acres across the U.S. Approximately 90% of that land lies in a dozen or so western states, including my home state of Utah. In Utah, the federal government owns 70% of the land. In neighboring Nevada, it's about 76%.

In the early 1970s, a movement that started in Nevada quickly spread throughout many western states. This organized resistance to federal public land use policies became known as the Sagebrush Rebellion. The Sagebrush Rebellion's goal was to wrestle control of public lands away from the federal government and place it in the hands of state and local government. Supporters of the Sagebrush Rebellion have argued that federal lands rightfully belong to the states and that states, not the federal government, can more effectively manage these lands.

During the past thirty years, the Sagebrush Rebellion has lost momentum but has never completely gone away. The principal reason for the failure of the Sagebrush Rebellion was the inability of the movement's proponents to sustain the legal argument that federal public lands truly belong to the states. Thus, public lands have remained under the federal government's control through oversight by federal agencies such as the Bureau of Land Management.

Unfortunately the rancorous debate continues. Its intensity is still as strong as it was 30 years ago. As we go to press, I am reminded of the similarities between the ongoing public land use debate and the virulent diatribe surrounding the discussion of health care reform in America.

With the Sagebrush Rebellion as backdrop, I chose to create a fictitious character named John David (J.D.) Books. As the protagonist in the story, J.D. is employed as a Law Enforcement Ranger in the Bureau of Land Management (BLM), a branch of the Department of the Interior. The BLM has jurisdiction over more than 260 million acres of public land located primarily in the aforementioned dozen western states.

In telling this story, I attempted to keep my personal views outside the framework of the plot and story. I wanted to allow the characters to express their own opinions and points of view through the use of dialogue. Ultimately, you, as readers, will decide how well I accomplished that.

Michael Norman
Salt Lake City
October, 2009

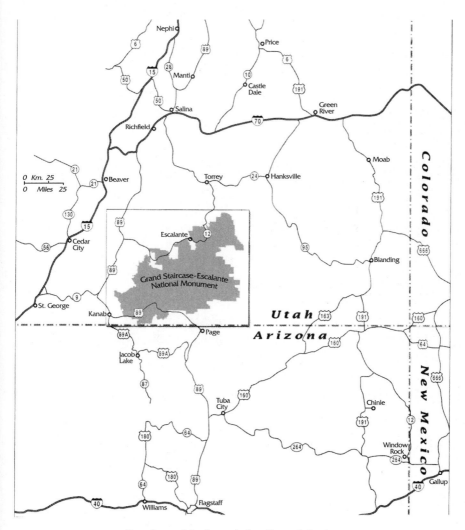

*Southern Utah and the Grand Staircase*

# Chapter One

Environmental activist David Greenbriar climbed steadily higher onto the Kaiparowits Plateau, unaware that this would be his last sojourn into Utah's southern wilderness.

Greenbriar had departed well before dawn, hoping to reach camp before the worst of the afternoon's fiery heat settled on the plateau. His rapid pace focused on the terrain ahead. The forty-nine-year-old retired college professor and president of the Escalante Environmental Wilderness Alliance (EEWA) prized these solitary journeys into the Grand Staircase-Escalante National Monument.

A fierce and dangerous place, summer heat and precious little water made the plateau one of the harshest terrains in the lower forty-eight states. Natural arches and conical spires colored in rich, earth tone hues formed millions of years ago by wind, water, and erosion, reached upward toward a cloudless blue sky.

As the sun climbed into the eastern sky and warmed the cracked, copper-colored sandstone, Greenbriar gave wide birth to a coiled Great Basin rattlesnake that had come out to warm itself on the sun-drenched rock. Overhead, an endangered peregrine falcon circled unhurried on the plateau's windy updrafts, canvassing the ground below for its next meal. Greenbriar stopped periodically to catch his breath and mop perspiration from his sweat-stained face and neck. His tanned, deeply lined face was hidden behind sunglasses and a floppy nylon polyester hiking hat.

By early afternoon, he had reached his destination and quickly set up camp. The expensive North Face backpacking tent would provide a measure of relief from the unforgiving sun. He camped atop Nipple Bench, which afforded spectacular vistas of Lake Powell, Fifty-Mile Bench, and the small town of Big Water. Although a poster child for environmental exploitation and excess, Lake Powell was the most magnificent lake he had ever seen.

From the modest shelter of his tent, Greenbriar napped most of the afternoon and woke to find a whiptail lizard staring at him from just outside the flap. He lit his propane stove and prepared a dinner of freeze-dried food to enjoy while the evening sun slipped lower in the western sky, painting the red Vermilion Cliffs in contrasting shades of bright sunlight and deepening shadows. After dinner he cleaned up and took a short walk to a rocky outcrop overlooking a boundless valley that stretched as far as the eye could see. The lengthening shadows climbed ever so slowly up the cliff faces, until only the highest pinnacles remained bathed in sunlight. With full darkness came the recurring realization that the plateau was a foreboding place of overpowering desolation and solitude.

As always, his enjoyment of the breathtaking landscape gave way to worries about the perpetual and sometimes virulent battles for the protection of the West's wild country from the shenanigans of groups like the Citizens for a Free West. He couldn't imagine a more insidious group of morons than Neil and Boyd Eddins and some of their ranching cronies. Livestock grazing on public lands produced more environmental damage than any other form of land use.

The immediate battle involved the expansion of roads on federal land, particularly in wilderness study areas. If the CFW and groups like them prevailed, road expansion would jeopardize the likelihood of getting additional federal lands designated wilderness study areas. Increases in logging, oil drilling, strip mining, and all-terrain vehicle use always followed road expansion.

Environmental groups like his could not afford to let that happen. And while the EEWA was not into blowing up buildings, he saw little harm in shooting an occasional stray cow. After all, ranchers had little problem killing bears, wolves, coyotes—anything that threatened their stinking cattle. As Greenbriar saw it, the ends justified the means. He considered himself an environmental disciple of the late Ed Abbey. His bible was Abbey's *The Monkey Wrench Gang.* He'd lost count of the number of times he'd read the book.

Greenbriar's environmental activism began when he was a young professor at Berkeley. Several colleagues had invited him to the home of a charismatic political science professor, head of the California chapter of the Nature Conservancy. The two became close friends. In time, Greenbriar became fervently committed to a variety of environmental issues.

Youthful idealism gradually turned to cynicism. Increasingly, he found himself at odds with the policy direction taken by the Nature Conservancy. The organization seemed far too willing to compromise its principles with groups whose sole purpose was to exploit the land, water, and air for economic gain. These groups were openly hostile to people like himself who wanted only to safeguard public lands for the enjoyment of future generations. In the end, he parted ways with the Nature Conservancy and developed the philosophical foundation for what would eventually become the Escalante Environmental Wilderness Alliance. Now he was fighting some members of his own board of directors. He had become the voice of moderation and compromise instead of escalation and confrontation. The irony was not lost on him.

As he settled into his tent and drowsiness took hold, he missed his young wife, Darby. They'd met at Cal Berkeley seven years earlier. To her, he was the handsome, intelligent, and witty university professor. To him, she was his beautiful, flirtatious, and bright graduate student. He'd fallen in love with her the instant they met. Within months of Darby's completing her master's degree in microbiology, he had divorced his wife of sixteen years and married her. Now, six years later, the luster had begun to wear off.

Darby had always been an insatiable flirt and was never very subtle about it. Lately, she acted more and more aloof, making excuses to spend time away from him. Was she cheating? He suspected so, but there was no way to know for sure. Perhaps he was foolish to believe that a man his age could hold the attention of a gorgeous, twenty-eight year old woman.

◇◇◇

John David (J.D.) Books, new Bureau of Land Management (BLM) law enforcement ranger, should have felt elated at the prospect of returning to his home town. But for him, did Billie Letts have it right that home is *Where the Heart Is?* He'd spent all of his adolescence in the small Kane County town of Kanab, Utah. He still had family there. When Books had been offered the job, it seemed natural that he should return to his roots. The tragic incident that ended his eleven-year career as a member of the Denver Police Department's elite robbery/homicide squad lay almost a year behind him, but it was still as fresh in his psyche as though it had happened yesterday.

Kanab is located in south-central Utah near the Arizona border. In the early 1920s, the town's cattle-ranching industry received a boost when Hollywood film companies began making Western movies in the area. Since the first Tom Mix silent Western, more than two hundred movies and numerous television series had been filmed around Kanab, giving rise to the town's nickname, "Little Hollywood."

What was the old saying? The more things change, the more they stay the same. That was Books' impression of Kanab as he arrived on a hot Friday afternoon in August, pulling a U-Haul trailer behind his Ford pickup. In some ways, the town had changed significantly in the years since he'd left. The main drag was a mix of old and new. Some old buildings had undergone a facelift, giving them a more contemporary look. In others, old storefronts hadn't changed in decades. He noticed a smattering of new businesses, lodging, real estate offices, and a new bank or two. Many of these changes reflected the economic reality that ranching was giving way to tourism and that retirees were moving into the area in large numbers. T-shirt shops, a trading post, and gift stores that catered to seasonal visitors were scattered throughout the downtown business district.

He had spent the past six months completing the arduous BLM law enforcement training academy in Glencoe, Georgia. He wasn't scheduled to report to work until Monday morning, but he had plenty to do before then.

Near the center of town, Books pulled into a crowded Chevron service station. He uncoiled his lean, six-foot-five-inch frame from the truck cab. The pickup was running on fumes, and he was in a junk food state of mind. He ate, gassed up, and on impulse, bought a mixed bouquet of flowers from a water-filled plastic bucket sitting on the floor next to the cash register. He drove across dried-up Kanab creek into the west side of town and cruised down the familiar street where he had spent his childhood. The old house hadn't changed much. The burnt lawn and weed-infested flower beds seemed neglected, and the faded chocolate brown exterior hadn't seen a fresh coat of paint in years. His dad's beat-up Toyota Land Cruiser sat in the driveway. The old man was nowhere in sight, and that suited Books just fine. They would have their awkward reunion, but it needn't be today.

Next Books drove to the cemetery. The afternoon sun baked the landscape, but a gusty northwest wind made it feel cooler. He walked to his mother's grave to leave the flowers, knowing they wouldn't survive long in the intense heat. To his surprise, the area around the grave was neatly manicured. A vase contained flowers that couldn't have been more than a day old. This struck him as odd, considering his father always avoided funerals and cemeteries. Somebody else, probably his sister Maggie, must be caring for the grave. Books added his flowers to those already in the vase, then spent a few minutes talking with his mother.

Seven miles east of Kanab, off State Highway 89, lay the fifteen-hundred-acre Case Cattle Company. It was home to Books' sister Maggie, her husband Bobby, and his two nephews. This would be his temporary home until he found something to rent. Unlike Books, Maggie had never left Kane County. She had married her high-school sweetheart, the son of one of the most influential families in Kane County.

Books had promised Maggie he would make it to the ranch in time for dinner. When he arrived, the smell of steaks cooking on the barbeque triggered memories of times long past when the family made a Saturday night tradition of grilling steaks during the summer months. Life was simpler then, or so it seemed.

Maggie prepared a big dinner in his honor. T-bone steaks, baked potatoes, corn on the cob, and home-made biscuits filled each plate. Apple pie à la mode completed the fare. After dinner, the kids ran off to play in the evening twilight while the adults sat on the front porch, happy to catch up after Books' nearly two year absence. He hadn't been home since his mother's funeral. By the time dusk gave way to full darkness, everybody had gone to bed except Maggie and Books. They sipped brandy and reminisced. Eventually, the discussion turned to their father.

"How is the old bird?" asked Books.

"Health-wise he seems to be doing okay," said Maggie. "But I'm worried about him. He spends too much time in Las Vegas. He'll disappear for days at a time without telling anybody. I think he's gambling and drinking quite a bit. I've started checking on him daily by calling Harrah's—that's where he always stays. I think he's pretty annoyed with me—hovering, that's what he calls it."

"Well, Sis, I wouldn't lose too much sleep over it. What'll you bet he's got a bevy of women stashed away down there?"

"Have you dropped by to see him?"

"Not yet. Hell, Maggs, I just got into town." He sounded defensive, something he hadn't intended.

She sighed. "You need to let go of it, J.D. It's history now. What's done is done. He's moved on, and so should you."

Maggie's remark angered Books. "I'm sure he hasn't had any problem moving on. I think he managed to do that even before mother died. The old fart was screwing anything in a skirt for years, and everybody in town knew about it, including mother.

She died of shame and a broken heart long before the cancer killed her."

"Jesus, J.D., that's not true. Don't blame dad's marital indiscretions for mom's cancer. That doesn't make any sense. The two aren't connected."

Maggie was right. "I know that, Sis. I guess I'm just angry at him for being so unfaithful for so damned long."

There was a brief lull in the conversation before Maggie said, "Carrie's called a couple of times now. I think she's really feeling devastated. She says you won't return her calls or answer the letters she's sent."

Carrie was Books' soon-to-be ex-wife. "I don't want to talk to her at all. The papers have been filed, and the divorce will be final in a couple of months. It can't be over soon enough to suit me."

"I'm so sorry, J.D." She glanced at him. "I haven't told you this, but it's really nice having you back home."

"Thanks, Maggs. It feels good to be home."

They talked a while longer about life on the ranch with Bobby and the boys and how difficult it was trying to make a decent living in the cattle business. He thanked her for doing such a good job of tending to their mother's grave. She gave him a sheepish look. "I'd love to take the credit, but I haven't been to the cemetery since the Memorial Day weekend."

Books was puzzled. Somebody was caring for the grave site. Could he have misjudged the old man? Maybe, but he didn't think so.

After Maggie went to bed, Books remained on the porch for an hour. He watched a full moon rise and cast its dark shadow over the black mountains to the north. Stars filled the night sky in every direction as far as the eye could see. Soon, overcome by fatigue, he settled down on the couch in the ranch house for what turned out to be a restless night of sleep.

Books was up and in town early Saturday morning. He had plenty of things to do. High on the list was finding a place to live. On his way out of the post office, he ran into Ned Hunsaker, a longtime family friend. Without a word, Hunsaker broke into a broad grin and gave him a good old-fashioned bear hug.

"Nice to have you back, son. I was delighted when I picked up the local rag and read that you were coming home. It's where you belong. Your mother would be pleased."

Hunsaker had been the Kane County librarian for thirty-three years. Book's mother had worked with him as the assistant librarian for twenty-seven of those years. They'd had a close friendship that had lasted until her death.

"Thanks, Ned. I'm not settled in yet, but it's already starting to feel like home. The last year's been tough."

"I was sorry to hear about that. Have you found a place to live?"

"Not yet. For the time being, I'm staying with Maggie and Bobby until I find something to rent. I'm supposed to look at one place later this morning."

"This might not interest you, but I've got an old double-wide mobile home sitting on my property. It needs a little paint, but it wouldn't take much to turn it into a cozy little place. And I guarantee you won't beat the price."

That piqued Books' interest. "How much do you want for it?"

"How about $200 a month and utilities?"

"Done."

"Geez, don't you want to see it first?"

"Nope. I'll take your word for it. When can I start moving in?"

"Right away if you want. I can hook up the propane tank and fire up the swamp cooler this afternoon."

# Chapter Two

Early the next morning David Greenbriar woke from a troubled sleep to the sound of a gusty wind that blew along the ridge-line of the plateau. He emerged from the tent just before the sun peeked above the eastern horizon. Even at the height of summer, a morning chill was common on the Kaiparowits Plateau. The cold didn't fool him. By midmorning the desert cool would give way to a blistering heat that would send most living things scurrying to the cover of shade. He broke camp without delay after a breakfast of dried fruit, cereal, and instant coffee. The return hike to his Suburban would take most of the day.

If nothing else, the trip had cleared his head. Greenbriar had made two important decisions. He knew the direction he intended to take the organization, and he'd also decided what course of action to follow with his unhappy marriage.

By late afternoon Greenbriar looked down through the shimmering heat and observed the welcome sight of his Suburban. The afternoon heat had been relentless. He stopped for a moment, removed his floppy hat, and poured water over his head and neck. As the crow flies, the Suburban wasn't far away. His path, however, wouldn't take him as the crow flies. Instead, the single-track trail meandered down the mountain, traversing a maze of switchbacks and depressions, until it finally brought him out on an old dirt road about a quarter mile away. He increased his pace, eager to feel the blast of cool air that awaited him from the truck's air conditioner. When he reached the Suburban, he slipped off the backpack and began rummaging through its side pocket for the keys.

For an instant, Greenbriar had the unnerving feeling that someone or something was watching him. He stood up and looked around. Above him to the west, something reflected off the sun. He hesitated, trying to decide what he was looking at. The report of the rifle echoed throughout the canyon at the precise moment Greenbriar realized that he was staring into the barrel of a gun. The bullet struck him in the chest, ripped through his heart, exited out his back, and struck the rear passenger door of the Suburban, showering it with blood and tissue. The force of the blast slammed his body back into the side of the truck. Greenbriar's legs buckled and his head slumped forward onto his chest as though he were taking an afternoon nap. The vermilion sandstone under him turned a dark shade of crimson as he quickly bled out.

◇◇◇

Books rose early Monday morning, showered, put on his new BLM uniform, and headed into town. The BLM office was located in the old junior high school. The red brick building was flanked by two side-by-side portable offices, testimony to the growing number of federal employees assigned to the Kanab field office.

He had an eight o'clock meeting with his new boss, Alexis Runyon, and then planned to head into the field for his first full day on the job. Since they had never met, he felt uneasy. She probably felt the same. He'd been hired by BLM law enforcement managers in the Salt Lake City regional office, not by Runyon.

Books arrived a few minutes ahead of his scheduled meeting. As he pulled into the gravel parking lot, he saw six sign-toting picketers marching in a small circle across the street from the BLM office. The messages on the signs struck a similar theme: eliminate mining, logging, and livestock grazing from all public lands. On another corner, a couple of hecklers watched with mild disinterest and barked an occasional insult. One of them waved a sign that read, "Eliminate tree-huggers, not cattle ranchers."

Alexis Runyon was not what Books had expected. Her small office could only be described as austere. She sat behind an old metal desk in a decrepit chair that must have knocked around government offices for years. One wall displayed a framed aerial photograph of the Grand Canyon. Other than that, the surfaces were bare. No diplomas, training certificates, or awards. Whatever ego she might possess wasn't on display in her office.

Runyon stood, introduced herself, and invited Books to sit in one of three metal folding chairs lined up in front of her desk. Dressed in work-casual blue jeans, a red-checkered chambray shirt, and hiking boots, she looked to be in her late thirties. Short, dark hair showed flecks of gray around the temples, and a pair of wire-rimmed reading glasses perched on the end of her nose. So far she seemed a very unpretentious lady—a good quality, thought Books.

"Hope you enjoyed the welcoming committee across the street?" She smiled.

Books smiled back. "They needn't have gone to all that trouble on my account."

"Trust me, they didn't. They do this sort of thing on a semi-regular basis. And sometimes the local ranchers mount a counter-demonstration, the Eddins brothers and their Citizens for a Free West, the CFW. If you haven't heard of them, you will."

"I know the Eddins family. Don't forget, I grew up here."

"The good news is that the two groups don't often protest on the same day. More often than not, it's Dr. David Greenbriar and his Escalante Environmental Wilderness Alliance, the EEWA, doing most of the sign-toting. That's not to say your arrival has gone unnoticed." She opened the center drawer of her desk and handed Books a newspaper article. "This appeared in the *Kane County Citizen* last week."

Books scanned the story. The caption above the article read, 'Books Returns to Kanab as BLM's First Law Enforcement Ranger.' He folded the newspaper article and stuck it in his pants pocket. "Bedtime reading."

"Suit yourself." Runyon gave him a clinical once-over. "I'm going to speak candidly. It's how I do things."

"Fair enough."

"I want to be clear with you that I'm one hundred percent behind the notion of having a law enforcement presence here in the Kanab office. In fact, it's long overdue. That said, you should also know that there are people in the office who believe that bringing a federal ranger into an already tense area is both unnecessary and dangerous."

Wonderful, thought Books. He expected hostility from some elements in the community, but he hadn't counted on it from his coworkers.

"I'm sure I don't have to remind you that you no longer work in a police department. Most of your fellow employees are botanists, geologists, foresters, and an occasional paleontologist. What they collectively know about law enforcement wouldn't fill a thimble. So it's going to be incumbent upon you to be patient. They'll adjust, but it's going to take some time."

"And you're telling me this because…?"

"I'm telling you this so you'll understand what you're getting into and because I have some concerns."

"And those would be?"

"In reviewing your résumé, as well as reading the newspaper coverage of your exploits, I see some things I like and some things I don't. What I'm most concerned about are the two fatal shootings you've been involved in and the cloud that hung over your departure from the Denver Police Department."

When Books didn't respond, Runyon pressed on. "The job you're about to take on requires far different skills from those in the police department. Here it's all about people skills, and I'm worried that your background doesn't lend itself well to the demands of this job."

"You ever worked in law enforcement?"

She shook her head.

"Police work is really all about good people skills."

"Maybe so," said Runyon, "but make no mistake about it, the complexities here are very real. We've got environmental groups of every ilk pitted against mining and timber interests and the ATV crowd, while an angry group of ranchers watches its lifestyle disappear. It's a tinder box just waiting for a match. You'll see everything from poachers to people harvesting timber to marijuana growers to pot hunters who don't give a second thought about destroying ancient archeological sites so long as they get their trophy."

"Sounds like a challenge."

Runyon regarded him for a moment, "Are you really that understated, Mr. Books, or are you just jerking me around?"

Books smiled and shrugged his shoulders. In the end, he left the meeting believing that he understood the job and the community a lot better than Alexis Runyon thought he did. She'd made her point though. His homicide investigation skills wouldn't be his best qualification for this job. Or so he thought.

# Chapter Three

After meeting Runyon, Books attended her Monday morning staff breakfast to meet some of his fellow BLM employees and get a feel for his place in the organization.

Most people were cordial. A few were not.

By nine-thirty, Books was driving east on Highway 89 from Kanab toward Lake Powell. He'd been asked to drop off topo maps and supplies at the BLM's new visitors' center in the controversial small town of Big Water. The hour-long drive took him past multicolored sandstone formations in colors ranging from dirty white to red, orange, and pink. The copper-colored clay-enriched soil was home to native sage, pinyon and juniper pine, as well as the invasive cheetgrass.

Big Water was located sixty miles east of Kanab near the Arizona border. The town became a magnet for people with nonconventional family values, such as the polygamist clan once headed by the late Alex Joseph. The town ended up in hot water by passing an ordinance that decriminalized both possession of marijuana and possession of drug paraphernalia. Under pressure from the state, the town council rescinded the ordinance but not before the press and Kane County residents started calling Big Water "Bong Water" and "Doobyville."

Books had just left the Big Water office when the county dispatcher asked him to return and call Alexis Runyon.

"I just got a call from the sheriff's office," said Runyon. "The EEWA office just filed a missing persons report on David

Greenbriar. Apparently, he failed to show up this morning for an eight o'clock staff meeting. He was supposed to have spent the weekend hiking in the Monument."

"Was he out there alone?"

"Yes."

"Not a very good idea. Anybody checked his home?"

"The sheriff has a deputy there now. Nobody's there and both family vehicles are gone. The secretary at the EEWA office recalls Greenbriar mentioning that his wife was planning to spend the weekend out of town with friends."

Runyon gave him a description of Greenbriar's SUV, knowing that it would be like looking for the proverbial needle in a haystack. They agreed that he would start searching the main roads on the east side of the Grand Staircase Escalante National Monument.

Thirty minutes later, Runyon called again. "I just got a call from Sheriff Sutter. A group of German tourists flagged down a highway patrol trooper on State Highway 89 and led her to a dead body at the old Paria ghost town. Sutter says it's the body of David Greenbriar."

"Foul play or accidental death?"

There was a long pause. "At the moment, he's calling it a suspicious death."

Books hesitated, figuring that he might not like the answer to his next question. "And why is that?"

"The tourists found Greenbriar hanging from a two-by-six beam outside the barn at the old West movie set. It also looks like he's been shot. The sheriff would like you to take a look at the crime scene. It's the county's jurisdiction, but I told him I'd ask you to stop by. Help 'em if you can, but keep us out of it if possible."

Easier said than done, thought Books.

◇◇◇

When Books reached the scene forty minutes later, the corpse of David Greenbriar was a hanging silhouette against the rising Vermilion Cliffs to the east. He could see that Greenbriar's arms and ankles were secured with duct tape. A hot, gusty wind caused the body to sway gently back and forth as it dangled four feet off the ground, an eerie image reminiscent of vigilante justice in frontier times. Maybe that's what was intended, thought Books.

Two Kane County Sheriff's Department vehicles formed a loose perimeter around the area. Books recognized Sheriff Charley Sutter but didn't know the other officer. A small knot of tourists huddled off to one side, several snapping pictures. Books realized that these folks had received a stronger dose of the American Wild West than anything they'd read in their tourist brochures.

He parked behind the sheriff's vehicles and walked a short distance to the crime scene. Sutter hurried over and extended a hand, "Greetings, J.D. Welcome home. This must feel like old times, what with a murder and all." Books nodded but didn't say anything. Sutter introduced him to his chief deputy, Brian Call. Sutter explained that Call acted as his second-in-command and also served as the department's only detective. Books guessed that Sutter intended to place Call in charge of the investigation.

One look at Brian Call didn't inspire a great deal of confidence. He looked to be several years older than Books, forty perhaps. The most distinctive thing about his appearance, aside from a pot belly that hung generously over his belt, was a waxed handlebar mustache. Dressed in period clothes, he'd have made a fine caricature of a frontier lawman in a B-grade western movie.

"Anybody gone in for a closer look?" asked Books.

"Nope," replied Sutter. "We established the perimeter and have been waiting for help to get here. I've got a CSI unit on the way from St. George, and the state medical examiner's office has dispatched a deputy ME from their Provo office."

"All right, let's take a look." He and Sutter entered the crime scene and walked to the body. Sutter said, "There's a note pinned to the front of his shirt." He squinted into the sun. "I think it says, 'one less tree hugger'."

"Yeah, I can't see it clearly, but I think you're right," said Books. "I can see a gunshot wound near the heart, and a larger exit wound out the back."

"That means we're looking for some type of hunting rifle," said the sheriff.

Books agreed.

"Was he shot first and then hanged, or the other way around?" asked Sutter.

"He wasn't killed here, Charley. He was shot somewhere else, and then moved here and strung up. There's not enough blood here."

"That means I've got another crime scene someplace else."

They studied the ground around the body. "What do you think, Charley?"

"Looks to me like his body was dragged several feet along the ground, probably by his shoulders. See where the heels of his boots dug into the sandstone as he was pulled along?"

"Plain as day."

"And you can see faint tire impressions that stop just short of where the poor buzzard was hanged. Those tires look pretty big—probably from a large truck or SUV. Your turn, Books."

"Had he been shot here, he would have bled out. And look at the dirt and crud on his hiking boots. It doesn't match what's here. The stuff on his boots has an alkali look about it. It's much lighter than the dark, copper-colored sandstone found in this part of the monument."

Sutter was taking notes. "Okay, anything else?"

"A couple of things. Greenbriar's body had to have come into contact with the shooter. That means that trace evidence will have been transferred from the killer to your victim and vice versa. Make sure the medical examiner handles the victim's clothing carefully—bag each article separately. I'd also bet that you've got either multiple perps or one strong male. Greenbriar isn't a big guy, but dead weight is hard to pack around. I doubt you're looking for a female."

"I'll pass that information along to Chief Deputy Call and make sure he follows up."

"Be sure the CSI team photographs the tire impressions and drag marks. I don't think the tire impressions are deep enough for a mold, but if they are, get one. And take soil samples from both sites."

The sheriff sighed. "I don't get it, J.D. Why would somebody go to all the trouble and risk of moving the body? Why not leave him at the kill site?"

"Good question. Maybe the perp brought him here for a symbolic hanging complete with the threatening note pinned to his chest."

"What do you mean?"

"In a small percentage of homicides, the offender poses the victim in order to satisfy some kinky, perverted need. Sometimes that's true of serial killers. Somebody's posed Greenbriar like this for a reason."

"Are you saying I've got a serial killer on my hands?"

"I don't think so. What I am saying is that if someone is intent on picking a fight, killing David Greenbriar makes for a solid first volley. Who knows if there's more to come? That might depend on how the environmental community reacts to this killing."

Sutter gazed off into the distance with his brow furrowed, trying to digest the implications of what he'd just heard. "If you're right, I could end up with a modern day range war on my hands—local ranchers against the Greens."

"I doubt it, but it's not altogether impossible. Have you notified his family?"

"Not yet. His office thinks his wife may be out of town. We keep trying their home number but nobody answers. The calls just kick into their voice messaging system."

Glancing again at the body, Sutter said, "How long do you think he's been dead?"

"Hard to say. Calculating time of death isn't an exact science, and it's even harder when you're dealing with an outdoor crime scene. Temperature variations and weather conditions change things. The ME will help you with that, but judging from the condition of the body, I'd say he's been dead for around twenty-four hours."

They retraced their steps as the CSI unit arrived, which Books took as his cue to leave. Driving away, he had no idea he was about to become embroiled in a murder investigation where he would be unable to distinguish friend from foe—a case in which the unfortunate death of David Greenbriar served the interests of so many.

# Chapter Four

Within minutes of his leaving Sheriff Sutter, county dispatch asked Books to drive the Smoky Mountain Road in search of Greenbriar's Chevrolet Suburban. A volunteer in the EEWA office told the sheriff that Greenbriar had mentioned a weekend hike to the Kaiparowits Plateau with a return Sunday evening.

It didn't take Books long to find the Suburban parked near a trailhead about five miles up the road. He could see blood and tissue smears on the rear passenger door on the driver's side with a pool of dried blood in the dirt right below. It looked like the bullet had passed through the victim and entered the door. He asked dispatch to have the sheriff call him on his mobile.

"Find anything, J.D.?"

"Yup, I've got your other crime scene, about five miles up Smoky Mountain Road. The vic's Suburban is parked in the turnout near the trail head. He must have hiked in from here. You'll want to send a deputy and a different CSI crew."

There was a pause. "What do you mean a different CSI crew? Afraid this is the only one we've got."

"Never mind, just send the one you've got."

Policing in Denver had taught Books that whenever you had two crime scenes, it was better for a different forensics team to process the second one. That way an astute defense lawyer couldn't claim cross-contamination of evidence from one scene to the next. But he'd forgotten one little detail: this wasn't Denver P.D.

"Sit tight," said Sutter. "I'll send Call over right away. The crime scene unit will come just as soon as they're finished here."

The location of the bullet as well as the blood splatter gave Books a general idea of where the shooter might have hidden. The rocky cliffs above and to the west of the Suburban would have provided a clear field of fire from an easy distance. He spent the next half-hour looking around before he found the spot.

The shooter had been careless, leaving two empty Guinness beer cans and a sandwich baggie on the ground. Best of all, Books found a single shell casing tucked under a shaded sandstone outcropping. The shooter hadn't cleaned up his brass—sloppy, but not altogether unusual.

By the time he returned to his vehicle, Call and members of the CSI team had arrived. Books led Call to the location where the killer had fired the fatal shot.

◇◇◇

Later in the afternoon, Books was summoned to a meeting at BLM headquarters. Alexis Runyon and Sheriff Sutter were there.

Sutter was a slight, almost dainty-looking man in his early fifties, with receding red hair. He'd been a member of the sheriff's department for twenty-five years and was now serving his fourth term as sheriff.

Looking at Books, Runyon said, "J.D., Charley has asked for your help investigating Greenbriar's murder. I'm inclined to deny his request, but I thought we should talk before making a final decision."

Volunteering to be thrust into a murder investigation in a polarized community didn't strike Books as prudent. The victim was the leader of a prominent environmental group, with his likely killer some radical right-wing local with an axe to grind.

"It looks like a can of worms, and I'd prefer not to become involved. And if that's the sole purpose of this meeting, I'd like to get back to work."

Books started to rise when Sutter spoke. "Would both of you hold on a minute and hear me out before you make up your mind?"

Books glanced at Runyon and dropped back in his chair.

"This is what I propose," said Sutter. "I'll commission J.D. a deputy in the sheriff's department. He'll have law enforcement authority on federal and state land. I'll give him complete autonomy to run the investigation any way he sees fit. In return, I expect to be kept appraised of the status of the case. And, if you want, I'll assign Chief Deputy Call as his assistant."

Before Books could reply, Runyon spoke. "Look, Charley, I can appreciate the seriousness of the situation, but I have major reservations about the propriety of the BLM getting involved in a murder case with local jurisdiction. What's in it for us besides a lot of time, money, and headaches?"

A good question, Books thought. You didn't have to be the brightest bulb in the box to understand where Charley Sutter got his political support, and consequently, where his loyalty lay. And it wasn't with the BLM. It had to come from the local ranch community, including the CFW.

"For starters," said Sutter, "you'd create a lot of political goodwill here in the county. I've already spoken to the county commissioners and they're one hundred percent behind the idea. In fact, they've already agreed to reimburse the BLM for J.D.'s time."

He'd annoyed Runyon. "You've already taken this to the commissioners?" It was like she'd caught the sheriff red-handed dumping a fresh cow pie all over her office floor. Sutter recognized the look and went straight to Plan B.

"Look, I'm between a rock and a hard place. I need your help. Not counting myself and Call, I got six deputies to cover over 4,300 square miles. This county is bigger than Rhode Island, Delaware, and the District of Columbia combined."

Fine. Now tell us something we don't know, thought Books.

"Besides, we don't have much experience handling murder investigations. In my seventeen years as sheriff, I can count the number of murders we've had on one hand. And most of them were domestic violence cases turned ugly. Nothing complicated like this one.

"J.D is here. He knows the community, and most important, he's a first-rate homicide detective. I know because I called his old boss in Denver, a captain named Howard Cornell. Recent problems aside, this Cornell described J.D. as one of the best homicide detectives he'd ever seen."

Books gave Sutter credit. The sheriff had done his homework in the few short hours since they'd parted company at the first crime scene.

Before either Runyon or Books could respond, her phone rang. She answered and handed the phone to Sutter. "It's for you."

"Yeah. Oh, Christ, When? Where are they now? Stall them until I get there. I don't know how long, maybe a half-hour or so."

He handed the receiver back to Runyon, a frown etched on his face. "That was my secretary. There's a crew from KSL-TV in Salt Lake City camped in front of my office. How could they have gotten wind of this so fast?"

It seemed like a rhetorical question, and neither Runyon nor Books responded.

Runyon glanced at Books. "What's your pleasure, J.D.?"

Reluctantly, Books nodded his assent. If he was going to be involved, he might as well run the investigation instead of trying to provide advice from the outside.

"Against my better judgment, Charley, I'm going to approve Ranger Books' assistance in this investigation, subject to a couple of stipulations. First, the county reimburses my budget for J.D.'s salary during the investigation as well as any secretarial support he requires. Second, everybody understands that my decision could be reversed at any time by the regional office in Salt Lake City. Are we all clear?"

Relieved, Sutter nodded. For better or for worse, Books now stood at the center of a volatile murder case in a bitterly divided community.

# Chapter Five

The local district court judge conducted a brief swearing-in ceremony in which Books became a Kane County deputy sheriff. The county commissioners offered him an office in a small conference room in the county courthouse, complete with a desk-top computer, a printer that looked about a hundred years old, a metal four-drawer file cabinet, and a telephone. For support staff, they offered Chief Deputy Call and a secretary who worked for the commissioners.

With the exception of Call, Books turned the rest down. He'd decided to run the investigation from his office at the BLM using a secretary provided by Runyon. Information from the investigation would be difficult enough to control without working from a courthouse conference room he couldn't secure, with a secretary who had a direct pipeline into the county commissioners' office.

Sutter held a brief press conference in which he read a short statement confirming that his office was investigating a suspicious death. He declined to answer any other questions, including who was running the investigation. Books hoped this might give him a little extra time to follow leads without having to dodge the media.

Books contacted Call and arranged to meet him in the office as soon as he returned from the field. In part, Books wanted to get a sense of whether Call was competent and if he was someone Books could trust. He was worried about both.

Over two cups of burnt coffee, the men talked. "I'm a Kanab native," Books smiled. "What's your excuse?"

Call smiled back. "I've always been a hunter and an outdoor enthusiast. When I was a kid growing up in Las Vegas, my dad used to take us to Kane County on hunting trips—great trophy deer around these parts, but I guess you'd know that."

"So you're originally from Las Vegas?"

"Yup, born and raised. I moved to Kanab thirteen years ago and set up shop as a hunting guide and outfitter."

"Makes sense."

"Maybe so. Problem was I damn near starved to death. Outside the hunting season, there just wasn't enough business to make much of a living."

"Why did you get into law enforcement?"

"Probably for the same reason you did. I needed a job. I'd worked a while in the Las Vegas Metropolitan Jail, so when a position opened up here, I jumped at the chance—good benefits, decent pay, and best of all, steady work."

"And you've worked for Charley ever since?"

"Ten years, almost eleven, now. Charley Sutter's a good man and a damn fine sheriff."

"Charley's been the sheriff a long time. I'm sure he doesn't remember this, but he wrote me my first traffic ticket when I was a senior in high school—pissed my old man off big time."

Call nodded. "Now if I've made it through the interview, I'd like to know how I can help with the investigation."

"I think you have, Deputy Call. I'd like you to get started on a couple of things. First, get hold of the medical examiner's office and find out when Greenbriar's autopsy is scheduled. I want you to attend. We need the medical examiner's report as soon as possible."

"Okay. What else?"

"Then get a list of all the CFW members as well as any CFW wannabes. Do the same with the EEWA. Keep your eyes and ears open. Talk to people. See if you can identify anybody with a grudge against Greenbriar. Better yet, see if you can identify anybody who may have threatened him."

Call was smiling now.

"I didn't realize I'd said something funny. Care to clue me in?" The grin disappeared.

"Only that you're going to end up with a long list of suspects. Most people outside the Green movement hated the guy, but I'll ask around."

"I'm curious. Does that 'most people' include you?"

Call gave Books a hard stare. "Tell you the truth, I didn't care much for the guy—trouble-maker if you ask me. But I'll work just as hard to find Greenbriar's killer as I would if the victim had been somebody from the CFW. I don't take kindly to murder in this community, regardless of who did it."

Books stared back at him for a long moment. "Fair enough."

# Chapter Six

When Books arrived at the sheriff's department, Darby Greenbriar was sitting at a round conference table in Sutter's office holding the hand of an older woman, who, at first glance, looked enough like her to have been her mother. It turned out that the woman was a neighbor of the Greenbriars and a volunteer in the EEWA office.

Darby Greenbriar was a knockout and looked to be about half the age of her now deceased husband. She had shown up unannounced in response to the phone message left at her home.

"How did she take the news, Charley?"

"Not as upset as I thought she might be. She saw the media outside, and I think she knew something was wrong. She just wasn't sure what."

Sutter had delivered the bad news in the privacy of his office prior to Books' arrival. At the moment, the widow looked composed, although Books could see that she was clutching a handful of Kleenex and occasionally dabbed at tear-filled, puffy eyes.

The sheriff introduced him to the two women and explained that Books would be assisting the sheriff's department with the investigation. They excused the friend and sat down for what would turn out to be the first of several interviews with Darby Greenbriar.

Books offered his condolences and then explained how important it was to have her cooperation if they were going to catch her husband's killer. He also had to figure out whether she was somehow involved in the murder without alienating her in the process. In murder cases family members often got the first look. That meant finding out whether she had the means, motive, and opportunity to have murdered Greenbriar herself, or whether she might have hired someone else to do it.

"Mrs. Greenbriar, may I call you Darby?"

She nodded.

"Tell me, Darby, had David expressed any recent concerns about his personal safety, or did he ever mention specific incidents in which somebody threatened him?"

"We've been receiving threats almost from the time we moved here. They occur so often in fact, that after a while you just learn to ignore them. Most of the threats come from anonymous e-mails sent to our Web site or crank phone calls to the EEWA office or our home. Sometimes callers leave obscene voice messages. Other times, all you can hear is heavy breathing—nobody says anything."

"Any idea whose been sending the messages?"

"Nobody in particular, but we assumed the threats had to be coming from locals who are associated with the Citizens for a Free West."

"Did you report the crank calls and anonymous e-mails to the police?"

She forced a laugh. "You must be kidding, Ranger Books."

"Please, call me J.D."

"Okay. We did at first, but it didn't take long to realize the sheriff's office didn't have the slightest interest."

Sutter bristled but didn't say anything.

"What makes you say that?"

"Well, why should they? Most of them either belong to the CFW or are CFW sympathizers."

"That's not true," said Sutter. "My men investigated every one of those incidents just as we do all citizen complaints that come into this office."

Books turned to Sutter. "Were you able to identify any suspects?"

"No, never did, but it wasn't because we didn't try."

Books shifted his attention back to Darby. "Has anyone ever threatened you or your husband directly?"

She started to shake her head and then paused. "Come to think of it, there was an incident about two, maybe three months ago involving that gorilla who works for Neil Eddins. Tommy something-or-other, I think his name is."

Books glanced at Sutter. "Help me here, Charley."

"McClain, she's talking about Tommy McClain."

"Yeah, that's him. Big guy, tall, with very yellow teeth and stinky breath you can smell clear across a room."

Sutter fidgeted in his chair, not caring for Greenbriar's characterization of Tommy McClain.

Books suppressed a smile. "Well, I'll be damned. Tommy 'Trees' McClain—haven't heard that name in a few years." Books had played basketball with McClain in high school. Trees had sprouted to six-feet-seven by the end of tenth grade. For a small-town high-school basketball team to have a six-seven center was akin to Shaq O'Neill playing for a local church team. Unlike O'Neill, Trees couldn't walk and chew bubble gum at the same time. McClain must have decided to remain in Kanab and work for Neil Eddins.

"Tell me what happened, Darby."

"David and I had just finished dinner at the Stagecoach Grill. It was a Friday or Saturday night, I think. We were in the parking lot about to get into our truck when this Tommy and some other guy I didn't recognize stopped us. They'd been drinking and were headed into the Stagecoach Bar when they saw us. After a couple of sexual innuendos directed at me, McClain asked David if he knew what happened to tree-huggers in Kane County. When David didn't answer, he laughed and asked us if we'd seen the movie *Fargo*. As I recall, he found it quite amusing telling us that ground-up body parts from a wood-chipper provided an excellent source of protein when mixed into hog feed."

Charley Sutter had heard enough. "If this incident happened as you say it did, why didn't you report it?"

"Hello, haven't you been listening? We don't report this kind of harassment because your office refuses to do anything about it."

Books interrupted to stop the acrimonious exchange from going further. "Aside from members of the CFW, can you think of anyone else who might have wanted to see your husband dead?"

"Nobody."

"What about members of the EEWA? Were there any members who seemed opposed to the direction your husband was taking the organization?"

That gave her pause. "The alliance is governed by a seven-person board, with David as the chairman. The vice-chairman, a guy named Barry Struthers, sometimes expressed frustration that David refused to approve more aggressive forms of protest."

Like acts of eco-terrorism, thought Books.

"But I can't see him getting involved in a plot to kill David. I just don't see it."

Books would need to find out more about Barry Struthers but that would have to wait. Instead, he turned the interview in a new direction. "How did you and David meet?"

"I met David when I was a grad student at Berkeley. David was the chair of my master's degree thesis committee. He was a professor in the microbiology department. Later, I became his graduate assistant. We grew close, and, over time, one thing led to another until we fell in love. David's marriage had been on the rocks for years."

"So after his divorce, the two of you decided to marry?"

"Not right away, but after a time, yes. We married in Las Vegas a little over four years ago." Her voice remained steady, but she used Kleenex to wipe tears from her eyes.

"Would you like to take a short break?" said Books.

She took a deep breath and shook her head.

"All right. What kind of relationship did David have with his former spouse?"

"Okay, as far as I could tell. They haven't had much to do with each other since the split. Lillian is a professor of English literature at Berkeley. The divorce was amicable considering the circumstances. They divided the personal property, split the proceeds from the sale of their home, and went their separate ways. They never had children."

"Can you tell me about your husband's estate? Did he have a will or perhaps a trust?

"David never talked to me much about stuff like that."

"And you never asked him?"

"Not really. Financial stuff bores me. He did mention once that he was working with his attorney on a will."

"When did he mention that to you?"

She hesitated, "Maybe a year or so after we married."

"Is his attorney local?"

"No. Even after we moved, David kept his Berkeley attorney—the same guy who handled the divorce. I can get you his name and number later if you want it."

"I'll need that, thanks. Did David ever ask you to sign a prenuptial agreement?"

"No, and if he had, I would've refused."

"Why is that?"

"There's something creepy about starting a new life with someone and having the cloud of a prenup hanging over everything. I would never have married David, or anyone else for that matter, if a prenuptial agreement was part of the deal."

"Was there a life insurance policy?"

"There was, but again, I don't know the specifics. I can look into it and get back to you."

"I'll need that information as well. Can you provide me with the insurance information when you get back to me with the name of David's lawyer?"

"Sure."

"Please don't be offended with my next question, but I'll need you to tell me where you've been the past forty-eight hours."

"I'm not offended at all. I know why you're asking and I understand. I spent the weekend in Las Vegas. It was kind of a spur-of-the-moment thing. I knew David wouldn't be back until Sunday night, and I was bored. I love to shop, so I drove down Saturday morning and came back today."

"So you spent two nights in Vegas?"

"Yes."

"Where did you stay?"

"The Hard Rock. It's my favorite casino hotel."

"Anybody go with you?"

"I went alone. I've got an old high-school girlfriend who lives in Las Vegas. I tried calling her before I left and after I got to the Hard Rock. I kept leaving messages, but I never reached her. She must have been out of town."

"So you spent the weekend by yourself?"

"Yes."

"I'll need your girlfriend's name and phone number?"

"Her name is Erin Rogers. The number is (702)678-9924. That's her cell."

"What does Ms. Rogers do for a living?"

"She's a dancer at the Mirage."

"How about receipts?" said J.D. "Would you happen to have receipts—credit card charges or the hotel receipt?"

"Um, not with me, but I can get them for you."

"Add that to your list. You said you left for Las Vegas on Saturday morning. What time was that?"

"Maybe nine o'clock."

"And returned today at...."

"I got back by early afternoon, two, maybe two-thirty."

"When was the last time you saw your husband alive?"

"David left the EEWA office around four o'clock Friday afternoon. That's the last time." She choked off a sob.

Books handed her a fresh tissue. "Sorry, Darby, just another question or two, and then I'll be finished."

She nodded and dabbed at her eyes.

"What did you do on Friday evening after David left?"

"I worked until about six and then went out to dinner with Celia Foxworthy. Celia's the lady who's here with me today. She's a volunteer at the office, and she's also our next-door neighbor."

"So you went to dinner with Ms. Foxworthy and got home at about what time?"

"You can check with her, but I think around eight-thirty."

"And what did you do for the rest of the evening?"

"I just tucked in, watched TV, and read until I fell asleep."

Books ended the interview by asking Darby for permission to search her husband's EEWA office. She consented but demanded to be present during the search.

# Chapter Seven

Books followed Darby to the EEWA office. The organization leased space in an old pueblo-style complex on the north end of town just off Main Street. He was struck by the security measures inside the office. The public entered a large, sparsely furnished foyer with an array of environmental publications stacked on a coffee table in front of a leather couch. The inner office was separated by a wall with a steel door at one end and a small plexiglass window in the center, through which a visitor could speak to a receptionist. Access to the inner sanctum was controlled from the window.

As soon as they entered the foyer, the receptionist buzzed them through the locked door and immediately gave Darby a tearful embrace. The two exchanged whispered words of comfort. The inner office consisted of a conference room and two small private offices, one of which had belonged to David Greenbriar.

Books spent the next hour searching the victim's office with Darby looking on. Citing privacy concerns, she refused to allow him to remove hard copies of documents or provide him with a list of EEWA members. For that he would need to get a warrant. He paid special attention to the e-mail messages Greenbriar sent and received as well as the files on his hard drive and on a CD Rom.

He hadn't expected the search to yield a smoking gun and it didn't. That's not to say that the search was for naught. Two things struck him. The first was the general tenor of Greenbriar's correspondence. During the past several months, he seemed preoccupied with the issue of road expansion into wilderness areas. When Books asked Darby about this, she confirmed it.

"The environmental issues we focus on shift periodically depending on what our political adversaries are up to," she explained. "Around here, livestock grazing often becomes the focus of much of our time and energy. At other times, our emphasis shifts to logging, mining, or all-terrain vehicle use in sensitive ecosystems. For the last maybe six to nine months, our attention has been devoted almost exclusively to the roads issue. That's what you're seeing in David's correspondence."

"What makes the roads issue so important?"

"The big concern is that if environmental groups lose on the roads issue, we risk forfeiting federal control of public lands to state and local government. That would be a disaster for the environmental movement. If states were to gain control of public lands, they'll open all kinds of sensitive wilderness areas to economic development."

"Is that such a bad thing?"

"Depends on your point of view, I guess." Darby glanced away looking as though she had lost interest in the conversation.

The other thing that attracted Books' attention was an e-mail that Greenbriar sent to one of his chief lieutenants, Barry Struthers, two weeks prior to his murder. Struthers was the EEWA member who Darby mentioned had been in conflict with the victim in the weeks and months before his death. The e-mail read:

*Barry,*

*I find myself increasingly frustrated with your angry rhetoric and outbursts during recent board meetings. In addition, you should understand that I will not be swayed by your personal attacks directed at me. Vague threats and innuendos will not change the direction of the organization.*

*If, as I suspect, your intent is to wrest control of the organization from me, then I urge you to follow the protocol established in our by-laws. You have the right to petition the board of directors for a special session in which you seek a vote of no confidence in my leadership. The chairman can be removed by a majority vote of the board.*

*You should understand that I am adamantly opposed to more radical forms of protest within the organization. To do so will further polarize the community and invite dangerous forms of retaliation from the other side.*

*Sincerely,*

*David W. Greenbriar, Ph.D.*
*President*
*Escalante Environmental Wilderness Alliance*

Books wondered what kind of "vague threats and innuendos" Greenbriar referred to. When he asked Darby about it, she shrugged.

Books had learned long ago that good homicide cops tended to have reliable instincts about people. His initial impressions of Darby Greenbriar were mixed. On one hand, she seemed cooperative, forthcoming, and genuinely distraught over the death of her husband. On the other, she seemed terribly uninformed about everything related to the family estate. That struck him as unusual, particularly in a marriage where a beautiful, young woman married a guy nearly twice her age. What did Darby stand to gain financially from her husband's death? And what about her weekend in Las Vegas?

Some murder investigations were straightforward—physical evidence connects a suspect with the crime, an eyewitness identifies a suspect, or a motive is so clear that it smacks you square in the face. That wasn't this case. Books could ill afford to ignore the chance that someone close to Greenbriar, an ally perhaps, had killed him and hatched an elaborate plot to cast blame on an obvious foe like the CFW.

Barry Struthers and Tommy McLain had become persons of interest in the Greenbriar murder. Both had motive and means.

That left opportunity. Books also considered the possibility that Greenbriar's murder could, in some way, be connected to the EEWA's opposition to road expansion on federal land. He knew virtually nothing about who would have the most to gain if federal road expansion restrictions were eased? While Books couldn't answer that question, he knew who could.

# Chapter Eight

Books caught up with Ned Hunsaker that evening working out-side in his garden. Hunsaker was still a handsome man, Books guessed, although it was hard to tell. He was tall, maybe six-five, and slim, with a swarthy complexion, leathery-looking skin, and a full head of silver hair—the direct consequence of years spent trekking across the southern Utah desert under a blistering sun. His solitary wanderings were the stuff of legend around Kane County. He knew the monuments and national parks far better than most people, because he'd spent a lifetime exploring them.

Since Books had neglected to leave the swamp cooler on when he left for work, the double-wide was going to be uninhabitable for the next half-hour. Ned interrupted his gardening and brought out iced tea. They sat in the shade of his covered front porch.

Hunsaker raised his glass. "Getting settled in the trailer?"

"Slowly, yeah, but it's going to take a little while—more shit to unpack than I thought."

"Well, son, there's no rush. You got plenty of time."

"True enough."

Ned sipped his iced tea before continuing. "The scuttlebutt around town is that you got yourself mixed up in Greenbriar's murder case. That true?"

"Yup."

"How're you feelin about that?"

"I didn't expect it, that's for sure. And talk about bad timing—first day on the job, no less."

"Some things are just fated, I guess," said Hunsaker.

"Maybe so. When I took this job, I assumed my days chasing murder suspects were over. I'd been trying to wrap my head around the notion of a simpler life commiserating with nature and being a good steward for public land."

Ned frowned. "Not that simple, is it? The word is that the BLM has taken over the investigation. If it's true, I'm surprised Alexis would go along. I can't imagine what's in it for the BLM except a gut full of heartburn."

"Tell you the truth, so was I. My sense is that Alexis saw a chance to improve relations with the county by working cooperatively on something instead of the usual bickering and conflict."

"That makes sense. Hope she's right."

"Me, too." They sat quietly for a couple of minutes enjoying the evening shade and the cold, berry-flavored tea.

"Let me ask you a question, Ned. It appears in the months leading up to his murder, Greenbriar was focused on trying to prevent road expansion into wilderness areas. Who are the major stakeholders on that issue? Who stands to gain the most from road expansion?"

Ned pondered the question. "First off there's the ranchers. They're going to oppose most environmental initiatives just on principle. Many of them hunt and fish using their all-terrain vehicles. If they're running livestock, you can bet your britches they're on federal land, using grazing permits that have been in their family for generations."

"Welfare ranching, that's what the environmental groups call it?"

"They do. Then there's the off-road vehicle organizations. They're always whining about more access to back-country. They'd love to see state and local government win on that issue. Greenies want to restrict ATV access to wilderness areas because of noise, air pollution, soil erosion, and damage to plant and wildlife.

"Then you've got anybody holding timber or mineral rights on public lands. Look at the number of logging operations around the West that have gone out of business in recent years because it's no longer cost-effective. What's the point of cutting timber in remote areas if you can't easily get in or out because you don't have roads?"

"So there's plenty at stake with several different groups having something to gain," said Books.

"Or lose, as the case may be." Hunsaker went into the house and came back with the pitcher of iced tea and refilled their glasses.

Books continued. "What's the legal basis for state and county governments to demand more back-country roads?"

"You're full of good questions tonight; hard ones, too. State and local governments are using an old federal law known as Revised Statute 2477, dating back to 1866. The statute granted public right-of-way across federal land. The problem is that when Congress repealed the law in 1976, existing roads were grand-fathered in. So the question becomes, what constitutes a road?

"Conservation groups believe that these so-called roads are nothing more than dirt tracks, and, in some instances, game trails. Greenbriar and his EEWA cohorts argue that this isn't about highways or transportation at all but a plain-and-simple land grab by Western states. In the end, I suppose the federal courts will have to sort it out."

"What about you, Ned, what do you think?"

"For what it's worth, I tend to agree with the conservation groups on this one. Mind you, I don't claim to have seen all the so-called roads Utah is claiming under RS 2477, but the ones I have seen hardly seem like roads to me. There isn't one I've been on that wouldn't require a substantial four-wheel or off-road vehicle to get you through."

Ned paused, took a large swallow of tea then belched. "You think it's the road issue that got Greenbriar killed?"

"I wish I knew. Unfortunately, it's only one of several possible theories."

◇◇◇

Early the next morning, Books stopped at the Ranch Inn & Café for breakfast. It was a small mom-and-pop motel with an attached restaurant that had been part of the Kanab scene for as long as he could remember. The restaurant was unofficially off-limits to BLM employees, because it catered to the local ranch community and, presumably, to the CFW crowd. He wasn't sure what kind of reception awaited him, but he figured that it might be a good place to hear the local scuttlebutt about Greenbriar's murder.

Rusty and Dixie Steed, who owned the business, had at one time operated a large cattle ranch a few miles outside of town. The Steeds had always treated Books well, even though his father worked for the federal government. He had seen them only once since he left town.

As a kid, Books remembered hearing that the Steed Cattle Company ran upwards of eight hundred head, mostly on BLM land, using federal grazing permits. Over time, the ranch, like many others in the area, became less and less profitable. Eventually, the Steeds purchased the motel and restaurant in town. They gradually reduced the size of their herd, sold off most of the grazing permits as well as some of their land, and became business owners instead of ranchers. Many locals, including the Steeds, blamed excessive federal regulations for the demise not only of the cattle industry but of an entire way of life.

Books took a seat at one end of the counter after a quick scan of customers scattered around the restaurant. He spotted Tommy McClain sitting in a corner booth with a guy he hadn't seen before. The man was younger than Books, with a beer belly that made him look nine months pregnant. Books wondered if it might be the same clown who had threatened David and Darby Greenbriar outside the Stagecoach Bar in the months before the murder.

The years hadn't been kind to McClain. Only a year older than Books, he looked closer to fifty. While still lean, he had thickened noticeably in the face, neck, and upper torso. Books guessed his present weight at something around two-thirty. His wrinkled skin was typical of a hard life spent outdoors laboring in dry, hot summers and windy, cold winters. The scowl on his face only deepened the lines on his forehead.

Books nodded. McClain ignored him. Then, Trees and Fatso gave Books the most hostile stares they could muster. A guy on the stool next to him nodded as he sat down but didn't speak. Rusty interrupted a conversation he was having at the other end of the counter and sauntered over to Books. He smiled and extended a hand.

"Hello, J.D., good to have you back in town, even if you are workin for the feds."

Books ignored the feds comment. "Thanks, Rusty. How have you been? I don't think I've seen you and Dixie since Mom's funeral."

"Think you're right. Oh, for a couple of old geezers, we're gettin' along just fine. About my only complaint these days are these arthritic old knees. Some days they just ache like hell, but that's mostly during the winter months."

"You know the old saying, Rusty. Getting old isn't for sissies."

"Ain't that the truth."

Rusty stayed long enough to drop a menu in front of him, pour his coffee, and take his order. He then shuffled back to the other end of the counter and resumed his conversation. It was loud enough to overhear. No mention of the murder, but plenty of complaints about the price of hay and other commodities.

A few minutes later, Rusty brought him a plate of huevos rancheros and tortillas and refilled the coffee.

"What's the local gossip about the murder, Rusty?"

"Mining for information, are you, J.D.?"

"Yeah, I guess."

"Really haven't heard much of anything. Everybody's being pretty tight-lipped about it. That said, you'd have to be a moron not to have a pretty good idea who the authorities are going to come looking for, don't you think?"

"What makes you say that, Rusty?"

"It's no secret that most people outside of the Greens hated the guy and his organization—no tears being spilled over his demise, that's for sure. But it's still hard for me to swallow the notion that anybody in this town hated the man enough to bushwhack him." Steed glanced up and slid down the counter muttering, "Speaking of morons......"

The strong hand of Tommy McClain gripped Books' right shoulder and squeezed hard. Would Trees prefer to use those beefy hands around his neck? McClain stood on one side with Fatso on the other. Both wore silly-assed grins.

"Well, if it isn't Beavis and Butthead," said Books. "Do you mind removing your hand from my shoulder? I think you forgot the Right Guard this morning. What brings you boys to town anyway—run out of glue to sniff?"

The stupid grins disappeared. "No reason to act hostile, Ranger Books. We just came by to say hello and welcome you back to town. We were also hopin' we might run across that pretty young widow of Greenbriar's so that we can extend our personal condolences—and I do mean personal, right, Chase?" McClain said, slapping Chase on the shoulder. Both men laughed.

Still grinning, McClain continued. "Now if there's anything I can do to help catch this nasty criminal, Ranger Books, you don't hesitate to ask, ya hear?"

"I'll remember that. There is one thing you can do to help me out."

"Yeah, what's that?"

"You can confess to the murder right now and save me the time and trouble of hunting down the lowlife bushwhacker who did this. And if your friend here helped you out, there's plenty of room in the jail for him too."

McClain frowned and headed to the door. Without breaking stride, he said, "Be seein you real soon, Ranger Books."

"Sooner than you think, moron," said Books.

McClain stopped and turned. His friend Chase grabbed him by the arm and pushed him out the door, muttering, "Leave it, Trees. There'll be plenty of time to catch up with him later."

# Chapter Nine

As Books crossed the restaurant parking lot, he heard the unmistakable sound of a cat-call whistle, followed by a distinctly female voice saying, "What's your hurry, cowboy?" Certain that the whistle and suggestive tone weren't directed at him, he continued without turning.

Then he heard the same female voice again, closer this time, "I'm talkin' to you, cowboy." Embarrassed, Books glanced tentatively over his shoulder. It took him a moment to place the attractive woman smiling at him from a few feet away.

"Rebecca Eddins, all grown up." Books returned the smile.

"You had me a little worried, J.D. I was afraid you might have lost your hearing."

"Cutting me a little slack might be nice, don't you think? It's been what, twelve, maybe thirteen years since we last saw each other?"

"Something like that, yeah. You were a senior in high school and the star of the football and basketball teams. I was the skinny little freckled-face girl in the tenth grade who had an enormous crush on you but couldn't get your attention."

"Sorry, Becky. I can be a little slow on the uptake sometimes."

"Forget it—ancient history now anyway."

"Guess so."

She definitely had Books' attention now. No longer a skinny high school tenth grader, standing in front of him now was a beautiful, fully grown, and fully developed young woman. She was tall, five-eight or nine, he guessed, with long black hair and penetrating green eyes that looked at him with bemused curiosity. She was bare-legged, wearing a denim skirt, pink blouse, and sandals. Her squash-blossom necklace was accented by matching turquoise earrings.

Becky Eddins looked fine.

He glanced down at her left hand and didn't see a wedding ring. She noticed the look. "I was married once, but it didn't last. We met in law school and got hitched at the end of our first year."

"Children?"

"One. A beautiful little boy. He's six now and looks every bit a member of the Eddins clan. Speaking of family, how's yours?"

"I'm sure you see more of them than I do. Sis and her family seem to be doing just fine. Maggie always sent pictures of my nephews, Jeff and Chad. I swear they've grown like weeds. We stayed in touch."

"What about your father?"

"Good question. I haven't seen or spoken to him since I got back."

"Ah. Sorry about your mom. I know she was really sick those last few weeks. And I felt bad that I wasn't here for the funeral. I was in Europe at the time. Dad called me in London with the news."

"Your folks came to the funeral, and they extended condolences on your behalf," said Books. "Your dad's a good man. I always liked Neil, although he and dad sure went the rounds."

"That's for sure."

"Has anything changed on that front?"

"Not really. The land management issues always take on a life of their own. You know that. After Clinton and his gang of thugs declared the Grand Staircase a national monument without any local input, the BLM has caught most of the flack. It's a never-ending battle—only the players change. Since your dad retired, he's no longer on the receiving end of the criticism. That privilege now belongs to your new boss, Alexis Runyon."

"And what's the local gossip saying about my return to town?"

"You want it straight?"

"No reason to sugarcoat it."

"Okay. Some locals will give you the benefit of the doubt because you grew up here, but not everybody. Some radical members of the movement don't care that you were raised here. To them, you represent a federal bureaucracy they hate. You're the first BLM law enforcement officer assigned here, and a lot of folks resent it. And it sure doesn't help that your first official act is to plant yourself square in the middle of a murder investigation. The best advice I can give you is to keep your eyes open and watch your back."

"By 'movement,' you mean that group of local ranchers and business people headed by your father, Neil, and your uncle, Boyd—the Citizens for a Free West."

She nodded.

"Well, I asked you not to sugarcoat it."

"Sorry," she said. "I didn't mean it to sound so harsh."

"It's okay, really, it is. What's the local gossip saying about me?"

She stiffened at the question and momentarily looked away. "This is a small town, J.D. People like to talk. The story going around is that you were forced out of the Denver police department because of two fatal shootings. Rumor has it that after the second one, you went home and caught your wife in bed with another guy and almost killed him."

"Except for a couple of details, the local gossip is pretty much on target."

They promised to get together after things calmed down.

◇◇◇

Books drove to the office and began organizing the murder book. He divided a three-ring binder into sections. In Denver, he'd learned the value of recording every thought, note, and report pertinent to the investigation in the book, no exceptions. It helped him stay focused and organized.

As much as he hated to admit it, his penchant for organization was a learned trait driven into him by his father. Bernie was obsessed about organization. It didn't matter whether it was clothes in his closet, which were always neatly arranged, or tools in the garage. Everything for Bernie had its place. Books learned from an early age that if he borrowed a screwdriver from Bernie's workbench, he'd better put it back. It didn't take long for Bernie to notice any misplaced tool. Unpleasant consequences always followed.

From the start several things about this case had Books concerned. He could feel the town hunkering down, waiting for the out-of-town press to leave and for the heat from the ongoing investigation to blow over. He needed to do something that encouraged people with information to step forward and cooperate.

And then there was the homicide itself. He wondered why anybody would risk moving the body miles from the kill site. Hanging a dead man and pinning a note to his shirt was symbolic, designed to frighten and perhaps paralyze not only the Escalante Environmental Wilderness Alliance but other environmental groups as well. As the news of Greenbriar's murder swept across other Western states, it might have a chilling effect on the environmental movement. Maybe that's what the killer intended. On the other hand, the killing might provoke an angry, violent response from environmental activists.

And there was more. How did the killer know where to find Greenbriar? Had he been followed? Had somebody with inside knowledge tipped the killer by providing Greenbriar's hiking itinerary? Books decided to contact Darby and find out who, besides herself, would have known where and when the victim went hiking.

The killer also had to know that the police would have little difficulty locating the spot where the fatal shot was fired. So why leave traceable physical evidence at the murder scene? The murder had an amateurish feel about it that didn't make sense.

It was time to stir the community pot, and Books had an idea what might do it. He also wanted the names of EEWA and

CFW members. Citing privacy concerns, Darby Greenbriar had already refused, and Books expected Neil Eddins would do the same. He placed a call to Sheriff Sutter. After a couple of minutes on hold, the sheriff picked up.

"Morning J.D., what's up?"

"I need your help on a couple of things, Charley."

"Shoot."

"I'd like you to schedule a press conference this afternoon. I'll prepare a written statement, but I'd like you to be there with me."

"Suits me. They've been hanging around my office like vultures circling a dead carcass. Maybe this will get them off my back for a while."

"Maybe, but I wouldn't count on it. I've got a couple of them camped in front of my office, too."

"What are we going to tell them?"

"I'm working on that, but let's agree on what we're not going to tell them. We're not going to reveal any specifics about the crime scenes or any evidence we've collected."

"Okay. It's your show. What else?" asked Sutter.

"Has your department monitored the activities of the EEWA and the CFW?"

"Call tries to keep track of the EEWA. He might even have surveillance photos."

"Good, get them for me. I'd like to see them. What about the CFW? Do you have surveillance photos of them as well?"

Sutter fumbled for an answer. "Well, I'm not exactly sure."

"Find out, Charley, and then sit down with Call and make a list of everybody you know or even think might be a member of either organization."

"I don't see why you need all that—almost seems like an invasion of privacy if you ask me."

"Humor me, Charley. It's important to identify the members of each group. It might lead us to our killer."

"But…"

"Charley, just get me the lists. Okay."

There was a long pause before Sutter spoke. "How soon do you need them?"

"Yesterday. I'll see you at your office a few minutes before the news conference."

"I'll see what I can do." Sutter's line went dead.

Books sensed that Sutter's reluctance to identify members of the rival groups applied only to the CFW. He was certain that Sutter would be more than willing to identify suspected EEWA members. Was Sutter a card-carrying member of the CFW?

◇◇◇

Books spent the next little while pouring over his case notes. There was a lot to do.

Assuming everything checked out, Darby's weekend trip to Las Vegas would provide her with a rock-solid alibi. Books also wanted to find out a little more about Darby's Las Vegas girlfriend, Erin Rogers.

He called an old acquaintance from the homicide unit of the Las Vegas Metropolitan Police Department. Books had assisted Detective Sergeant Grant Weatherby on an old murder case, so Weatherby owed him one. Books asked him to check credit card receipts from the Hard Rock Hotel Casino to corroborate Darby Greenbriar's presence there and run a background check on Erin Rogers. Weatherby promised to get back to him as soon as he had something.

◇◇◇

At one-thirty, Books and Sheriff Sutter met with the assembled media in the Kane County Commission chambers. Sutter hadn't been exaggerating when he complained about the amount of interest the case was receiving from various news sources. There were print, radio, and television representatives from all over Utah as well as from Las Vegas and Denver.

The sheriff made the introductions and explained that the investigation would be a joint operation between his office and the BLM. He then turned to Books, who agreed to answer questions after reading a brief statement:

*"As you know, the BLM, in cooperation with the Kane County Sheriff's Office, is conducting a death investigation involving a local resident, Dr. David Greenbriar. Dr. Greenbriar's body was discovered yesterday morning by a group of tourists visiting the old West movie set at the Paria townsite east of Kanab. While we are awaiting an official report from the Utah state medical examiner's office as to the specific cause of death, we have reason to believe foul play was involved. Therefore, we are treating the case as a homicide. We'll take your questions now."*

Hands popped up all over the room. Books had been involved in these kinds of news conferences many times in Denver, so he wasn't surprised by the questions. The press wanted to know what kind of evidence they had, whether any suspects had been identified, and how close they were to making an arrest. Books answered some questions and declined to answer others.

One reporter caught him off-guard. The moment this guy began asking questions, Books realized someone close to the case had already leaked sensitive information. The reporter knew specifics about the investigation that hadn't been made public: that there were two separate crime scenes; that there was a note pinned to the victim's shirt; even that they found a shell casing and other physical evidence.

The investigation had already been compromised, and Books was angry. Near the end of the news conference, he finally got the question he was hoping for. A female reporter seated near the back of the room asked if they had developed a motive for the murder.

"While we want to emphasize that we are keeping an open mind concerning possible reasons for Dr. Greenbriar's murder, it's no secret that his involvement in the environmental movement as president and chairman of the board of the Escalante Environmental Wilderness Alliance might have provided the motive," said Books. "It is also clear that there are elements in the local community who were hostile toward Dr. Greenbriar and his organization. We urge everyone in our community to put differences aside and help us solve this horrific crime. If anyone has information pertinent to our investigation, please contact either Sheriff Sutter or me."

Books never mentioned the CFW by name, but he didn't have to. Moments after the press conference, a visibly angry Charley Sutter cornered him in the hallway outside the commission chambers. Books had noticed that when Sutter got upset, there was a visible twitch in the cheek on the left side of his face.

"Do you have any idea what you just did in there?" He didn't wait for an answer. "You did everything but accuse members of the CFW of complicity in Greenbriar's murder."

Books listened patiently to Sutter's tirade before firing back. "Somebody in this town knows what happened to David Greenbriar, and they need to come forward. And I would think, Charley, that you ought to be more concerned about finding his killer and less concerned about whether we ruffle some feathers in the process."

Sutter snorted, "Maybe so, but you better understand, you've just set us up for a shit-storm of public criticism."

"I'll try not to lose sleep over it, Charley, and neither should you. By the way, who was the reporter sitting in the front row who asked the pointed questions about our case?"

Now his cheek was twitching like crazy. "That was Lamont Christensen. He's the editor of the local newspaper, the *Kane County Citizen*."

"Somebody's leaked information to him, Charley. Was it you?"

"I sure as hell didn't. He called me at home last evening, but I refused to answer his questions."

"Well, somebody sure as hell did," said Books. "He had to have gotten that information from a source close to the investigation, and that's a damn short list." If not the sheriff, Books wondered about Brian Call.

Sutter was right about one thing. CFW members and their sympathizers wasted little time before placing a deluge of angry phone calls to the BLM, the sheriff's office, the Kanab Town Council, and the Kane County Commission. Books didn't give a damn about the criticism, so long as it resulted in somebody coming forward with new information that would advance the investigation. And it actually didn't take long.

# Chapter Ten

Books spent the rest of the afternoon in his office dealing with voice messages and phone calls from angry citizens and government bureaucrats. A couple of anonymous messages were predictably threatening, but most weren't. Sutter managed to disappear after leaving instructions at the sheriff's office to forward every cranky citizen call to Books. For the most part he listened patiently, allowing callers to vent and hoping for a kernel of helpful information.

Alexis Runyon phoned to express concern over how quickly Books had managed to alienate so many locals in such a short period of time. She reminded him that success on the job meant maintaining good public relations and, that so far his performance was less than satisfactory.

The help Books was seeking came in a late afternoon call from Celia Foxworthy, the EEWA volunteer who had accompanied Darby Greenbriar to the previous day's interview. She seemed reluctant to discuss specifics over the phone, so Books suggested a private face-to-face meeting later in the evening at his office. She agreed.

Soon after the call from Foxworthy, Darby Greenbriar called. She had located receipts from her Vegas trip and also wanted to give Books the name and phone number of her husband's lawyer. There was something else he wanted to ask her about, so he jumped into the Yukon and drove to the EEWA office.

The sullen widow greeted him with a strained half smile. "You look exhausted," said Books. "Get yourself eight hours of uninterrupted sleep."

"You're right. I am exhausted. I'm going to need some sleep meds if this goes on much longer. I heard you rattled some cages at a news conference this afternoon."

"Had your spies over there, did you?"

"You bet. Consider yourself living in a fishbowl for the duration."

That didn't seem unreasonable to Books, considering the untidy mess he'd gotten himself into. They sat opposite each other at a rectangular mahogany table in the conference room.

She handed him a slip of paper with a name and phone number on it. "My husband's lawyer is Victor Stein. That's his Berkeley office number."

Books thanked her. "What were you able to find out about David's estate? Did you locate a will or trust, anything on his life insurance?"

She shook her head. "I couldn't find anything. The more I thought about it though, I think David maintained a safety deposit box in town. He was always paranoid about somebody breaking into our home and snooping into our personal affairs."

"Which bank?"

"Wells Fargo, I think. That's where we bank. Victor would know for sure."

"You mean your name isn't on the safety deposit box."

She hesitated. "I don't think so."

Books couldn't recall a murder case he'd worked where the spouse knew less about the family estate than Darby did. He wondered if she was telling the truth.

"I've been thinking about something," said Books. "Who, besides you, knew that David was hiking in the Kaiparowitz Plateau?"

"The only person I recall telling was Celia, and I think I mentioned it during dinner on Friday night."

"The night before you left for Las Vegas?"

"Right. Of course David could have told any number of people."

That was true.

"If you don't mind, I'd like to ask the office secretary," said Books. "Maybe she shared David's hiking plans with somebody."

"All right. Let me get Cathy before she locks up and goes home."

"While you're up, there's something else."

"What's that?"

"I recall seeing David's day planner in his office. Mind if I borrow it?"

"Sure, if you think it'll help. I'll send Cathy in and go get the planner for you."

Books had spoken with Cathy Carpenter previously but hadn't officially met her. She had been a part of the EEWA from the beginning, first as a volunteer and then as office manager once the organization could afford a full-time, paid employee. Books asked her whether she had shared David's weekend hiking plans with anyone besides Darby.

"As a matter of fact, I did. One of our members, Lance Clayburn, called Friday afternoon looking for David. When I told him David wasn't in, he wanted to know whether David planned to come into the office on Saturday."

"What did you tell him?"

"That David was hiking the Kaiparowitz and wouldn't be back until Sunday evening."

"What did Mr. Clayburn want?"

"He never said. I mean it's not unusual. People call all the time wanting to talk with David—members and nonmembers."

"Okay, anybody else?"

She started to say no and then stopped. "Come to think of it, there was another call. I remember it because I was standing at the front door ready to lock up when the phone rang. I debated about whether or not to answer it."

"Who was it?"

"Don't know. The guy didn't give his name."

"What did he want?"

"He said he was one of David's old colleagues from Berkeley and that he was passing through town and hoped to see him."

"What did you tell him?"

She paused momentarily trying to recall the conversation. "I'm pretty sure I told him David was out of town for the weekend."

"Did he ask where David was?"

She paused again. "Damn. I don't recall that he did, but I'm not sure."

"And you're sure this guy didn't leave a name or a call-back number?"

She shook her head. "No, he didn't. I'm certain of that."

"Did you notice anything unusual or anyone hanging around the EEWA office in the days leading up to the murder?"

"Not that I recall."

Books had one last question.

"In the days before David's death, did you notice anything different about him? Was he behaving differently, acting fearful, anything like that?"

"No, and I think I would have noticed. Other than Darby, I knew David as well as anybody. I didn't see any change in him."

Books thanked her, gave her his business card, and asked her to call if she remembered anything else.

Darby returned and handed the planner to Books. "You'll get this back to me when you're through with it?"

"You bet."

She opened a file folder and looked at him. "I want to ask you something, and I'd like a straight answer."

"Sure thing."

"If I were to give you a copy of the EEWA membership list, would I have your word that it would be for your eyes only—that it wouldn't end up in the hands of the press, the CFW, or anybody else?"

"You have my word on it. I'm curious, though, why the change of heart?"

She hesitated a moment as though carefully composing what she wanted to say. "I don't know whether you can understand this, Ranger Books, but my husband had a dream. His dream was to preserve these wild lands in their natural state for the enjoyment of this and future generations. He understood that to fulfill that dream, he'd have to take on groups like the CFW and the ATV crowd. He was willing to do that, and in the end, it cost him his life. I intend to make sure his death doesn't put an end to his dream. If my turning over our membership list helps you find his killer, then it'll have been worth it."

He thanked her for her cooperation and her trust.

The compliment brought a weak smile. "I'm also being pragmatic. I suspect you could compel us to surrender the list with a court order."

She was right about that. If Books couldn't obtain membership lists from each group voluntarily, he had planned to go to court. At least now he wouldn't have to do that with the EEWA. He intended to use this gesture from Darby to brow-beat Neil Eddins into voluntarily surrendering the CFW membership list.

"Was Cathy able to provide any assistance?"

Books told her about the anonymous caller claiming to be an old university colleague. "That doesn't sound right to me," said Darby. "In all the years we've lived here, David has never had so much as a phone call from any of his old colleagues, much less from one passing through town wanting to stop in for a visit."

Books shrugged. "If you'll give me a list of his closest friends from the university, I'll call and inquire if any of them phoned David."

"I'll do that, but you should also ask David's ex. She would know his former colleagues a lot better than I do."

"What can you tell me about an EEWA member named Lance Clayburn?"

The mention of his name brought a subtle and yet visible reaction to her face—shock or surprise, maybe. "How did Lance's name come up?"

"He was the other person who called Cathy asking about David's weekend schedule. Why? Does that surprise you?"

"No, not really. I can't tell you much about Lance because I don't know him all that well. He joined the EEWA about a year and a half ago. He doesn't miss many meetings. Other members seem to like him quite well."

Books had never heard of him. "Where's he from, do you know?"

"Seems like he mentioned Vermont or Connecticut, somewhere in New England. I'm not really sure."

"What does he do for a living?"

"From what I hear, he isn't employed. He's a trust baby who comes from a family with a boatload of money."

"Did he get along with David?"

"He seems to get along with everybody, including David."

Books told her he'd pay Clayburn a visit, thanked her, and left. When he got back to the office, he found Celia Foxworthy waiting in the reception area. She was a few minutes early. He also found a voice message from Sergeant Grant Weatherby asking that he call as soon as possible. That might mean Weatherby had discovered information about Darby's trip to Las Vegas, although the receipts she had provided seemed to show her presence in Sin City.

# Chapter Eleven

Celia Foxworthy was a transplanted Californian who had moved to southern Utah more than four years before. The roots of her environmental activism began years earlier with the Sierra Club when she'd lived in Lake Tahoe. She was an EEWA volunteer and a neighbor of the Greenbriars. After several minutes of getting-to-know-you small talk, Books brought the conversation around to the investigation.

"Thanks for contacting me, Celia. If we're going to solve David's murder, we need citizen help. So what brings you to see me today?"

"Well, it might be nothing, but I felt someone should tell you."

"Tell me what?"

"During the past year, there's been a lot of internal conflict in the EEWA, a power struggle I guess you'd call it."

This was the second time Books had heard this. "Please go on."

"You may know the EEWA is governed by a board of directors, with David serving as chairman. In recent months, he and another board member, Barry Struthers, have been in a great deal of conflict over the direction of the organization."

"What kind of conflict?"

"Verbal mostly, raised voices, shouting on a couple of occasions during board meetings."

"What were they fighting about?"

"I'm not sure how to say this, but Barry, I think, has grown frustrated over the past year that goals in the organization aren't being as aggressively pursued as he thinks they should be."

Books frowned. "Are you trying to tell me that Struthers advocated using more extreme tactics that might include breaking the law?"

"I wouldn't go that far. Let me put it another way. David was far more patient than Barry. He was tenacious in pursuing EEWA goals, but he was willing to take the long road to get there. Not so with Barry. Barry is an impatient guy who expects results yesterday—different styles, I guess you could say."

"As far as you know, had Struthers ever threatened David?"

"Not that I heard. But at our spring picnic in May, everyone had been drinking. David and Barry exchanged words, and the two had to be separated."

Books looked surprised. Darby hadn't mentioned this. "Did you overhear the exchange?"

"No. By the time I noticed what was going on, David and Barry were tangled in a wrestling match, and other members were separating them. Unfortunately, the incident put a damper on what should have been a pleasant social outing."

"I'll bet. In your opinion, was David in danger of losing control of the organization?"

"I don't think so. It's a seven-person governing board, and Barry had one other member solidly behind him. That still gave David a commanding five-to-two majority in board voting. But things had become so disruptive in recent months that other board members were talking among themselves about whether the organization would be better off if David stepped aside."

"That couldn't have made him very happy. Who was the other board member supporting Struthers?"

"An ex-BLM guy by the name of Richard Hill. Rich retired from the BLM a couple of years ago and immediately joined the EEWA."

Books decided to change direction, and his next question caught Foxworthy off-guard. "How was the marriage between David and his wife?"

She shrugged her shoulders, avoiding eye contact. "Like most marriages, I think they had their ups and downs."

"What kind of ups and downs?"

"I'm not sure that's a question I'm qualified to answer."

"It might turn out to be important."

"Maybe, but it would only be speculation on my part—nothing I know for sure. It makes me feel like a gossip."

"If it makes it any easier, I promise that I'll hold anything you tell me in confidence."

She gave him an exasperated look. "Are you always so persistent?" It sounded like a rhetorical question. He waited.

After an uncomfortable period of silence, she said, "Darby is a beautiful young woman, outgoing, and always flirtatious in an innocent sort of way, I think. And of course, they were years apart in age." She paused, carefully gauging what she wanted to say next. Books had a pretty good idea where this conversation was headed. Personal experience made it painful to hear nonetheless. "Rumor has it that Darby has been having an affair with a fellow EEWA member."

"And who might that be?"

"His name is Lance Clayburn."

Books didn't react. "Anything specific to substantiate the rumor?"

"Nothing very concrete—the way they look at each other and the amount of time they spend together. I have seen Lance's truck at the Greenbriars' house a couple of times when David was out of town."

"You live next door, right?"

"Yes."

"Two questions," said Books. "How long do you think the relationship has been going on, and do you think David knew about it?"

"Seven or eight months, and I doubt that David knew."

"What makes you so sure?"

"Well, I'm not one hundred percent sure, but I just don't think most guys would notice. There's been a glow about Darby these past months—like there's something new and exciting going on in her life. Call it woman's intuition, if you like."

Books' own intuition told him that Celia Foxworthy knew something else she wasn't telling him, but he decided to let it go for now.

Foxworthy confirmed having had dinner with Darby the previous Friday night. The timeline was consistent with everything Darby had told him. Two things piqued his interest. The first, and arguably most significant, was that Darby might be having an affair with the guy Books knew was trying to track the whereabouts of her husband shortly before his murder. That might also explain her unease and evasiveness when he mentioned Clayburn's name. The second was why Darby seemed to have deliberately downplayed the seriousness of the conflict between her husband and Barry Struthers.

# Chapter Twelve

It happened again. It was the third time in the past month that Becky Eddins had returned home late to find the same heavy-breathing, no-voice phone calls on her answering machine. The calls, coupled with an incident a few days earlier, were starting to scare her.

That night, she picked Cody up from her parents, drove home, fed him dinner, and settled him into bed. Her pueblo-style home, which sat on two acres, backed into red rock cliffs that afforded maximum privacy from nosy neighbors. It also provided stunning views from the home's covered rear portico. Until now, Eddins had enjoyed the seclusion and thought nothing about pouring a glass of wine, starting a fire in the outdoor kiva fireplace, and relaxing in the hot tub.

She poured a glass of Rosemount Shiraz, stripped out of her clothes, grabbed a towel, and walked outside for a long soak. She stayed in the hot, swirling water until she felt the stress of the day ebb away.

Her thoughts drifted to J.D. Books. If anything, he looked better now than he did a dozen years before when he moved away from Kanab. He carried what she guessed was two hundred pounds on a six-five frame. He was lean and muscular, not showing any sign of the middle-life paunch carried by a lot of men his age. His only sacrifice to middle age was the flecks of gray showing at the temples of his short-cropped black hair. She felt happy to have him back in town, although she wasn't sure why. Whatever puppy-love feelings she'd had for him in high school were long over. It probably didn't matter anyway. What interest would a man coming out of a bitter marriage have in a divorced woman raising a six-year-old boy?

Eddins climbed out of the hot tub and lay on the beach towel she had spread on the redwood deck. The cool evening breeze gave her goose bumps but felt good against her wet, naked skin. She remained motionless on her back for several minutes allowing the evening breeze to dry her. She ran her hands slowly over her breasts until the nipples stiffened. Her right hand moved lower across her abdomen until her fingers began a slow, rhythmic movement that grew faster and more urgent until she shuddered in a powerful orgasm.

As her breathing returned to normal, she heard it. It was the scratching sound that only a shoe or boot would make as it scraped across sandstone. She sat up and froze, heart pounding. She stared into the darkness for what seemed like an eternity without hearing the sound again. For just an instant, she thought she saw a flash of movement among the juniper and pinon pine near her bedroom by the corner of the house.

Eddins grabbed the towel, ran inside the house and doused the lights. Slipping on a terry cloth robe, she headed straight for the gun cabinet where she selected a Browning pump-action shotgun. At close range, this would do the job regardless of whether the critter was two-legged or four. She had grown up in a family of hunters. Guns were second nature to her.

She loaded the weapon and moved quickly through the darkened house until she reached the back patio. For a minute, she sat perfectly still, allowing her eyes to adjust to the dark. Nothing moved. Everything was quiet. She turned on the outside flood lights. They lit up the back yard and the lower cliffs like a Christmas tree. Whoever or whatever had been out there was gone. She would look for tracks in the morning.

Becky spent the remainder of a restless night in Wes' bedroom, the shotgun within easy reach. Early the next morning, she discovered a partial boot print in the red clay where she thought she'd seen movement the night before.

She hadn't told anyone, not even her parents, about the crank phone calls or the peeping-Tom incident. Until now, she had convinced herself that the calls were the work of some harmless local crackpot or the mischievous pranks of teenagers, either of whom she might have encountered in her law practice. In all likelihood, she thought, the incidents were unrelated. Still, it was time to file a report with the police department. There was little they could do, but at least there would be a record.

For the first time she felt vulnerable living alone with her son, Cody, and Felix, the family cat.

# Chapter Thirteen

When Books got home, the message light on his ancient answering machine was blinking. He had four messages. One was from Neil Eddins. He knew what that one would be about. He also had a pretty good idea what the call from Douglas Case, Chairman of the Kane County Commission and Maggie's father-in-law, would be about.

The third call was from an angry Lamont Christensen, editor of the local newspaper. Christensen left Books a testy message accusing him of trying to suppress the public's right to know by using Draconian methods in dealing with the media. Ironic, since Christensen had a pipeline inside the investigation.

The fourth and the most interesting call came from Lillian Greenbriar, the victim's former spouse. She left her home phone and a cell number and asked him to call her back. Lillian Greenbriar was out of breath when she answered the phone. Books introduced himself and told her he would call back later if the time was inconvenient.

"Not at all. Sorry I'm so out of breath," she said. "I just got back from a run with my dog. She's a middle-aged, overweight lab that my vet told me needs to lose some pounds. To tell you the truth, I'm not sure who's exercising whom anymore. Anyway, thanks for getting back to me so fast."

"No problem. I'm very sorry about David, by the way."

"Thank you. It was a real blow to all of us."

"I'll bet it was. So how can I help you?"

"I called the sheriff's office this afternoon to find out who was in charge of the case. The deputy gave me your name and number. I hope it was okay to call you at home."

"No problem." Books lied. Actually, it was a problem. At Denver P.D., and every other police department he was aware of, providing an officer's home number to a citizen was a big no-no. A little chat with Sheriff Sutter on the subject seemed in order.

"I wanted to find out what's going on in the investigation. Have you arrested anyone? Also, I'm trying to find out about funeral arrangements. Darby hasn't given me the details."

"I doubt it's intentional. She's in a state of shock like you and everyone else. This little community doesn't see many homicides."

"I'm sure that's true."

"As to your first question, I can tell you that it's still early in the investigation. We do have some physical evidence, and we're busy chasing a number of leads."

"What kind of leads?"

"Sorry, but at the moment, I can't get into that."

"I take it then that you haven't identified the killer?"

"That's right."

"Can you tell me anything else?"

"Not much, I'm afraid. But I will say this. I think we're going to solve David's murder, and, I think, sooner than later."

"I'm relieved to hear that. What about funeral arrangements?"

To Books, Lillian Grenbriar sounded stoic over the phone, emotions well in check. "I haven't heard anything. You'll want to speak to Darby about that. Nothing is imminent, I'm sure of that. The medical examiner hasn't released the body yet." Books explained that that would happen in the next day or two once the autopsy was completed.

"I take it you're planning to attend the funeral?" he added.

"I am. As a matter of fact, several of David's old Berkeley colleagues are planning to make the trip. His lawyer plans to attend as well."

"That would be Victor Stein?"

"Yes. Victor and I will travel together."

"Glad to hear it. That'll save me the time of having to fly to Berkeley. I'd like to talk to both of you."

"That shouldn't be difficult to arrange."

"Appreciate it. Can you answer a couple of questions for me now?"

"I'll try."

"Did you and David stay in touch after the divorce?"

"Not right away. I don't know, Mr. Books, whether you've ever experienced marital infidelity. At first, there was such a sense of hurt and betrayal that we communicated only through our respective attorneys. Then the hurt turned to anger. Eventually, those emotions receded. After a while, David and I began to talk, and in the last year or two, we've been in touch every few weeks."

Books knew exactly how she felt, except he hadn't reached the healing part yet. He was still angry. The memory still burned.

He had just been suspended from duty because of his involvement in a fatal shooting. When he arrived home, Carrie's Explorer was nowhere in sight. Instead, an unfamiliar, silver BMW was sitting in the driveway. He parked down the street and walked behind the house, entering quietly through the back door, gun in hand. He heard them before he saw anything—the unmistakable sound of two people making love; the playful giggles, the heavy breathing, the pleasurable moans of a couple in the throes of sexual heat.

Books pushed the bedroom door open with the barrel of his gun. The stranger was lying naked on his back, and Carrie was sitting astride him rocking slowly up and down, moaning with every stroke. Books froze, like a voyeur watching a peep show, until something made Carrie glance over her shoulder. She gasped and rolled off the guy and stood to face him.

Then he lost it. Books pushed Carrie aside and threw a roundhouse left hook that grazed the side of the stranger's head. The guy had jumped off the bed and was standing there with his dick at half-mast. The straight right that followed connected with the middle of his face. Books heard the distinct sound of breaking bone as his fist shattered the stranger's nose. Screaming in pain as blood spurted everywhere, the man fell face down on the bed and grabbed the sheet with both hands in a futile attempt to stop the flow of blood.

The last thing Books recalled was Carrie trying to restrain him from behind. She yelled, "Christ, J.D., stop it. Leave him alone."

Books walked down the hall, out the front door, and out of Carrie's life. They didn't see or speak again except through their lawyers.

"Ranger Books, are you still there?" said Lillian Greenbriar.

"Oh, sorry. Something distracted me for a moment. When was the last time you spoke with David?"

"I thought I'd lost you," she said. "Probably a week, maybe ten days ago."

He asked her the usual questions. Had David expressed any recent fear about his own safety? Had he ever mentioned being threatened by anyone? The answers were no and no.

"How about his marriage to Darby—did he ever discuss that with you?"

"No. The subject of Darby was strictly off-limits in any context. We hadn't reached a comfort level where discussing Darby was tolerable for either of us. It was unspoken, but something, I think, we both intuitively understood."

"What about his work. Did you talk about that?"

"We did. That was safer ground for us. David often wanted to know what was going on in the campus community, particularly when it involved any of his old colleagues. And I would feign interest in his environmental activities."

"Feign interest—an odd choice of words. I take it you weren't a fan of David's environmental activism."

"Not really. David was into protecting the environment and I'm all about rescuing animals, dogs for the most part."

"Both noble causes."

"I think so."

"In your recent conversations with David, did he ever discuss what he was working on?"

"As a matter of fact, he did. David was passionate about a broad range of environmental issues, and I could always count on receiving a blow-by-blow description of whatever he was involved in at any given time."

"So what was he doing?"

She answered without missing a beat. "Road expansion seemed to be the latest issue. At least that's what he talked the most about during the past few months. David had a real burr up his backside on that one."

"Do you know why?"

"Not really. Tell you the truth, David would get me on the phone and prattle on and on about some issue I didn't much care about. It went in one ear and out the other."

"I understand."

"Why are you asking me this, anyway? Do you think it might have something to do with his murder?"

"Not sure. I do know this, though. In a murder case, if you can figure out motive, it's often easier to find a suspect."

Books asked Lillian for the names of David's closest friends in Berkeley. It was a short list. He intended to have Brian Call contact each of them and ask whether they had tried to reach David at the EEWA office a couple of days prior to his murder. Somebody had, and maybe that somebody was the killer.

Lillian Greenbriar promised to contact him if she remembered anything else that might be important. They agreed to meet after the funeral.

# Chapter Fourteen

After talking to Lillian Greenbriar, Books nuked a frozen dinner in the microwave, cracked a bottle of Corona, and began studying the murder book.

He had always been a visual sort of cop. In his former Colorado home, he filled his office walls with flip charts. In his new digs space was at a premium. He had stopped at the local hardware store, purchased some cork board, and mounted it on a small wall in his combined kitche and dining room.

He reviewed everything—crime scene sketches and photographs, police reports, newspaper clippings, and witness statements. It was premature for the lab reports, but he'd add them as soon as they came in. He was searching for any small detail that might have been overlooked. He couldn't find anything. He created four charts for his makeshift office wall, including a list of all the physical evidence recovered from the crime scenes; a list of possible suspects; a prioritized list of investigative leads that still needed follow-up; and finally, a list of completed tasks.

By the time he'd finished, it was after midnight and he had just polished off his third Corona and his second papaya enzyme tablet. He'd been getting it a lot lately—a burning sensation deep in his gut after eating just about any kind of food. Consuming any of his other regular vices, such as booze and coffee, only added to his discomfort.

As fatigue took over, he knew that clear thinking would not be possible until he grabbed some shut-eye. He crawled into bed without so much as brushing his teeth. Since his life had been turned upside nine months earlier, he often went to bed bone tired and then found sleep about as elusive as the Holy Grail.

Books had been in bed about half an hour when he heard something outside his bedroom window. It sounded like someone walking on loose gravel. He reached across the bed to a nightstand, picked up his holstered 357-magnum Smith & Wesson, and quietly removed it from its holster. Unfortunately, the box spring he was sleeping on must have been a relic from the Spanish American War—the slightest movement made the damned thing squeak loud enough to wake up Las Vegas. Books lay still and listened. It was eerily quiet.

The trailer had no outside lighting, but a full moon decorated a cloudless sky. Through the flimsy curtain, he watched a shadow move slowly toward the front door. Someone turned the door knob.

Books jumped out of bed and ran toward the door just as a large rock, about the size of a softball, smashed his front window. Shards of glass scattered everywhere. He got out the door in time to see the taillights of a pickup truck in rapid retreat toward the county road. In the dark, Books couldn't make out the color of the rig, much less the number of occupants. One thing for sure: the engine had the gravelly sound of a big diesel.

The lights inside Ned Hunsaker's home flicked on, and Books saw the old man trotting in his direction carrying a pump action shotgun. "You okay, J.D.? I dialed 911 as soon as I heard the commotion."

"Yeah, I'm fine. Did you happen to get a look at that pickup truck?"

"Not a close one," said Hunsaker, "but good enough to think that it just might belong to one of Tommy McClain's nitwit friends, Derek Lebeau."

"How certain are you?"

"Fairly. Lebeau owns a silver Dodge pickup, a high-rider with big tires, similar to the one that just roared out of here."

"Does Lebeau's have a diesel engine?"

"Not sure, but I think so."

Was McClain along for the ride? Books intended to find out. "Do you know where Lebeau lives?"

Ned frowned. "I hope you're not thinking of going over there right now. That wouldn't be such a good idea."

"Damn straight, I am."

"Well then, count me in. I'm going with you. I don't want you going over there by yourself."

At that moment, a Kanab City police car pulled on to the property with its emergency lights flashing.

Ned glanced over and said, "Son, you might want to go inside and put some pants on."

Books glanced down and felt a bit foolish. He was standing there holding a firearm, wearing only a T-shirt and Jockey shorts. When Books returned, he was carrying a fist sized rock with a note taped to it. He removed the tape and gingerly opened the note with a pair of tweezers to avoid adding his own fingerprints to the paper he hoped might contain the suspects'. The note read: *'Go back where you came from, killer—you ain't wanted here.'* Short and to the point—a clear reference to his recent troubles in Denver.

Ned exchanged greetings with the Kanab cop and then introduced him to Books. His name was Lloyd Wiggins. Wiggins was a barrel-chested man in his mid- to late forties who seemed unconcerned, almost amused by the incident.

"Probably just teenagers," he said. "A lot of them take their cues from Mom and Dad —hate the feds. You know how it is."

"I'm learning real fast," said Books.

"Sorry I can't take a report for ya," said Wiggins, "out of my jurisdiction, ya know."

Books glanced at Ned, wondering why Officer Wiggins had bothered to show up at all. Ned explained. "I live right on the edge of the town limits, J.D., but just outside. It's actually the sheriff's jurisdiction by a few hundred yards."

Despite Ned's explanation, Books continued. "I'm curious about something, Lloyd. How come you responded?"

"It's close to the town limit, and I thought Ned might be in some kind of trouble—didn't realize you lived out here, though. Besides, you might not see a sheriff's deputy for quite awhile. There's only one on duty during the graveyard shift, and he could be eighty miles from here. You just never know."

The implication was clear. Wiggins came out of concern for Ned's well-being, not his. Although Wiggins didn't come right out and say it, Books was left with the distinct impression that Officer Wiggins wouldn't have come to his aid.

"Did you get a look at who did it?" asked Wiggins.

"Never saw a thing. All I heard was the sound of shattering glass and a vehicle making a hasty exit."

"Too bad," muttered Wiggins. "Like I said, it's probably just teenage pranksters out havin a little fun." With that, he climbed back into his cruiser and drove away.

Books glanced at Ned and shook his head. "Now there's a piece of police work straight from the pages of Mayberry and Deputy Barney Fife."

Ned chuckled, "Congratulations, J.D. You just met one of Kanab P.D.'s finest. As you can tell, they're here to serve and protect."

Books shook his head and walked back to the doublewide.

He got into his uniform while Ned swept up the broken glass and rigged a piece of cardboard to plug the hole where the front window had been. A record check on Derek Lebeau revealed several prior arrests, all misdemeanors. Most involved alcohol—drunk and disorderly, DUI, domestic violence, and an assault beef resulting from a bar fight. Books also discovered an outstanding $250.00 arrest warrant from Salt Lake County on a traffic ticket Lebeau had failed to pay.

On the drive to Lebeau's home, Hunsaker broke a long silence. "I know you're busy as a bird dog right now, but I heard something in town this afternoon that you might want to know."

Books arched an eyebrow. "And that would be?"

"When I went into the county building this afternoon to renew my truck plates, I ran into Beulah Wood."

"Who's Beulah Wood?"

"One of the sheriff's dispatchers."

"And?"

"She told me that Becky Eddins filed a police report this morning claiming somebody may be stalking her. It seems she had an unwanted visitor of the two-legged variety at her house last night."

"A prowler?"

"Prowler, a peeping Tom, I'm not sure which."

"What happened?"

"Don't know for sure."

"Boy, that's not good," said Books, "considering she lives alone with her son. I wonder if she got a look at the guy."

"Don't know that either. I hear she's been getting some strange phone calls lately—heavy breathers, no voice, that sort of thing."

"Maybe she ought to consider moving home for a while."

"I guess Neil wants her to, but she won't have any part of it. Stubborn gal, that one."

"I'll drop by and see her as soon as I can. In the meantime, I'll try to keep an eye on her home."

"I'll do the same," added Ned.

Lebeau lived in a mobile home several miles east of Kanab off Highway 89. The lights were still on when Books and Ned arrived. A 2004 Dodge pickup truck registered to him was parked next to the house. The truck was jacked up so high that Yao Ming couldn't have gotten into it without a stepladder. The truck also had a diesel engine.

"Does this look like the rig you saw running from my place?"

Hunsaker nodded. "Sure does. Tall one, isn't it?"

"Wait here while I pay our friend a visit." Ned looked like he was about to argue but changed his mind.

Books ran his hand over the hood of the truck on his way to the porch. The engine was still warm. He climbed two makeshift steps to a rickety front porch and rapped on the front door.

"Who's there?"

"Mr. Lebeau, it's the police. Open up."

Books heard the door unlock and then it opened a crack. Obviously intoxicated, Lebeau stood on the other side of the screen door wearing a white muscle shirt and a pair of blue jeans. He was holding an open can of Budweiser. He hadn't shaved in several days and reeked of BO and alcohol.

"Who are you, and what the hell do ya want?" slurred Lebeau.

"Answers to a few questions. I'm investigating a vandalism complaint that happened at my home a while ago. Your pickup was observed leaving the scene not more than an hour ago. What can you tell me about that?"

"Bullshit. That truck's been parked right here since I got home about six o'clock this evening. You're that new fuckin ranger, aren't ya?"

Books ignored the question. "That's odd because the engine is still warm. Somebody drove it, and recently, too. You didn't happen to lend it to someone, did you?"

"You callin me a liar," he said, stepping out on the small front porch.

"Yup, as a matter of fact, I am."

Lebeau caught Books off guard. He lunged at him and threw a wild left hook. Books tried to duck, but the blow caught the top of his forehead just below the hairline. He was thrown off balance and started to bleed where Lebeau's ring hit him. Books swung his oversized mag flashlight and caught Lebeau flush on the shin bone of his left leg just below the knee. The man cursed and began hopping up and down on his good leg. Books swung the flashlight again and connected with the shin bone on the other leg. Lebeau howled in pain but managed to get off a wild punch that struck Books high on the left shoulder.

Books feinted to his left, came up under Lebeau, and struck him under the chin with the grip end of the flashlight. Lebeau staggered and his knees started to buckle. He cursed some more. Books tackled him and they went down in a tangled mass of arms and legs. Despite the pain, Lebeau still had fight left in him.

Ned jumped into the fray and pulled Lebeau away. Together, the men managed to get Lebeau's hands behind his back and slap him in handcuffs.

Books spent the next two hours getting medical treatment for Lebeau at the community hospital in Kanab and then booked him into the Kane County Jail. By the time Lebeau sobered up and the pain subsided, he'd realize that he was neck deep in cow dung. Besides the outstanding arrest warrant, he would also be charged with assault on a police officer, resisting arrest, and vandalism, assuming Books could pull the case together.

Books made it home at four in the morning, slept for three hours, and was back in his office by eight.

# Chapter Fifteen

Chief Deputy Brian Call sat across from Books' desk in an old beat-up leather recliner that another BLM employee had donated to him. Call looked decidedly uncomfortable. Maybe it had something to do with the fact that they hadn't had time to develop trust in one other and in their new alliance.

Books arranged to meet early so Call would still have time to make the seventy-five mile drive to St. George to attend David Greenbriar's autopsy later in the morning.

"Heard you had a run-in with Derek Lebeau last night," said Call.

"News sure travels fast in a small town—not exactly used to it, either."

"It ain't like the big city, that's for sure."

Call reached across the desk and handed Books a file. "You asked for a list of possible EEWA members. This is what I came up with."

Books scanned the list. He didn't bother to tell Call that Darby Greenbriar had provided an official EEWA membership list the day before. Now he would have the opportunity to compare the official list with the one Call had produced. There were about twenty names on Call's list. Some were familiar, many weren't.

"Has the sheriff had a chance to see these names?"

"Yeah, I gave them to him yesterday and asked if he could think of anybody else who ought to be on it. He came up with a couple of additional people I wouldn't have thought of."

"What was the source of your information?"

Call frowned. "What do you mean?"

"Who gave you these names?"

"Oh, sorry, didn't follow you there for a minute," said Call. "The department maintains an intelligence file on the EEWA."

"That's good. I assume you have a similar one for the CFW."

Call drew back. "I don't know. You'll have to talk with Sheriff Sutter about that."

"So you don't have the CFW list?"

"Uh, no, I don't. Sheriff Sutter wanted to put that list together himself."

"Okay, I'll talk to Charley about it when he gets in."

Call nodded.

"Let's start with ballistics. We should have one shell casing and a recovered slug from the murder scene undergoing ballistics testing. Is that right?"

"That's right. I asked them to check the shell casing for prints before it went to ballistics."

"Good thinking. Glad you remembered to do that."

Books continued down the list of evidence. "I'm showing that we've got two empty beer cans, Guinness, one plastic baggie, and the note that was pinned to Greenbriar's shirt, all being run for latents."

"That's right. What do you want me to do with the soil samples we took from the crime scenes?"

"Nothing for now. Just hang on to them. If we need to have them analyzed later, we can."

"Okay. While I'm in St. George today, I'll drop by the lab and press the techs for test results."

"It may be too soon, but tell 'em we needed those lab results yesterday."

◇◇◇

Books sat at his desk thinking about the investigation and about Brian Call. Maybe he'd underestimated the guy. So far he was pulling his own weight, showing himself to be a guy with a solid grasp of investigative procedures and a good head for details.

Books had sensed that getting a list of EEWA members from the locals would be a damned sight easier than getting one on the CFW. Charley Sutter had taken it upon himself to put the CFW list together, and Call seemed more than happy to put distance between himself and the sheriff on that issue. How long would the sheriff stonewall him before he produced something?

The phone rang. It was Grant Weatherby from Las Vegas P.D. "Good morning, Ranger Books. I'm having a difficult time getting hold of your new handle."

"You're not the only one, Grant. How are things in Sin City?"

"Same shit, different day. Things move so damn fast in this town that it's impossible to stay ahead of the curve."

"It's that kind of town all right. What did you find out for me?"

"Several things. For starters, Darby Greenbriar was a guest at the Hard Rock for two nights, Saturday and Sunday. She registered as a single. Her bill shows several room charges, phone calls mostly, a gift shop purchase, and several meals."

"That jibes with what she told us. Got a list of the phone numbers she called?"

"Sure do, all right here in front of me. She called Erin Rogers twice, once on Saturday night and again early Sunday afternoon."

"That's what she told me, too. Claimed she never got hold of Rogers."

"That's true. She left messages both times. Rogers confirmed that. I spoke with her late yesterday afternoon. She just got back from LA, where she'd spent the weekend with her boyfriend. When she returned, there were two messages from Greenbriar, hoping they could get together while she was in town."

"Okay, anything else?"

"Yeah, one thing, and I think you'll find it interesting."

"Hmm, and that would be….."

"Mrs. Greenbriar had a male guest for dinner Saturday night in her room, an intimate dinner for two, or so I was told by the room service staff. Probably a sleepover, I'm thinking. What do you make of that?"

"The loyal wife—husband goes hiking while the Mrs. goes trolling in Vegas—very interesting. You didn't happen to come up with a name for me, did you?"

"Sorry, hoping you might be able to fill in the blanks on that one."

"Afraid not, at least not at the moment."

"It appears that no expense was spared on the dinner—champagne, caviar, all rather pricey, and probably not something you'd do for your Uncle Burt. The whole thing was charged to Darby's hotel bill."

"So I take it we have no idea who her knight in shining armor is?"

"I'm working on it. I spoke to the room service attendant who delivered the fancy dinner."

"And."

"The attendant said Casanova answered the door in one of the hotel's fluffy bathrobes. His hair was wet, like he'd just gotten out of the shower. The attendant said he was a Caucasian male, early thirties, slim build, medium height, with short, sandy blond hair. Casino security is checking their tapes to see if the room service staff can identify the guy. I'll have to get back with you on that one."

"Not quite as good as a name, but close."

"My sentiments, exactly."

"And your take on Darby's friend, Erin Rogers?"

"A real classy dame, I can tell you that. And a damn fine-looking one too—registered a solid nine on the Weatherby ten-point peter meter. She's thirty-one, a Las Vegas native, and a show girl at the Venetian."

"I had her working for the Mirage."

"Used to, but she moved to the Venetian about two months ago—not unusual for Vegas show girls. They tend to be quite mobile."

"Any priors?"

"Nothing recent except a couple of traffic tickets. She got popped about seven years ago for possession of cocaine. The charge was reduced to misdemeanor possession. She served a year on probation and paid a fine."

Weatherby promised that he'd dig a little deeper into Erin Rogers' background and get back with Books if he learned anything new.

# Chapter Sixteen

Alexis Runyon walked in and closed the door. She didn't look happy.

"Morning, Alexis. What's up?"

She gave him a curt nod. "When I walked into the office this morning I found three urgent messages, one from Doug Case, another from Lamont Christensen, and the third from Thomas Boggs. I got the general drift of their concerns, but I thought I'd better hear your side before I call them back."

He knew who Doug Case and Lamont Christensen were, but he'd never heard of Thomas Boggs. "I assume this is more whining about the press conference. Charley wasn't too happy about it either. Who's this Thomas Boggs, anyway—afraid I don't know him?"

"He's a local attorney hired to represent the guy you assaulted last night, Derek Lebeau."

"Whoa, time out. You mean 'allegedly' assaulted, don't you? Actually, he's the guy who was injured last night while resisting a lawful arrest. There was a warrant for him out of Salt Lake County."

She looked somewhat relieved. "Tell me about it. Who is Derek Lebeau and how did you manage to get tangled up with him?"

Books spent the next few minutes walking Runyon through the events of the previous night. When he finished, she still didn't look pleased.

"It sounds like we're on solid ground so far as the treatment of Lebeau is concerned," said Runyon, "but now you've given me something else to worry about."

"And what would that be?"

"This is the first time we've ever had a BLM employee attacked in his own home. That kind of thing has happened in Arizona, Nevada, and some places in California, but never here. It's a disturbing trend."

"Let's not get carried away. First off, it's not a trend. It's one isolated incident that may have a lot to do with Greenbriar's murder and my involvement in the investigation. This is what happens when you stir the pot. Creeps like Derek Lebeau start coming out from under rocks."

"That's my other concern. You seem to be a lightening rod for these kinds of incidents. I'm sure you've heard the old saying that perception is reality."

Books nodded.

"This is a small town, J.D. You arrived with plenty of baggage to begin with, and this latest incident only reinforces that perception among locals. Keep that in mind as you go about your business."

◇◇◇

After the exchange with Runyon, Books felt he'd be wise to get on the phone with Neil Eddins and Doug Case to see if he could smooth things over. However, at the moment he had bigger fish to fry.

Books hopped in the Yukon and headed north on Highway 89. Lance Clayburn owned a home in Angel Canyon. His name had come up several times in the investigation. It was time to see what he had to say.

Clayburn owned a large, single-level home that, at first glance, looked like the typical imitation adobe commonly used in the Southwest. Upon closer inspection, Books concluded that the uneven texture was adobe rather than stucco. Building it had to have cost a fortune. The house stood on several acres with unobstructed views of the Grand Staircase to the east. Books could see solar panels on the roof. A Toyota Prius was parked in a circular gravel driveway next to a ratty old Chevy pickup. It was just the kind of home a wealthy trust baby might own.

He parked the Yukon behind the Prius and got out. One bay of the detached double car garage had the door up, and Books could hear the buzz of a power saw cutting lumber. Moments later, a guy in jeans and a black muscle shirt wearing safety goggles appeared. He wiped his sweaty face with the end of his muscle shirt. He gave Books the once-over, and extended a hand.

"Lance Clayburn. And you are?"

Books introduced himself and explained the reason for his visit. Clayburn nodded as if he'd been expecting somebody else. He invited Books inside, leading the way through a long tiled entryway and into the home's great room. Expensive oriental area rugs provided a pleasant contrast against dark brown Saltillo tile. Books sat in a fine-grain leather chair while Clayburn washed his hands in the kitchen sink.

Grant Weatherby's physical description of the unknown subject who'd had dinner and breakfast with Darby Greenbriar at the Hard Rock was a dead ringer for Clayburn.

"Can I offer you something to drink, Ranger Books?"

"What have you got?"

"About anything you want—ice tea, soda, water or beer."

"In this heat, a beer sounds awful good."

He smiled. "Good choice." He disappeared into the kitchen and returned moments later with two cans of Guinness. He handed one to Books and took a seat on a leather sofa directly opposite.

"Now," he said, "about those questions."

They exchanged polite niceties over the tragic murder of David Greenbriar. Clayburn's demeanor suggested genuine sorrow over the death. Books asked Clayburn where he was from and how long he had lived in the Kanab area.

"I'm originally from New Hampshire; at least that's where my family is from. I discovered Southern Utah ten years ago, when some of my Princeton University frat brothers and I came out to Moab during spring break for some mountain biking. I fell in love with the place. After I graduated, I moved to Moab, but it was a bit touristy for my taste. I settled permanently in Kanab."

It was true that much of southern Utah was undergoing a transformation with tourism driving the economic engine.

"And your family in New Hampshire, are they pleased you've settled here?"

He grunted. "Hardly. Look Ranger Books...."

Books interrupted. "Why don't you call me, J.D, most people do."

"Okay, J.D. As I was saying, I come from a long line of blue-blood Clayburns from New England. My family made its fortune in the financial services industry, and they've got more money than God. My father, Reginald Clayburn, is so conservative that he makes Rush Limbaugh look like a flaming liberal. He hates my lifestyle and what it represents."

Books shrugged. "Well, the money can't be all bad."

"Damn straight, it's not. It gives me a luxury most people don't have."

"And that would be....?"

"Time and freedom, J.D.—freedom to dedicate myself to the kinds of political and social issues that are important to me, and the time to engage those passions fully."

"That would explain your environmental activism and your involvement with the EEWA."

"Right."

Books shifted gears. "The EEWA office told me you called Friday afternoon inquiring about the whereabouts of David Greenbriar. Is that true?"

"It is. I chair a committee for the EEWA that's in charge of fundraising activity. I was trying to reach David to schedule a meeting with him."

"A meeting concerning fundraising activities?"

"Exactly. There's some grant money coming available in the next few months that I thought we should discuss."

"And are you also the organization's grant writer?"

"No, I'm not," said Clayburn. "I could, but it's not necessary. We are fortunate to have a member who once managed a nonprofit, and she's a good grant writer."

"Please don't be offended at my next question, but I'll need you to account for your time this past weekend."

"Not a problem. I was home most of Friday working around the house. On Saturday morning, I got up early and drove to Vegas to do some shopping. Don't get me wrong, I love Kanab but if you're in the market for some new clothes, this isn't the place."

"You're right about that. Anybody go with you?"

"No, I went by myself."

"Did you happen to see anybody in Las Vegas you knew—somebody who could verify your presence?" Someone like Darby Greenbriar?

Clayburn waited, maintaining eye contact and trying to figure out whether Books knew something he wasn't saying. "You got me. Afraid I don't have an alibi. Are you going to arrest me?"

Books smiled. "Not today, I'm afraid. How about receipts for items you purchased? You must have some of those lying around."

"Now those I've got." He got up and walked over to a large rectangular dining room table, where he rummaged through a stack of mail and assorted papers. He returned with several receipts.

Books thanked him. "Can I hang onto these for a while?"

"Sure. Keep them. I won't need them back."

"So what did you do the rest of the weekend?"

"I drove back to Kanab late Saturday night—got in just before midnight. I slept in on Sunday and then grabbed a late lunch at Escobar's. I picked up a few groceries at the Jubilee and then came home. I was here until late Monday morning, when I went into town to run some errands. That's when I heard about David."

"What time did you have lunch at Escobar's?"

"Around two o'clock or thereabouts."

"Were you alone from the time you arrived home Saturday night until you came into town Monday afternoon?"

"Afraid so. Wish I had somebody who could verify that for you."

"Oh, I wouldn't worry about it too much. I think we can work around it."

"Hope so."

"Any ideas about who might have killed David?"

Clayburn shook his head. "Sorry, I wish I did. David was a polarizing kind of figure. People either liked him or they didn't. At times his style came across as abrasive, even to people in the movement."

"What do you mean?"

"I think it was just his personality. David knew what he wanted to accomplish, and he didn't always listen attentively to others, particularly if their views were contrary to his own. I don't think he intended to, but sometimes he projected an attitude that said 'I'm a hell of a lot smarter than you'll ever be.' And some people resented him for it."

Books listened without interruption until Clayburn finished. "You know, Lance, you seem to be making a pretty good case that David might have been killed by somebody inside the environmental movement."

"As opposed to…"

"As opposed to some angry rancher who hates environmental groups like the EEWA."

"That's not what I meant. David could just be hard to get along with. I didn't mean to imply that one of our own would've killed him. I don't believe that."

Books had one last question. "Which issue or issues was the EEWA focused on at the time of David's murder?"

Clayburn had to think about that for a moment. "I'd have to say grazing. That's the one issue that never seems to go away. That's because we live in the West where cattle grazing is king. The local welfare ranchers with their federal grazing permits cause many of the problems. Their filthy cattle erode the soil, destroy plant life, and pollute the water. The miserable critters piss and shit everywhere."

Clayburn sounded downright angry, thought Books. "Anything else?"

Clayburn sighed. "Yeah, roads, I guess would be the other issue. The local crackpots are trying to claim that every game trail or cow path is a navigable road that belongs to the state of Utah. It's just another attempt to open the back country to more kinds of economic exploitation. Anything to make a buck, you know, and to hell with the land and the creatures that live on it."

Books liked Lance Clayburn. He seemed genuine, dedicated to the things he believed in. He struck Books as a guy who was willing to walk the walk. On the other hand, Books felt certain that Clayburn was lying about not seeing Darby Greenbriar in Las Vegas. And then there was the matter of the Guinness beer. Two empty Guinness beer cans had been found at the kill site. Would the prints from those cans match the prints Books planned to have lifted from the beer can he just took from Lance Clayburn's home?

# Chapter Seventeen

Back in the Yukon, Books placed the empty can of Guinness into an evidence bag and tagged it. He glanced at his watch and then tried to raise Brian Call on the radio and then on his cell phone. Call answered his cell.

"This is Call."

"Brian, it's J.D. Are you still in St. George?"

"That's affirmative—just getting ready to head back." The call was breaking up.

"What did you find out from the crime lab?"

"We got some good news. The fingerprint technician reported finding a comparable thumb print on the plastic sandwich baggie and prints galore on the two beer cans. Nothing on the shell casing or the note, though. They ran the prints locally and through the state system—no hits."

"What about the FBI?"

"They submitted them to the Integrated Automated Fingerprint Identification System earlier this morning and haven't received a response."

Books told Call about his interview with Lance Clayburn and about the Guinness beer can from Clayburn's home. "I'll meet you part way between Kanab and St. George. I'd like you to take the beer can back to the lab and see if Clayburn's prints are on it. If they are, let's see if we got a match with the prints on the sandwich baggie and the beer cans recovered from the crime scene."

"How did you manage to get an empty beer can out of Clayburn's house?"

"The old fashioned way. I told him I was thirsty. He offered me a choice of beverages. I chose beer, and he handed me a can of Guinness. Simple."

"You sneaky bastard." Call was obviously pleased.

"It seemed like the right thing to do at the time. Hear anything from ballistics?"

"Not yet. The slug they removed from Greenbriar's Suburban was pretty badly damaged. The rifling grooves may not be comparable even if we do come up with the murder weapon."

"We've got a shell casing. At least that gives us the manufacturer of the ammo and the caliber of the bullet."

◇◇◇

Books returned to his office. He placed a call to the sheriff. Sutter's secretary told him the sheriff was out. Books asked her to raise him on the radio and have him stop by.

His secretary handed him telephone messages from Doug Case and Neil Eddins, as well as an envelope addressed to him. The flower-covered envelope had the distinct smell of lavender. He opened it and found a note from Rebecca Eddins inviting him to a barbeque in his honor at the home of her parents on Wednesday evening. She indicated that his sister and brother-in-law, as well as his father, had accepted invitations. That stopped him cold. Since his return he'd managed to avoid having any contact with his father. Becky wrote her home phone number and asked him to RSVP.

Ordinarily, Books would never have attended a social event like this one while in the throes of a murder investigation. In this case, he decided to make an exception. Dinner at the home of the leader of the CFW might prove interesting. Perhaps David Greenbriar's killer would be there.

His phone rang. It was Grant Weatherby. "Afternoon, Grant. What's up?"

"Hey, J.D. I just got a call from a contact who works in security for the Hard Rock Resort and Casino. The security tapes reveal that Darby Greenbriar's mystery guest spent about three hours prior to dinner on Saturday afternoon at the black jack and craps tables. I guess he dropped some serious cash, too."

"Huh. Did they happen to show the security tape to the room service staff?"

"Sure did," said Weatherby. "The waiter made a positive identification. He says it's the same guy who answered the door to Darby's suite when he delivered dinner. Do you want the tape?"

"Maybe, but just have them hold on to it for now. I'll let you know."

Books left a message for Becky Eddins accepting her invitation to the barbeque. Reluctantly he returned phone calls to Neil Eddins and Doug Case. Both men objected to the tenor of the previous day's press conference, but for different reasons.

Eddins complained vehemently that Books left the media with the impression that David Greenbriar's killer, in all likelihood, would turn out to be a local, someone with a strong anti-environment point of view. Eddins didn't mention the CFW by name, but he didn't have to. However, he ended the call on a conciliatory note. He welcomed J.D. back to Kanab and wished him well in his newfound career. He made it clear that he was looking forward to continuing their discussion at Wednesday night's barbeque.

Doug Case took a different but still critical approach. As Chairman of the Kane County Commission, Case was concerned that the press conference had created the false impression that there was a conspiracy in the community to hide the identity of the killer until the case became old news and simply disappeared off the media's radar screen.

While Books didn't disagree with either man, he tried harder to mollify Doug Case, because Case was his sister Maggie's father-in-law. Mostly he kept his mouth shut, assumed an apologetic tone, and allowed them to vent. The press conference had accomplished what he intended. His comments had stirred the community pot and provided new information that helped advance the investigation.

While he waited for word from Brian Call in St. George, Books ran criminal history checks on Lance Clayburn and Barry Struthers. Neither man had a record, not in Utah and not nationally. From his conversation with Clayburn, Books doubted that he had served in the military. That would make a latent print match from IAFIS impossible. If Clayburn was mixed up in Greenbriar's murder, the best bet for linking him to the murder was a print match from the beer can taken from his home.

Books knew even less about Barry Struthers. While his criminal record was clean, the physical skirmish he'd had with Greenbriar and the generally testy nature of their relationship had piqued Books' interest. He wanted to get better acquainted with Struthers, and the best way to do that would be a face-to-face sit-down.

He was about to dial Struthers' home phone number when Charley Sutter waltzed into his office as if he didn't have a care in the world.

"Afternoon, Charley. You look like a happy man. What's the occasion?"

"A discussion I just had with Chief Deputy Call." Sutter sounded downright pleased with himself.

"Don't keep me in suspense. What'd he have to say?"

"He called from the crime lab in St. George. They just matched the latent prints off the beer can you took out of Clayburn's house to the sandwich baggie and empty beer cans found at the murder scene."

Books leaned back in his chair as Sutter paced back-and-forth. "That is good news, Charley."

"Damned straight it is. The spoiled-ass rich boy is about to take a fall on a murder beef. Isn't it ironic that Greenbriar's killer turns out to be somebody inside his own organization?"

"Let's not get ahead of ourselves," cautioned Books.

"What do you mean?"

"Just what I said. The print match is a nice start, but we've still got plenty of work to do. I've seen homicide cases taken to trial with this kind of evidence, but I've never met a prosecutor yet who didn't want a lot more."

"So what is it you think we should do now?"

"For starters, I'd like to talk with Clayburn again—give him the opportunity to explain how those beer cans with his prints on them ended up at the murder scene. I also think he lied about his trip to Las Vegas last weekend."

"You think he hooked up with Darby Greenbriar?"

"Yup."

"Seems to me that might be a pretty strong motive for murder," said Sutter.

"Could be. I want to get a search warrant for Clayburn's home. We've got more than enough probable cause for me to go to work on the affidavit."

"Anything I can do?"

Brian Call poked his head through the office door. "Okay if I come in?"

Before Books could answer, Sutter said, "Absolutely. Get your sorry ass in here, Brian." The sheriff slapped his chief deputy on the back. Sutter was acting giddy. What a relief for him if Lance Clayburn turned out to be the killer. And to have the whole thing wrapped up in a couple of days couldn't have turned out any better.

Books was about to place a damper on his giddy celebration.

# Chapter Eighteen

When Sutter and Call had finished their self-congratulations, Books invited them to sit. "We've got a lot of work left to do, so let's get to it. Charley, you asked if there was anything you could do, and, as a matter of fact, there is."

Sutter looked slightly less giddy now.

"Clayburn told me that he ate lunch around two o'clock at Escobar's Sunday afternoon. Would you drop over there and find out if anybody remembers seeing him."

"Sure, but I don't see the point."

"I'm trying to establish a timeline for Clayburn's whereabouts the weekend leading up to the murder. We know he called the EEWA office Friday evening trying to locate our vic. We can place him in Las Vegas on Saturday by his own admission as well as through receipts and witnesses...."

"Including Darby Greenbriar, right?" said Sutter.

"Possibly, yes. More likely, though, from surveillance tape shot of him at the gaming tables in the Hard Rock Saturday afternoon. A waiter from the casino's room service staff also saw him in Darby's hotel suite that evening."

"We need to interview Darby again," said Call, "see if she's ready to fess up to having an affair with Clayburn."

"I'll do that," said Books. "In the meantime, Brian, I'm going to give you a list of David Greenbriar's colleagues from Berkeley. I'd like you to call them and find out if anybody called the EEWA office Friday afternoon trying to locate David. The secretary remembers a call from someone who identified himself as an old colleague of David's. The caller said he was coming through Kanab and wanted to stop and see him. Maybe that caller was our killer."

"Afraid I don't get it," said Sutter. "That call was made by Lance Clayburn. We already know that."

"Clayburn did call Friday afternoon," said Books, "but the secretary says this was a different call, and whoever made it didn't want to leave a name or a phone number."

"And she's sure it wasn't Clayburn," said Sutter.

"She insisted it was somebody else—a different voice."

"All right, I'll check it out. You got the list?" Books rummaged through the case file until he found the names Lillian Greenbriar had provided. He passed them to Call.

"You want to hear about the autopsy?"

"No need, not unless the ME came up with some unusual finding that might alter the direction of our investigation."

"Nothin' we didn't expect. The ME said he'd dictate the report right away. We should have a copy in the next day or two."

Books hesitated. "On second thought, I would be interested in what the ME had to say about the time of death."

Call removed a small spiral notebook from his shirt pocket and began turning pages. "The ME estimated the time of death between noon and eight P.M. Sunday."

"Sounds about right," said Books.

As the meeting adjourned, Books asked Sheriff Sutter to stick around.

"Charley, I want to be sure you and I are on the same page going forward."

Sutter nodded but didn't say anything.

"Short of a confession from Clayburn, I intend to continue looking at other possible suspects until we can eliminate them."

"I don't see why that's necessary. We've got our man; I'm certain of it."

"You might be right, but I've been at this long enough to know that it's a big mistake to focus exclusively on one suspect to the exclusion of others who may also have had motive. And even if it is Clayburn, we need to find out whether he was acting alone or in concert with somebody else."

"Like Darby Greenbriar?"

"Possibly."

"Anybody else?"

"At the moment, the short list includes Barry Struthers and Tommy McClain, and, as noted, Darby Greenbriar. That reminds me. I need your list of CFW members. Call already gave me the list of EEWA members that you and he put together."

"Again, I don't see the point. You don't have anything tying members of the CFW to the murder."

"Not directly, but one of our remaining suspects threatened the Greenbriars shortly before the murder, and he'd be a CFW member."

"You mean Trees McClain."

"Tommy and one of his yet-to-be-identified cohorts."

Sutter frowned, got up from his chair, walked to the window, and looked out over the BLM parking lot. He turned back to Books and dropped a folded sheet of paper on his desk.

"There you go—knock yourself out. But don't forget who's in charge of this investigation. I intend to keep you on a short leash."

# Chapter Nineteen

Books leaned back in his chair and reviewed the list of likely CFW members. It included some predictable names, some he didn't recognize, and a few that surprised him, such as Rusty Steed. Groups like the CFW had sprung up all around the West in response to real or perceived threats from environmental organizations. While Books knew little about the origin of the CFW, he guessed that it was mostly comprised of like-minded locals, intent on lobbying for state and county control of public lands.

Books intended to pressure Neil Eddins into surrendering an official CFW membership list much the way Darby Greenbriar had. He wasn't holding his breath that Eddins would choose to cooperate, however. In the meantime he added the list to a growing murder book.

He wanted to roust Barry Struthers and Trees McClain, but that would have to wait. Instead he needed to schedule another round of interviews with Darby Greenbriar and Lance Clayburn to find out the exact nature of their relationship. Both had lied to him during their first interviews.

His plan called for Sheriff Sutter and Deputy Call to execute the search warrant at Clayburn's home while he questioned Clayburn at the sheriff's office. If everything worked, he would extract a confession from Clayburn while a search of his home yielded additional evidence linking him to David Greenbriar's murder.

It was late in the afternoon when the telephone rang.

"Ranger Books, this is Assistant Medical Examiner Cornelia Wallace. I wanted to let you know that the body of Mr. Greenbriar is ready for release pending your approval."

"We don't have a problem with that. Would you like me to contact the family for you?"

"Please, that would be helpful. Any questions I can answer for you?"

Books thought for a moment. "I think I know the cause of death. Any other wounds?"

"Not much doubt about cause of death," said Wallace. "There was significant trauma to the area around the heart—relatively small entry wound but massive damage with the exit wound. He wouldn't have survived if he'd been shot in a hospital parking lot. As for other wounds, nothing major—some postmortem light bruising on both legs and one arm, probably caused when the body was moved."

Books thanked her and disconnected.

He dialed the EEWA office. Celia Foxworthy answered.

"Hi, Celia, this is J.D. Books. I'm looking for Darby. Is she in?"

"She left early this afternoon—poor girl—she was sick all morning."

"That's too bad. Her stress level's probably off the charts."

"Could be, but I don't think so. If I was a betting woman, I'd say she's pregnant. This wasn't the first morning she's spent with her head in the toilet. I had two boys. I know all about morning sickness."

"Don't know what to say about that. Bad timing, maybe, or a planned pregnancy. Did she or David ever mention wanting to start a family?"

"Subject never came up, not with either of them."

"One more thing for her to have to deal with, I guess."

"I'll look in on her tonight when I get home—maybe bring her something to eat."

"That would be nice."

Books then asked her to tell Darby that David's body was available at the ME's office in Provo.

"I'll let her know," said Foxworthy.

"Appreciate it," said Books. "You might also ask her to call Lillian in Berkeley and discuss the funeral arrangements. I think a small contingent of David's old friends plan to attend the service."

"Okay."

Books thought about Darby Greenbriar. While he could empathize with everything she must be going through, he could ill afford to let his feelings interfere with his next round of questions. There were things that only she and Lance Clayburn could answer. And as in every homicide case, time mattered.

He decided to contact David Greenbiar's attorney before he talked to Darby again. Stein would have answers to the estate questions that Darby was either ignorant of or deliberately lying about. When he called, the lawyer's secretary informed him that Stein was in conference with a client and would return the call as soon as he finished.

Thirty minutes later, the phone rang. "Good afternoon, Mr. Stein. Thanks for getting back to me so quickly."

"No problem, Ranger Books. How can I help you?"

"I just spoke with the medical examiner. She told me that David's body is ready for release. I assume a funeral service will be scheduled fairly soon."

"I'll pass that information along to Lillian."

"Appreciate it. As a part of our investigation, we're trying to determine the specifics of David's estate—figured you'd be the man to help me with that."

"Hold on a minute. I'll pull the file."

A minute later, Stein was back. "What specifically would you like to know?"

"Who stood to gain what in the event of David's death?"

There was a pause. Books could hear the sound of pages turning. Finally, Stein said, "Here we go. It looks like David left a quarter-million dollar life insurance policy with Darby listed as the primary beneficiary."

"Any secondary beneficiary?"

"Yes, in the event both he and Darby died, the policy proceeds would be split equally between Lillian and the Escalante Environmental Wilderness Alliance.

"Anything else?"

"Yes. There's also a will. I tried to get David to dump it and create a revocable trust, but he never got around to it."

"That means what?"

"That means nobody gets anything until the matter goes through probate," said Stein. "There's also the issue of estate taxes. The state of California will end up getting a piece of the estate."

"What was in the will?"

Stein sighed before continuing. "David left the bulk of his estate to Darby. However, he made several bequests to a small number of friends and to the EEWA."

"Translate that into dollars for me if you can."

"Sure. David's university retirement account held between three and four hundred thousand, I'd say closer to four, but I don't have any recent account statements."

"Not exactly chump change."

"No, it's not," said Stein. "He also maintained a small stock account with Charles Schwab. David liked to dabble in individual stocks and took great pride in his stock-picking acumen."

"And what was that account worth?"

"Just a guess, but I'd say somewhere in the range of fifty thousand."

"So, Darby stands to inherit roughly six hundred grand, counting the life insurance policy."

"That's ballpark, but yeah. And that doesn't include the house in Kanab, which she also gets."

"Tell me something else. Was Darby aware of what was in the estate and what she stood to gain in the event of David's death?"

"Oh, yes. Darby attended several meetings. I'd say she took more than a passing interest in the estate planning."

"That's odd," said Books. "The reason I'm calling you about the estate is that Darby professed almost total ignorance about what might be in it."

"That doesn't make any sense, unless she snoozed through our meetings, and I don't believe she did. She should have been able to fill you in on at least the rudiments of the plan, particularly in this kind of a marriage."

"What do you mean 'this kind' of marriage?"

"I do a lot of estate planning, Ranger Books, and my experience has been that in the case of trophy wife couples, the young lady often has, how can I discreetly put it, an intense interest in the details of the estate."

"And Darby was no exception."

"Most definitely not."

"Then let me ask you this. Did David ever consider asking Darby to sign a prenuptial agreement?"

"Oh, I suggested it to him on more than one occasion, but I'm afraid David was so smitten that he never seriously considered it. I doubt he and Darby ever discussed it."

"Is that unusual in trophy wife marriages?"

"Not really," said Stein. "I'd say in maybe half the cases I see, a prenup becomes part of the estate plan. And in this case, let's face it, David was not a terribly wealthy individual. I think he considered himself a very lucky man to have landed a beautiful young woman twenty years his junior."

"Let me ask you one more thing. Did David ever mention wanting to start a family with Darby?"

There was a lengthy pause. "Hmm, none of my business, you know, but I want to say that on one occasion, many years ago, Lillian expressed sadness that she had been unable to conceive. You'd better ask her about that."

"I'll do that. You've been most helpful, Mr. Stein, and I'll look forward to meeting you when you come out for the funeral."

"Likewise," said Stein, and the line went dead.

# Chapter Twenty

Books left the office and stopped at the post office to pick up his mail and buy stamps on his way home. He had a stack of unpaid bills lying around that required his immediate attention. After that, he'd go to work on the search warrant affidavit for Lance Clayburn's home.

On impulse he drove into west Kanab past the home of Rebecca Eddins. Her SUV was parked in the driveway. He stopped, got out of the Yukon, and knocked on the front door.

Moments later, Eddins opened the mission-style door. She broke into a broad smile when she recognized Books. "What a pleasant surprise! How are you, J.D.?"

"Good, Becky. And you?"

"Fine. Please come in. Your timing couldn't have been better."

"Yeah, how come?"

"You're just in time for dinner."

"I don't want to impose...."

"You're not imposing. In fact, I'm going to put you to work. Follow me." Books followed her into the kitchen.

"Nothing fancy, but Cody and I were just about to sit down to beef tacos and corn on the cob. You can shuck the corn."

He smiled. "You always this bossy?"

"Always," said Eddins. "In fact, that was one of my ex's biggest complaints about me—that I constantly drove his car, as he liked to call it."

"Did you?"

Becky sighed, "Yeah, I guess I did. But in my own defense, if ever there was a guy who needed somebody to drive his car, it was Clark Porter."

"Porter. That was your married name?"

She nodded. "Once I had the baby, it felt like I had to raise two kids."

"That couldn't have been much fun."

"Trust me. It wasn't."

Books stood over the sink and shucked three ears of corn. "There's nothing better than sweet Utah salt-and-pepper corn on the cob during late summer. I've been gone a long time, but I still remember that. You don't know it, but you saved me from another frozen TV dinner—they get old real fast if you're eating them often enough."

She smiled. It was a great smile. "We're glad you could join us. So what can I get you to drink? I'm drinking Australian Shiraz, or I can get you a beer or ice tea."

"A glass of the Shiraz, please. Tell me something, and pardon me for being so nosy, but what's a nice young woman who grew up in the Mormon faith doing with a refrigerator full of beer and a nice rack of wine?"

"I guess somebody in the family was destined to become a rebel, and it turned out to be me. Clark grew up in the church, but his family was never very active. After we married, neither of us showed much inclination to remain involved."

At that moment, a stranger walked in. He was wearing a two-gun rig around his waist, leather chaps over his jeans, a cowboy hat, and a sheriff's badge pinned to his shirt. Becky said, "Cody, I'd like to introduce you to an old friend of mine. Can you say hello to Mr. Books?"

Looking up, Cody said, "Hello, Mr. Books."

Books extended a hand and Cody tentatively reached out and shook it. "Nice to meet you, Cody. I really like that two-gun outfit you're wearing. Where'd you get it?"

"Grandpa gave it to me for my birthday."

"That's just what grandpas are for."

Books glanced from Cody to Becky. "I can sure see his mother in him."

"He's an Eddins from head to toe," said Becky.

They ate dinner outside under the covered portico. After dinner, Cody headed off to play while Books and Becky remained outside to enjoy pecan pie and coffee.

"By the way, thanks for organizing the homecoming party," said Books.

"Glad to do it. We're really looking forward to it.

"Heard you had a visitor the other night."

"Sure did. I'd spent a brutal day in juvenile court in St. George on an ugly child custody case. By the time I got home, I was beat. I'd put Cody to bed and was relaxing in the hot tub when I heard someone or something walking across the sandstone." She pointed to an area toward the back and side of the house.

"Did you see anybody?"

"Not really. When I looked at where the sound came from, I thought I saw something move in the shadows, but I wasn't sure."

"What'd you do?"

"I was out of the hot tub in a flash—ran back to the house, turned on the outside lights, and headed straight for the gun cabinet."

"You didn't dial 911?"

"Nope. I'm a big girl, and I can take care of myself, thank you very much." She sounded defensive. Books let it pass—none of his business anyway.

"Any idea who the visitor might have been?"

"Not a clue. I've also had some strange phone calls lately, no voice, heavy breathing, that sort of thing. I'd dismissed it as the work of some crackpot, maybe even some kid I'd dealt with in my law practice. Now I'm not so sure."

They talked a while longer. By the time he left, Books thought he'd convinced her to dial 911 if she experienced another incident. In turn, he promised to keep an eye on the house whenever he could. She seemed relieved and thanked him. At the front door, she put her arms around his neck and gave him a hug. She kissed him lightly on the lips, holding the kiss long enough that Books felt a stirring he hadn't experienced in nearly a year.

◇◇◇

Back home, Books began writing the search warrant affidavit for Lance Clayburn's home. It became clear that he'd overlooked something important. Did Lance Clayburn own a .30-06 caliber rifle? The shell casing found at the murder scene came from a .30-06. In the morning, he'd check the firearms registration records of the Utah Bureau of Criminal Identification.

The legal case against Clayburn already looked strong, and the possibility of complicity with Darby Greenbriar couldn't be ruled out either. Short of a confession, nothing would strengthen the state's case more than finding the actual murder weapon. There was no denying that physical evidence found at the murder scene put Clayburn there. Both he and Darby Greenbriar had lied about their relationship, and Darby stood to inherit significant financial assets from David's estate. From what Books had learned from Victor Stein, Darby had even lied to him about her knowledge of what was in the estate. And now there was the matter of a possible pregnancy. Was David Greenbriar the father or could the father be Lance Clayburn? He had to find out.

◇◇◇

Around midnight, Books surrendered to fatigue and went to bed. The nightmares started again as they did with alarming frequency—the adrenalin rush, the sound of gunfire, the agonizing screams of an innocent victim's bereaved widow as she held his head in her lap and rocked back and forth watching her husband's life blood stain the snow a dark crimson.

His memory of that awful day, his last day as a member of the Denver Police Department, remained as vivid as if it happened only yesterday:

Books and his partner, Detective Beth Guzelman, had just left police headquarters on their way to an east Denver hospital to interview the victim of a recent robbery. They drove south along Broadway until they reached Colfax Avenue. The state capitol rose up in front of them like some Gothic castle from medieval Europe. Its crowning gold dome sparkled like a smooth nugget etched into a clear blue sky, as if it had been painted on canvas. The January day was frigid but sunny. A blast of arctic air following a snow storm left a dusting of the white stuff.

Radio traffic seemed routine for a weekday morning—the usual assortment of fender benders, stalled cars, and traffic gridlock. And then it happened.

The radio crackled and was followed by three distinct beeps, a warning used only for in-progress felonies. The 911 dispatcher barked out the call to the patrol car: "Robbery in progress at the Stop & Shop convenience store, corner of Colfax Avenue and Pearl Street, shots fired, code three. Other units that can provide backup?"

Guzelman said, "For crissake, we're almost on top of it" as she tossed the last few swallows of a lukewarm cup of coffee out the car window. They would arrive ahead of any uniforms. It wasn't unusual in the winter months for robberies to happen during, or shortly after, snow storms. Inclement weather slowed police response time, something well understood by bad guys. But not this time.

Books grabbed the mike. "RH211, we're almost on scene. Any suspect descriptions?"

"Stand by," said the dispatcher.

There was no time to stand by. Nothing was more unnerving than rolling into an in-progress felony with no suspect information.

Beth maneuvered the Chevy Corsica into the icy convenience store lot and jammed it into park just as a suspect launched himself out the store's front door carrying a bag in one hand and a pistol in the other. She angled the vehicle so that Books could jump out the passenger side and remain protected by the car's engine block. That left Guzelman exposed, closer to the perp than Books, and with nothing more than the driver's side door for cover.

The perp fired three shots one of which shattered the driver's door window, showering Guzelman with fragments of glass.

"Christ," she yelled.

They returned fire and struck the suspect in the upper torso. He yelled something unintelligible as he went down. The handgun skittered away on the snow-covered parking lot. At the same instant, a second gun-toting suspect ran from the store in the same direction. He fired one round from a snub-nosed pistol, although Books later recalled thinking it was hard to discern where he was aiming. Books fired two shots in rapid succession from his nine-millimeter semiautomatic. The first shot missed, but the second struck the suspect in the chest. He ran several more unsteady steps and then collapsed on his side. The entire shooting incident was over in seconds.

The detectives moved cautiously forward in a low combat crouch ready to fire again if necessary. They kicked the handguns out of reach of the suspects. One lay on his side groaning. He slowly rotated his legs as if trying to command them to do something they couldn't. A brown paper bag was lying next to him. They could see loose cash inside. The second perp hadn't moved at all, and as Books and Guzelman moved closer, they could see a growing blood stain in the area near his heart. His mouth was open in a grotesque sort of way as though desperately seeking oxygen. His eyes had rolled back in his head.

As the adrenalin rush started to subside, a middle-aged woman rushed out of the store crying hysterically. She ran to the body of the second suspect. She knelt beside the man, cradling his head in her lap. She spoke rapidly in Spanish. Books couldn't understand what she said. Guzelman, however, did.

"Christ, J.D., the man we just shot is her husband. He wasn't one of the perps. He's the store owner. I think we just shot the victim."

Books felt numb, temporarily unable to think or move. He recalled two patrol cars arriving within seconds of the shootout, followed by paramedics, crime scene techs, and a team of detectives from robbery/homicide unit. The victim's wife had to be pulled away so paramedics could begin treatment.

Books turned to Beth and said, "Did you fire at the second guy or was it just me?"

"I didn't fire at the second guy, but I'm not sure why. Something just didn't seem right."

Books felt desperate. "Like what?"

"I don't know," said Beth. "I guess it was a hunch."

"I wish to God I'd had the same hunch."

A couple of hours later, the detectives had reconstructed the incident as best they could. They had been interviewed and re-interviewed by the internal affairs detectives. Both were placed on paid administrative leave pending a review of the incident by the department brass and by members of the Denver County District Attorney's Office.

Suspension from duty was routine in shooting incidents, but what wasn't routine was that Books had accidentally shot and killed a crime victim. It wouldn't help that this was the second fatal shooting he'd been involved in during his eleven years on the force.

The first incident occurred when Books was a rookie patrolman responding to a domestic violence call. A jilted ex-husband had broken into the home of his former wife, caught her and her new beau in the sack, and shot them both to death. Books and another officer killed him in a shootout after a high-speed chase. Shooting an armed suspect in the act of fleeing from a violent crime was one thing, but gunning down an innocent crime victim by mistake was something else entirely.

Books awoke and sat up in bed. The clock said it was three in the morning. His heart was pounding, his breathing labored like a man at the end of a long uphill run. Sweat poured from his forehead and soaked his tee shirt, leaving him chilled in the cool trailer.

He couldn't get back to sleep. He tossed and turned for a while, then got up, went to the refrigerator and grabbed a beer. He settled on an old recliner in the living room and spent the next two hours reflecting on his decision to become a cop in the first place, and his more recent decision to continue his career as a BLM law enforcement ranger.

When Books entered college, he hadn't the slightest idea what he wanted to do for a career. By chance he enrolled in a criminal justice class. After that, everything came into focus. He knew that he wanted a career in law enforcement. After two years of college, when he had reached the requisite age of twenty-one, Books saw a recruiting advertisement for officer positions with the Denver Police Department. He applied and was subsequently hired. Eleven years and two fatal shootings later, that job was over.

And as much as he hated to admit it, dear old dad probably had a hand in getting him the BLM position.

# Chapter Twenty-one

Early the next morning, Books put the final touches on the search warrant application in his office. Under normal circumstances, he would have taken the paperwork to a deputy district attorney to ensure that all the i's were dotted and the t's crossed before making an appearance before a judge. In this instance, he decided against following normal protocol. The DA's office in Kane County was a one-horse operation run by a guy named Virgil Bell, a part-time prosecutor who also ran a private law practice. Books didn't know him and therefore didn't trust him. What Books wanted to avoid at all costs was a leak about the search warrant to a hungry news media. For now, the fewer people who knew about the warrant, the better.

Books glanced up as Brian Call walked into his office carrying two steaming cups of black coffee and two apple fritters. "At the risk of sounding ungrateful, Brian, nothin like starting our day with a low fat, highly nutritious breakfast."

Call laughed. "Hell, J.D., I didn't want to spoil the public stereotype of cops sitting around drinking coffee and eating donuts on the taxpayer's nickel."

"Wouldn't want to do that. Pass me an apple fritter."

Call pushed a fritter across the desk and handed Books a cup of coffee. "Wasn't sure how you take your coffee. Hope black is okay."

"Black'll work just fine. Thanks."

Books set a meeting with Call and Sheriff Sutter for nine o'clock to create a coordinated plan of attack allowing him to conduct back-to-back interviews with Darby Greenbriar and Lance Clayburn. While Books interviewed Lance, Call, Sutter and a team of deputies would execute the search warrant at Clayburn's home. If the search produced additional incriminating evidence, Books intended to arrest Clayburn on the spot. If the search came up empty, he would temporarily release him and keep digging. They were close to breaking the case wide open.

Books dispatched Call to check firearms registration information from the Utah Bureau of Criminal Identification. If there was a record of Clayburn having purchased a .30-06 rifle, he wanted the gun for ballistics testing.

Books spent the next few minutes trying to locate Darby Greenbriar. He called her home, but nobody answered. He didn't leave a message. He then called the EEWA office. The office secretary, Cathy Carpenter, answered. "Good morning, J.D. What can I do for you?"

"Morning, Cathy. I'm looking for Darby. Has she been around this morning?"

Carpenter lowered her voice. "She's here, but I'm afraid I'm going to have to take a message. She's indisposed at the moment."

"I hope she's okay."

Carpenter hesitated. "She's not feeling well this morning. I've got her lying down on the couch in the conference room. Can I have her call you back?"

"Yeah, that's fine. Tell her it's important."

"I'll give her the message," said Carpenter. "Is there anything I can help you with?"

"Not really. I've got a few more questions I need to ask her."

"I'll tell her to call you ASAP. And by the way, there's going to be a memorial service for David at Blanchard's Mortuary the day after tomorrow at one in the afternoon."

"Appreciate the heads-up. I'd like to attend." He thanked her and hung up.

Books called Lance Clayburn's home phone but got no answer. He dialed his cell, and Clayburn answered on the first ring. "Talk to me," said Clayburn.

Books could hear a lot of background noise and wondered where Clayburn was. "Hi, Lance. This is J.D. Books. Can you hear me?"

"I can, J.D. Sorry about the noise but I'm on the highway to St. George—gotta meet somebody for lunch. What can I do for you?"

"I've got a few more questions. Do you think you could you drop by my office when you get back—should only take a few minutes?"

Clayburn paused before answering. "Sure, I can do that. How about three o'clock?"

"See you then."

Books replaced the receiver and sat back in his chair. The meeting was set. He sipped the coffee and ate a bite of the apple fritter. The coffee got a C–, the fritter an A+.

Sutter walked in with Brian Call at his side. Both men were smiling like two guys holding a winning lottery ticket. They sat down without a word. Call pushed a sheet of paper across the desk in front of Books. On it was a registration number for the purchase of a .30-06 Remington 700 SPS rifle. The gun had been purchased on March 26, 2008, from the Cabela's sporting goods store in Lehi, Utah. The owner was Lance Clayburn.

"Well, well, the noose grows tighter by the hour," said Books.

"So it seems," said Sutter. "Are the appointments set?"

"Clayburn'll be here at three. Darby hasn't returned my call, so I'm not sure about her."

"Any preference as to whom you want to question first?" asked Call.

"Doesn't matter," said Books. "What I want, though, is to interview them one after the other so there's no time for them to compare notes."

Sutter nodded. "So you want us to search Clayburn's place while you're questioning him?"

"That, or he can go out to the house with you after we're finished."

"I don't see the point in that," said Sutter. "He'd just be under foot." Call agreed.

"Maybe not," said Books. "If he has to stand around watching a bunch of cops turn his house inside out, it might be enough to push him over the edge. If he is involved with Darby in this thing, maybe he'll decide to give her up and try to cut a deal for himself."

"I doubt that. Besides, I'm not interested in cutting any deal with a killer," said Sutter.

"Your call on this, Charley, but I want to be smart about how we do it. What I don't want is to drop a search warrant in Clayburn's lap before I try to question him. He might panic and decide not to answer any of our questions. We don't want that."

"Makes sense to me, Charley," said Call. "If we hit the mother lode with the search, you can arrest him on the spot and hold a press conference afterward."

Sutter liked that idea. "Okay, J.D. We'll do it your way."

◇◇◇

By early afternoon the local district court judge had approved the search warrant. Books still hadn't heard anything from Darby Greenbriar and he was starting to get worried. If he didn't hear from her soon, he intended to go find her. Sheriff Sutter was standing by with a small contingent of deputies ready to execute the warrant once Books finished questioning Clayburn.

At one-thirty, Books grabbed the keys to the Yukon and drove to the EEWA office. The office was locked and there was no sign of Darby Greenbriar. He drove to her home. Nobody was around. It occurred to Books that maybe Lance Clayburn's lunch appointment in St. George had been with Darby. He hoped not. On his way back to town, his cell phone beeped. It was Charley Sutter telling him that Darby had just walked into his office looking for Books.

They met in a small conference room in the sheriff's office. Books laid a tape recorder on the table between them. "Hope you don't mind, but I'd like to tape-record our conversation today."

She shrugged, "Fine by me."

"Hot out there today, isn't it? Can I get you something to drink before we get started?"

Darby shook her head. "No, thanks."

"How are you feeling today, Darby?"

She looked at him quizzically before answering. "Fine, why do you ask?"

"When I called your office this morning, Cathy told me you were ill."

"Just a touch of indigestion, I think. I'm feeling much better now, thanks."

"Good."

Books turned on the tape recorder. "Darby, why did you tell me that you didn't know what was in David's estate?"

"Because I don't know, simple as that."

"You didn't participate in multiple meetings with David and Victor Stein concerning estate matters?"

"No, I didn't," she snapped.

"Victor Stein says otherwise."

"Then he's mistaken."

"Stein not only says you attended but that you took more than a passing interest in what was in the estate."

She sighed. "Let me tell you something about Victor Stein, Ranger Books. Victor has been a close personal friend of Lillian Greenbriar for many years. David even wondered if they were having an affair. Victor blamed me for the divorce and hasn't been civil to me since. It got so bad that David considered changing lawyers. Now I wish he had."

"You haven't spoken with Victor Stein since David's murder?"

"No."

"So you don't know the size of the estate or how much you're going to inherit. Is that what you're telling me?"

"That's right. Now let me ask you something. What do these questions have to do with solving David's murder?"

"It's a fair question, Darby. Let me answer it this way. People fall in love, get married, and, after a while, sometimes they fall out of love and get divorced. In a few cases, one spouse decides to kill the other or have someone else do it. It happens out of anger, hatred, greed, money, or falling in love with somebody else."

"What's your point?"

"Well, you stand to inherit a large sum of money. You claim to be oblivious about it. If I'm to believe what you're saying, I have to accept something that is counterintuitive for starters and is also contradicted by the estate attorney. It just doesn't track. Can't you understand how it looks?"

"And why can't you understand, Ranger Books, that, at this moment, I'm grieving for the loss of my husband, someone I loved very much. It's a matter of priorities. Whatever money there is isn't going any place. Right? It'll still be there next week, next month, or next year. It simply doesn't matter to me right now."

Books knew going in that this wouldn't be an easy conversation. "Look, I know it's a difficult time for you, but if I'm going to find out who killed David, I've got to stick my nose under every rock, including this one."

Darby rolled her eyes. "Are we about finished because…?"

"No, we're not," Books interrupted. "I have reason to believe that Lance Clayburn may have been involved in David's murder and that you're having an affair with him. Care to tell to me about that?"

A wave of shock, followed by guilt, etched her face. She broke eye contact and sank down as though she wanted to disappear into the woodwork. "Well?" Books prodded.

Darby ignored the question. "I don't believe Lance had anything to do with David's death. What makes you think he did?"

"Because we found physical evidence at the crime scene that directly links him to the murder. How long have you and Lance been involved?"

She stared at the floor and muttered, "About six or seven months. How did you find out?"

"Let's just say you haven't been as discreet as you might have thought. It's a small town, Darby, people talk. We've also got witnesses who can place Lance in your hotel room in Las Vegas this past weekend."

She didn't say anything.

"What time did Lance join you on Saturday?"

She hesitated, "I don't recall exactly. Noon, maybe."

"And he left Saturday night sometime?"

"No. He stayed over and left Sunday morning."

"What time did he leave Sunday?"

She was thinking about it. "Not sure, midmorning, maybe nine or ten."

Books nodded.

"I still don't believe he had anything to do with David's murder."

"We're about to find out about that. Were you planning to divorce David and marry Lance?"

"Of course not, and I didn't have anything to do with David's murder, either. That's what you're implying, isn't it? That I had Lance kill David so that I could have his inheritance and then run off with Lance."

"It's been known to happen."

"Well, it's not true—none of it is."

"Are you pregnant, Darby?"

Books hit a nerve. The tears came in buckets. Books left the conference room and returned with a box of tissues. She wiped her eyes.

"God, how I wish there was a single strand of something in my life that I could hold close and keep private, but I can't even protect my baby."

"I'm sorry, Darby. Would you like to take a short break?"

She shook her head. An awkward silence filled the room. Finally, Books asked, "How far along are you?"

"Eleven weeks."

"Is David the father?"

"Yes."

"How can you be sure of that?"

"The calendar, Ranger Books. I know when I was with David and I know when I was with Lance. David has to be the father."

Was she telling the truth or lying to cover up for Lance Clayburn? There was no way to tell short of a paternity test. Books wondered whether Darby would go along voluntarily, or whether he'd need a court order to force the test.

"Are you going to arrest me?"

"Not today. As to the future, I can't say. I learned a long time ago that it's about 20 percent common sense and 80 percent following the evidence. The evidence almost never lies."

Darby stood to leave. "It has in this case."

Books stood. "Look me in the eye, Darby, and answer two questions. Did you have anything to do with planning David's murder? And do you have any personal knowledge of whether Lance killed David?"

"No and No."

# Chapter Twenty-two

By the time Books finished questioning Darby and drove back to BLM headquarters, Lance Clayburn was waiting outside his office. Whether inadvertently, or by design, Darby had just blown a hole in the timeline of the murder. In doing so, she had also provided Clayburn with a possible alibi.

Follow the evidence, thought Books. The evidence almost never lies. The first seeds of doubt began to form.

Books conducted the interview with Lance Clayburn using a conference room in BLM headquarters. He got Clayburn a bottle of water and a Coke for himself.

"Lance, we've got a problem, and I'm afraid I'll need your help to sort it out."

"Fair enough." Clayburn was sweating and Books could tell that his discomfort quotient was definitely on the rise.

"I'm not going to sugar-coat this. Officially, you're a suspect in the murder of David Greenbriar, and before I can ask you any questions, I've got to advise you of your constitutional rights. I'd also like to tape-record our conversation."

Clayburn dropped his eyes and muttered, "I can't believe this is happening."

Books walked Clayburn through the Miranda warnings, unsure whether the growing sense of panic he saw on Clayburn's face would result in his refusal to talk.

"I need to tell you that I just finished interviewing Darby. We know all about the affair, so there's no need for you to lie to me again about that."

Clayburn winced but sat perfectly still, listening intently.

"Darby told us that you and she have been seeing each other for six or seven months. Is that accurate?"

He took a deep breath. "Yes, but for God's sake, that doesn't mean I killed David."

"That's true, but sometimes it becomes a motive for murder. The last time we talked, you told me that you went to Las Vegas on Saturday, shopped for much of the day, and then returned to Kanab late Saturday night. Do you remember that?"

Clayburn nodded.

"The recorder can't pick up a nod. You'll have to speak up."

"Yes, I remember."

"That's not what Darby says you did. She told me you spent Saturday night with her in Vegas and didn't return to Kanab until Sunday morning. Which is it?"

He sighed. "I spent Saturday night with her, had breakfast in the hotel room on Sunday morning, and then drove home."

"This is important," said Books. "What time did you leave Las Vegas on Sunday?"

"It's just a guess, but I'd say around nine-thirty in the morning."

"What did you do after you got home?"

"I hung around the house for a while, then drove into Kanab to run a few errands, and then ate a late lunch at Escobar's."

"What time did you eat at Escobar's?"

"Christ, you've asked me all this before."

"Indulge me. I'm asking you again."

"Three, maybe three-thirty. Why do we have to keep going over old ground?"

"Because it's important." Books let the silence hang in the air. It was an old interrogation tactic that worked especially well on nervous suspects. And Lance Clayburn was definitely nervous.

Finally, Clayburn said, "Look, I lied about my relationship with Darby. I'm sorry about that. But you've got to believe me, I didn't kill David Greenbriar. I wouldn't kill anyone, not ever."

"Not even if you could have the beautiful wife and the substantial estate she's about to inherit?"

"Absolutely not. Christ, J.D., think about it. I don't need her money. Whatever money David had is a pittance compared to what's in my trust." He was probably right about that, thought Books. "Did Darby tell you that she's pregnant?"

Clayburn put his head between his hands. "No, she hasn't said a word."

"Could you be the father?"

"I suppose it's possible, but we used condoms most of the time."

"Most of the time! Once is all it takes, my friend."

Books opened a cardboard box labeled "David Greenbirar Homicide, Case Number, 08-1794." From it, he removed three separately packaged items. There was a spent .30-06 shell casing, a plastic sandwich baggie, and two empty cans of Guinness beer.

Holding up the evidence bags, Books said, "These items were recovered from the murder scene. Can you explain how it is that your fingerprints are all over them?"

Clayburn was incredulous. "Christ, that's impossible. There's got to be a mistake. My prints can't be on that stuff. I keep telling you, I didn't have anything to do with David's murder."

Books held up a baggie containing the shell casing. "You own a .30-06 Remington hunting rifle, don't you?"

"Yes, and now I suppose you're gonna tell me that that shell casing came from my gun."

"Well, did it?"

"Hell, no, it didn't."

"Where's your rifle now, Lance?"

"It's at home. I keep it in my bedroom closet. It's unloaded, and I haven't fired it in months. I'd be happy to get it for you."

"That would definitely help clarify things."

Books held up the empty can of Guinness beer. "I know you drink Guinness. That's what you served me the other day at your house."

"I don't deny it. Everybody knows I drink Guinness. Plenty of people do."

"Unfortunately, there's only one set of prints on the cans, and they're yours."

Clayburn shrugged, resigned to an unexplainable set of circumstances that made him out to be a killer. "I want to cooperate to catch the person who murdered David. Is there anything else you'd like me to do?"

"Yeah, there is. For starters, look me in the eye and tell me you had nothing to do with either the planning or murder of David Greenbriar."

"I didn't, I swear it."

"What if I asked you to take a polygraph examination? Would you be willing to do it?" Books knew the results of a lie detector test were usually inadmissible in court; however, he'd seen more than one perp cave under the pressure and confess either before, during, or after the examination.

"Yes, anything," said Clayburn.

"I'll try to arrange that for tomorrow—that okay?"

"Sure."

"That's all I have for now, Lance. The sheriff is waiting outside for you. He's got a warrant authorizing us to search your home. He'll give you a copy of the warrant and a receipt for any items we take. Any questions I can answer for you?"

The last thing Lance Clayburn wanted to hear was that the sheriff's office was about to execute a search warrant on his home. He shook his head.

◇◇◇

Brian Call and two deputies conducted a systematic search of Lance Clayburn's home. Clayburn sat on a lawn chair watching the proceedings, lost in his own thoughts. Books and the sheriff conversed outside.

"Don't rush this, Charley, that's all I'm saying. I know you're anxious to make an arrest, but this would be a bad time to make a mistake. We've got time and Clayburn isn't going anywhere."

"So you say. As far as I'm concerned, this guy had the motive, means, and the opportunity to murder David Greenbriar."

"We might be able to prove motive and means," said Books, "but given the evidence we've got, opportunity is a hell of a stretch."

Brian Call emerged from the house and interrupted their conversation. "J.D., where did you say that .30-06 rifle was supposed to be?"

"In the master bedroom closet. At least that's where Lance said it would be."

"That's what I thought you said. I'll look again, but I didn't see it."

Call returned moments later shaking his head. "It's not there."

Books, Call, and Sutter walked over to where Clayburn was sitting. Books spoke. "Lance, Deputy Call can't find your rifle. Didn't you tell me it was in your bedroom closet?"

"That's exactly where it is."

"You're sure?"

"Absolutely. It's in the walk-in closet in my bedroom."

"We'd better all go have a look," said Books. Clayburn led the way into the house. The rifle wasn't there, and Clayburn was dumbfounded. He couldn't explain the missing weapon.

Sutter pulled Books aside. "Look, J.D., Greenbriar was killed with a .30-06 slug. This guy owns a .30-06 Remington that he assured you was here at the house. Now it's vanished, and he says he doesn't know where it is. I'll bet he does. I'll bet he used it to kill David Greenbriar and then dumped it someplace where we'll never find it."

"That's pure conjecture, Charley, and that's all it is. We still have to prove it in court."

"Murder cases have been won on less," said Sutter.

Books shrugged. "We don't have Clayburn's rifle, so we can't run a ballistics test. Do you have any idea how many folks in Kane County own a .30-06?" Books didn't wait for an answer.

"I don't know either, but I'm sure of one thing, there's plenty of 'em around—probably the most common weapon used to hunt deer and elk. A good defense lawyer is gonna rip us a new asshole and the jury's apt to laugh us right out of court." That was a stretch and Books knew it.

"But......"

"Wait, Charley, hear me out."

Sutter nodded.

"The weakest link in our case right now is the issue of opportunity. The timeline doesn't fit. The ME will testify that the time of death was noon to eight p.m. Sunday. Darby's going to testify that Lance spent Saturday night with her in Las Vegas and didn't leave for Kanab until midmorning Sunday. If that's true, he couldn't have made it back until at least one. Then he's got to drive into the Grand Staircase, find and kill Greenbriar, move the body, and make it back to Kanab in time for a late afternoon lunch at Escobar's. It just doesn't track."

"But you're forgetting something," said Sutter. "The first time you interviewed Clayburn, he told you he came back to Kanab late Saturday night. Now he's sayin' something different. Who's to say that he and Darby didn't get together and concoct this story to provide Lance with an alibi?"

"It's possible."

The search of Lance Clayburn's home turned up little of value. The Remington .30-06 rifle wasn't there, and Clayburn was unable to explain its disappearance. The sheriff's deputies seized two pair of his hiking boots. Both had dried mud and sandstone residue. They also took a set of truck tires from Clayburn's garage so they could compare the tire tread against photographs taken from the old West movie set where Greenbriar's body had been discovered. They also took his computer.

In the end, Books convinced Sutter to temporarily delay arresting Clayburn, that another day or two would provide sufficient time to investigate Clayburn's new alibi and to pursue several remaining leads.

# Chapter Twenty-three

That evening Ned Hunsaker knocked on the front door. Books waved him in.

"Evening, J.D. Another busy day, I'll bet."

"That's for sure, Ned. Sit yourself down for a minute. I was just getting ready to head out for the barbeque."

"Headed into the lion's den, huh?"

"Yeah, guess so. What'll you bet I won't make it out of there without a fireside chat with Neil?"

"I think you can depend on it."

Books removed two cans of Coors Lite from the refrigerator. He popped the top off one and offered the other to Ned. Hunsaker declined. "Hell, son, I've been on the wagon for almost a year now, and I intend to keep it that way. Actually, about the time of your mother's death, I started drinking pretty hard. I was boozing at night, and then getting up the next morning and feeling like I needed a shot or two of something just to get my day started. It came to a head about a year ago when I got busted by the Highway Patrol for DUI. I can't tell you how humiliated I felt. Everybody knew about it. They put me on probation, made me pay a hefty fine, and I lost my driver's license for six months. It turned out to be a real wake-up call."

"I'll bet it was. It does remind me though of something Dean Martin once said about teetotalers."

Ned was smiling. "Yeah, what's that?"

'Imagine waking up in the morning and knowing that's the best you're going to feel all day.'

Ned laughed. "I can identify with that."

So could Books.

"My daughter, Staci, and my son-in-law stepped in and provided lots of support. They even bought me a cell phone and insist that I carry the damn thing with me everywhere I go."

"Not a bad idea. Do you use it?"

He shrugged. "Not often. But I take it with me all the time just to keep them happy. I tossed it in an old Velveeta box, and I carry it in the glove compartment of the truck. The problem is I never remember to keep the damn thing charged, or if I remember to charge it, I forget to turn it on."

Books suppressed a smile. He always thought Ned Hunsaker was a little on the eccentric side.

"There are three rules you've got to remember when it comes to cell phones, Ned. First, you have to carry it with you; second, it has to be turned on; and third, you have to keep it charged. Sounds like you're good for two out of three."

"Got that right."

Books noticed that Ned was dressed for an evening on the town—not that an evening on the town in Kanab amounted to much. He was wearing neatly pressed black jeans, black cowboy boots, a long-sleeved denim shirt, and a Western tie. His black bolo had a beautiful turquoise stone in the center surrounded by an ornate silver border.

Books complimented him on the tie and asked where he was headed. Grinning, Hunsaker said, "I got an invite to a fancy barbeque to celebrate the return of some young buck to town after an extended absence."

"Ah. I should have remembered. You plan on driving yourself, or would you like to ride with me?"

"Thought you'd never ask. Becky called and invited me, so, I figured, what the hell, you might as well have at least one friend amongst all those CFW boys. Actually, that's not quite

right. Maggie and Bobby will be there, and oh, by the way, so
will your dad—wondered if you'd heard that?"

Books nodded. "I did."

◇◇◇

They turned off State Highway 89 and proceeded down a gravel
road about a half mile. The Eddins brothers had built almost
identical sprawling log homes a couple of hundred yards apart. A
large barn and fenced corral sat between and behind the homes.

The Eddins' ranch was one of the nicest and, from all appear-
ances, one of the few prosperous livestock spreads in Kane County.
Much of the land was privately owned and had been in the family
for several generations. The ranch was surrounded on three sides
by BLM land. It was natural for the Eddins clan to take advantage
of the available federal permits and graze a significant number of
steers on government land. Despite the apparent profitability of
the cattle company, both Neil and younger brother Boyd, had
been involved in real estate development around Kanab for as
long as Books could remember. The family owned Vermilion
Cliffs Realty and maintained an office on the town's main street.

Books' jangled nerves dissipated when he realized the gathering was smaller than he'd envisioned. With a couple of exceptions,
most of the guests were familiar—friends and neighbors from a
past life, a life for which he was slowly gaining new appreciation.

Becky came over and gave Ned a warm embrace. "Damn. We
need to have these little get-togethers more often," said Hunsaker.

She gave Books a peck on the cheek, placed her arm through
his, and walked him through the crowd over to his father, who
was embroiled in an animated conversation with Neil Eddins.
When he saw his son, he broke away from the tête-à-tête and
strode over. Books reached out to shake his hand. His father
brushed it aside and gave him an awkward hug. "How are you,
son? It's been, what, almost two years?"

"Since Mom's funeral. I'm fine, Bernie. How've you been?"
Books couldn't remember when he had stopped calling him dad,
but it had been a long time ago.

"Doing very well, thank you. Retirement suits me just fine."

"Glad to hear it." An awkward silence fell between the two men.

"I get to spend lots of time with your sister and the grandkids. Never hear much from you, though, except what I manage to pickup secondhand from Maggie."

"Well, Bernie, it's not like I'm living right here in town. Six hundred miles, I'm afraid, is a little more than a weekend jaunt. There is such a thing as a telephone. Ever heard of it?"

Before things could deteriorate further, Becky stepped in, as if on cue, and led him away. She walked him from one group to another until he'd made the rounds.

Becky smiled and said, "That wasn't so bad, now was it?"

"How did you know?"

"Call it woman's intuition. You've been uncomfortable at these kinds of shindigs for as long as I've known you."

"I thought I disguised it better than that."

"Most people probably don't notice. It's just that in those days, I thought you were so cute that I watched every move you made."

"And today?"

"I'll plead the fifth on that, thank you very much. Anyway, that was a long time ago, J.D. Life beats us all up. People change. I know I have, and so have you. Better leave it at that, don't you think?"

"Probably a good idea. And thanks for guiding me through that maze of people, including the clumsy encounter with Bernie."

"You're welcome. Now shall we find you something cold to drink?"

"I thought you'd never ask."

Since Kanab was settled by Mormon pioneers and the LDS faith remained the dominant religion in the area, Books was sure about two things at tonight's party. There wouldn't be any booze on the premises, and ice cream would be the only dessert. He was right on the latter count but delighted to find an ice-filled tub with bottles of Coors and Miller beer. He snatched a Coors and offered one to Becky. She gave him a conspiratorial wink and shook her head suggesting she would like a rain check. To imbibe at the home of her Mormon parents was probably a big no-no. Assuming he had Ned as designated driver, Books downed several Coors over the course of the evening and washed a grilled cheeseburger, potato salad, and baked beans down with the last two. He had an ice cream sundae for dessert.

After dinner, while the sun slowly disappeared in the western sky, folks stood around talking in pairs or small groups. Gradually, most people said their good-byes and disappeared into the gathering darkness. Books felt a large hand on his shoulder.

"Got a minute, J.D.?" Neil motioned toward the house. Seeing no avenue of escape, Books followed him inside. Eddins had always been a handsome man. He was in his early fifties, tall, narrow at the hips, and broad through the shoulders. He had a full head of salt-and-pepper hair.

Eddins ushered him into a spacious office with maple hardwood floors. A large oak roll-top desk sat in the center of the room on an expensive Two-Grey-Hills Navajo rug with a burgundy leather couch and matching chair in front. Charles Russell Western prints adorned the walls. On the corner of his desk sat a framed picture of a smiling Neil Eddins with his arm around former Secretary of the Interior James Watt. Watt, a former Reagan appointee, was the darling of ranchers and big oil but had been despised by every conservation and environmental group on the planet.

Eddins had been a politically powerful figure on the local scene for as long as Books could remember. He'd been a member of the Kanab City Council, and later, chairman of the Kane County Commission.

As soon as they sat down, Boyd Eddins and Tommy McLain walked in. Trees didn't seem happy to see him. In fact, he looked downright hostile.

After several minutes of perfunctory small talk, Neil brought the discussion around to the real purpose of the meeting.

"I'm not going to kid you, J.D. Part of the reason we invited you out was to have this opportunity to correct any misconceptions you might have about the CFW. God only knows what kind of wild stories you've been hearing from that new boss of yours, or worse yet, from the local environmental groups. That includes the late David Greenbriar and his granola-eating friends."

The comment didn't provoke any reaction from Boyd Eddins who sat chewing on a toothpick, but it brought a stupid grin to the face of Trees McLain.

"Look, Neil, you and I both know that the tension between locals and the Green community isn't anything new. It's been a part of the Kane County landscape for as long as I can remember. And, actually, Alexis Runyon hasn't said much to me about either group."

Books didn't express his concern that relations between ranchers, the federal government, and environmental groups were far more strained than anything he could recall as a kid.

"Perhaps I was unnecessarily concerned," said Eddins.

"Perhaps you were. As far as David Greenbriar is concerned, he was murdered shortly after I got here—never had the opportunity to meet him. But I am going to find out who killed him. It must have been some lowlife coward, a bushwhacker at that." He stared hard at Trees McLain, who stared back.

Neil Eddins looked from Books to McLain and then back to Books. He cleared his throat. "From what I hear, J.D., you're pretty close to making an arrest."

"Still chasing leads."

"Well, I hope you don't think anybody from the CFW had anything to do with it, because I can assure you they didn't."

"That's comforting, Neil, but tell me something. How can you be so sure?"

Eddins' face reddened. "Because I know the kind of people who belong to the CFW. They're good, hard workin' folks, people with good conservative values, Christian values. They wouldn't get involved in a murder. We have our differences with the Greenies but none of it so serious that anybody's going to resort to murder."

"Somebody sure did," said Books.

"I hear Greenbriar was killed by one of his own," said Eddins.

"Who're you gettin your information from, Neil?"

"None of your business, J.D."

"Fair enough. And while we're on the subject, the EEWA was kind enough to provide us with a list of their members. I'm sure you'd like to extend the same level of cooperation by giving me a list of CFW members."

That request brought a paternalistic smile to Neil Eddins' face. "Sorry, J.D., that information is private. Get me a court order, and I'll hand it over without delay.

Boyd, who'd been quiet, spoke up. "Even though you never had the chance to meet David Greenbriar, by now I'm sure you've had the opportunity to meet some of his extremist friends, one of whom apparently killed him. The word 'compromise' isn't in their vocabulary, J.D. They want all the federal land sealed up so that nobody can use it for anything. We don't intend to let that happen." McLain grunted his agreement.

"I'm afraid Boyd's right, J.D.," said Neil. "At least groups like the Sierra Club and the Southern Utah Wilderness Alliance are known quantities. On some issues, we can find common ground. They seem more moderate compared to the Escalante Environmental Wilderness Alliance."

Books listened intently as the Eddins brothers rattled on.

Neil continued. "Most of us have been here for several generations. You know that. We've established a way of life, and we intend to defend it. We're committed to using every legal means at our disposal to stop this radical group before they become any stronger."

"And maybe a few methods that aren't so legal," said McLain.

"Afraid I didn't hear that, Trees," said Books.

"You'd better hear it," said McLain, "cuz you're either for us or against us. What's it gonna be, Ranger Books?"

Before Books could answer, Neil cut in. "That'll be enough, Tommy. Consider yourself excused." Trees started to say something else but thought better of it.

"I'll be seeing you around, Books." He got up to leave, offering a weak smile that exposed yellow, tobacco-stained teeth.

"Sooner than you think," said Books.

"Please accept my apology, J.D. Tommy means well enough, but he tends to be short on manners sometimes. We didn't invite you here to insult you," said Neil.

"Forget it. Apology unnecessary, but tell me something, Neil, why *did* you invite me here?"

"Two reasons, actually. I happen to have a very persistent daughter who seems quite fond of you. Also, I wanted to find out where you stood on the issues."

"What you really want to know is whose side I'm on, right?"

He raised his eyebrows and shrugged. "Seems like a fair question."

"I think you already know the answer to that. For better or worse, the BLM is committed to the notion that federal land can serve multiple purposes. When reasonable people sit down and talk, solutions to problems can be found in ways that work for everybody. There's no reason the land can't serve the interests of everybody as long as it's done in a way that protects the ecosystem."

"Easier said than done," said Boyd.

Books looked directly at Boyd. "Your family is one of the most influential in Kane County, Boyd. You and Neil should be leaders in discussions that are going to have to take place sooner or later."

"Spoken like a true bureaucrat," said Neil. "As the old saying goes, it takes two to tango, and, at the moment, we don't seem to have a dance partner who wants to be reasonable."

"That's exactly what the environmental groups are saying about you," said Books. "Taking your dance analogy a bit further, at some point, people on both sides are going to have to find a dance partner and get out on the floor. Short of dialogue, the alternatives just aren't very good."

The conversation lasted almost an hour. By the time it was over, Books was exhausted and sober as a judge. He found Ned, iced tea in hand, doing his best to entertain Becky. The two men said their good-byes and left.

When he got home, Books found a voicemail from Lillian Greenbriar. She explained that she and Victor Stein would fly into Las Vegas early Friday morning, rent a car, and drive to Kanab in time for David's memorial service. A small cadre of David's friends and former colleagues opted to drive from Berkeley and would arrive sometime Thursday night. Lillian and Stein asked to meet Books at the sheriff's office at noon for an update on the status of the case.

# Chapter Twenty-four

Books arrived at the office early Friday morning to find Sutter and Brian Call waiting for him. Something was up; he just wasn't sure what. Both men looked uncomfortable.

"Morning, Charley, Brian. You boys don't look too happy, this morning. What's up?"

"We've had a development in the case," said Sutter.

Books' interest was instantly piqued. "What kind of development?"

"Not a very important one, at least we don't think so," said Call.

"But important enough for both of you to be sitting on my doorstep this morning. Tell me about it."

"You remember the Gadasky family, J.D.?" asked Sutter.

"Scrapiron Gadasky?"

Sutter nodded.

"Sure do. The old man operated a salvage business and towing service out of that decrepit old place they lived in outside town." Books recalled the place being a graveyard of rusted-out cars, trucks, farm equipment, even some old school buses.

"That's him," said Call. "Last night old man Gadasky called the sheriff's office and wanted to speak to a deputy."

"About?"

"The Greenbriar murder," said Call. "A deputy went out to the house and ended up taking a statement from Ivan's youngest son, kid by the name of Ronnie."

"And what did Ronnie have to say?"

"Boy said he was out on the Smoky Mountain Road last Sunday afternoon and says he got a look at the guy who shot Greenbriar," said Call.

Books' temper flared. "Jesus, why didn't I hear about this last night? It's kind of important, don't you think?"

"Hold on a minute, J.D. Don't get your tail in a knot," said Sutter. "Ronnie Gadasky's a loony-tune, and everybody in town knows it."

"Since you placed me in charge of the investigation, maybe you ought to let me be the judge of that?"

Sutter frowned. "And you will be, J.D. I just thought maybe you'd like a little insider information about the family, since you've been gone so long."

"You're right, Charlie, sorry. Tell me about Ronnie Gadasky."

Sutter continued. "What do you remember about the Gadasky family?"

"Not all that much. They had four or five kids. The oldest boys, Ernie and George, were at Kanab High School around the same time I was. The other kids were pretty young at the time...."

Sutter interrupted. "Here's the story, J.D. Ivan and his wife had five kids, four boys and a sweet little girl named Irina. You're right about the older boys. They were a year or two behind you in school. Ronnie is eighteen. He's the youngest. About seven, maybe eight years ago, Ivan's wife ran off with a construction worker—never did come back. Ivan did the best he could raising the kids, but things didn't work out very well."

"Skip the family history, and get to the point."

Sutter ignored him and continued. "Ronnie started getting into all kinds of mischief, and so did Irina. Rumor had it that Ernie was having his way with Irina, although we never could prove it. She eventually got pregnant and ran off with a Navaho boy—lives somewhere near Page, Arizona. Ronnie started sniffing glue when he was about thirteen. He's been in and out of juvenile court numerous times over the past couple years. You can ask Rebecca Eddins. Ivan hired her to represent the boy a time or two."

"Okay," said Books. "So what you're telling me is that we've got a possible murder witness with a juvenile court record and brain damage from spending too much time with his head in a plastic bag sniffing glue."

Call picked up the story. "It gets worse, J.D. About two years ago, Ronnie stole his brother Ernie's motorcycle. The kid was high on something. Anyway, he was racin' along Highway 89 toward Kanab, with Ernie in hot pursuit, when he came up behind George Detmer's plumbing supply truck. You remember George Detmer?"

"Detmer Plumbing, how could I forget," said Books. "The old man drove a ratty old panel truck around town with a sign on it that read, 'We're Number One in the Number Two Business.'"

"That's him. Anyway, it was an old flatbed truck that George used to haul plumbing supplies around when the weather was good. What happened was that old George was hauling several commodes for a job he was doin' in Orderville. About the time Ronnie rolls up behind him, a commode falls off the back end of the truck and lands smack in the middle of the highway. Ronnie does an Evel Knievel, hits the commode head on, goes airborne, and crashes the bike. He lands on his head and ends up with serious internal injuries and head trauma. The boy almost died."

"Jesus." Books shook his head. "What an epitaph that would make: 'Here lies Ronnie Gadasky, killed by a flying crapper.'"

Sutter and Call laughed.

"Point is, J.D., the kid's goofy," said Call. "He just isn't credible."

"Okay. Now what you're telling me is we've got a potential witness with a juvenile record and brain damage caused by sniffing glue as well as injuries sustained in a motorcycle accident. Is that it?"

Sutter looked frustrated. "There's not a juror in his right mind that's going to believe one word that comes out of that kid's mouth."

"Maybe, maybe not," said Books. "You can never tell what a jury will choose to believe—unpredictable, that's what they are."

"You'll be wasting your time," said Sutter.

"Let me worry about that. I definitely want to talk to him. Where can I find him?"

"Have it your way," said Sutter. "Best place to find Ronnie is at home. I don't think he works other than doing odd jobs for the old man. Since the accident, the kid disappears into the Grand Staircase, sometimes for days at a time. Nobody knows where he goes or how he survives. I suspect one of these days he'll walk into that wilderness and we'll just never see or hear from him again."

"That's why I should have been called last night." Having a disabled witness was difficult, thought Books, but having a disabled, missing witness was worse, much worse.

As Sutter and Call got up to leave, Sutter gave Books a final admonition. "Remember this, J.D., as far as I'm concerned, we've already identified our killer, and if you haven't come up with something else for me by tomorrow, I'll be going to the DA for a murder warrant on Lance Clayburn."

Books leaned back in his chair and finished his lukewarm coffee. Call and Sutter had already made up their minds about Clayburn's guilt, and they weren't about to allow the emergence of Ronnie Gadasky as a possible witness to influence their thinking.

◇◇◇

Books still had almost four hours until his noon meeting with Lillian Greenbriar and Victor Stein. It was time to start tying up loose ends, and he had several that required his immediate attention. First, he called Grant Weatherby and explained the problem with Lance Clayburn's alibi. If room service receipts or hotel employees could place Clayburn in Darby's suite on Sunday morning, the case against him would be weakened. Weatherby promised to get back to him after another visit to the Hard Rock Hotel and Casino.

Books hopped in the Yukon and drove to the sheriff's office. He wanted to pick up a copy of Ronnie Gadasky's statement.

What the statement said was that Gadasky had heard the report of a rifle along a stretch of the Smokey Mountain Road Sunday afternoon around four o'clock. He recalled seeing David Greenbriar's Chevrolet Suburban but claimed not to have seen Greenbriar. Gadasky told the deputy that he saw a man dressed in camouflage hiding in a rocky outcropping above and to the west of Greenbriar's Suburban. He had been unable to provide a physical description of the man other than he was white and older looking. A quarter mile further down the Smokey Mountain Road, Gadasky saw a shiny black car parked in a turnout. Although uncertain, he thought it had Nevada license plates.

What the police report failed to address was what Gadasky was doing in the area. What made him run? Why hadn't he bothered to report the incident to police?

With the statement in hand, Books drove to the Gadasky home. Little had changed over the years. The property remained a wasteland of rusting metal hulks of every sort. A narrow dirt road snaked through the debris over a small rise to an old two-story clapboard house nestled in a sea of sagebrush and rock. As Books parked, a three-legged black lab raced around the side of the house, making a sound that resembled a cross between a bark and a howl.

Ivan Gadasky climbed down from a backhoe he was using to dig fence post holes near the side of the house. Gadasky was a large man, thick through the neck, shoulders, and waist. He had a noticeable limp as he walked slowly toward Books. He mopped his brow with a blue gingham hankie he'd removed from the back pocket of his bib overalls. As he approached, Gadasky returned the hankie to his pocket and placed a Deere logo cap back on his head.

"Gonna get damn hot today," said Books.

"Already is." Gadasky extended a hand. Books shook it.

"How have you been, Mr. Gadasky. It's been a long time."

"Very long, indeed, J.D. Feeling old and a bit rundown at times, but, other than that, I'm doing fine. Think I know what brought you out here—Ronnie's not around."

Despite many years in the states, Ivan Gadasky still spoke with a pronounced Eastern European accent. The family was Polish Catholic, if Books remembered correctly.

"Where can I find him? It's important that I talk with him as soon as possible."

"I'm sure it is," said Gadasky, "but I have no idea where he is or when he might return. When I got up this morning, he was already gone."

"And you have no idea where he went?"

Gadasky sighed, "No, not really. The boy just up and disappears whenever it suits him. I think I upset him when I called the sheriff's office last night. He didn't want me to do that."

"How come?"

"Didn't want to get himself involved, I suspect. He's become a pretty reclusive boy since the accident—wanders off into the wilderness whenever he gets the urge. No telling when he's gonna go or when he might come back."

Books couldn't tell if Gadasky's tone was one of indifference, worry, or mere acceptance.

"Does Ronnie happen to own any guns, Mr. Gadasky?"

"He's got an old .25 caliber pistol that he hasn't used in years."

"Do you have firearms?"

"One. It's a 12-gauge Remington shotgun—keep it around to scare off varmints, two-legged or four."

"When Ronnie disappears, how does he get around?"

"Mostly on foot, but he's also got a dirt bike."

"What kind?"

"2000 Kawasaki, 250 cc, a red one. I hope he's not in trouble."

"He's not. I just need to talk with him about what he saw on the Smokey Mountain Road last Sunday afternoon."

"Think he's said about all he's gonna say about that."

Books handed Gadasky his business card. "That may be true, but I've still got to try. What he saw might be really important—appreciate it if you'd call me when you hear from him."

Gadasky took the card, nodded, and then lumbered off to the back-hoe.

Books returned to the Yukon and put out an immediate BOLO on Ronnie Gadasky and his red Kawasaki dirt bike. He also asked the dispatch office to notify State Fish and Game, the Forest Service, as well as the National Park Police. Given the vast expanse of the Grand Staircase Monument and nearby national parks, Books wasn't holding his breath that Ronnie would turn up until he was good and ready.

# Chapter Twenty-five

Peter "the Rose" Deluca heard the telephone ring. He was in the greenhouse tending his delicate rose bushes. Reluctantly, he took off his gloves, set the scissors down, and went inside. "Yes," he answered, trying to keep the annoyance out of his voice.

"We have a problem."

"Nothing new about that. What is it this time?"

"The job you did for us last weekend—somebody saw you."

Deluca sighed, "Well, I'm not surprised. I tried to tell you your plan was ill-conceived. That's why my fee was so high. The target should have been left where I found him."

"Maybe, but we didn't. Now we've got a problem, one I assume you can help us solve."

"Are you certain it's necessary?"

"Yes, it is. Failure to eliminate the problem could undermine everything we've done so far."

Deluca processed what he'd heard. He had never accepted a job that he hadn't finished. He had a reputation to uphold. And besides, unfinished loose ends had a way of coming back to bite you.

"All right, but my fee will be the same as the first time."

"Jesus, that's a little steep, don't you think, considering you're the one who got careless and let somebody see you?"

"Don't waste my time. Do you want my help or not?"

The line was silent. "All right, we'll pay your fee, but get the job done as quickly as possible. And don't let anyone see you this time."

Deluca wiped the sweat from his brow. "Think of it this way, if it makes you feel better. Much of your fee will be paid in tithe to the Catholic Church as part of my absolution for missing mass two weeks in a row. Besides, it's a sin to labor on the Sabbath. Any good Catholic knows that."

"I never realized you were such a pillar of the Church, a regular St. Peter, you might say."

"Don't mock me." Deluca's tone turned icy cold. "Father Gregory has asked me to consider studying to become a deacon in the parish."

"Will miracles never cease? Care to know who you're looking for?"

"Give me the information." Deluca received a home address, a physical description of Ronnie Gadasky, and a short history of his troubled past.

"One more thing."

"Yes," said Deluca.

"There's a cop running the investigation—a former Denver police detective, a real hotshot, they say."

"So?"

"He's the new BLM ranger. The local sheriff has turned the case over to him."

"And I should be quaking in my boots?"

"Not necessarily, but I'm told he's very good. He could become a problem."

There was a lengthy pause. "What's his name?"

"J.D. Books."

"I'll check him out." Deluca disconnected.

Peter Deluca was the only son of a Chicago florist. His parents had emigrated from Italy to the U.S. in the early 1930s after the rise of Benito Mussolini. The family operated a thriving floral business on Chicago's south side. Deluca's love affair with flowers began at a young age in the family greenhouse at the hands of a stern but loving father. His mother, Maria, had died during childbirth. He couldn't remember a time, other than a stint in the army, when flowers were not a part of his life.

For a man who had spent the past several decades killing others for a living, nurturing flowers from seedling to bloom provided him with a sense of grounding, a belief that his life amounted to something other than death and destruction.

◇◇◇

To Books, Lillian Greenbriar seemed the quintessential English literature professor, with long brown hair pulled back into a bun, glasses perched on the tip of her nose, and very little makeup. Victor Stein, on the other hand, looked like a lawyer for the stars. He could have passed for actor George Hamilton's brother—a thick head of silver hair with streaks of black; an artificial Hollywood suntan that had to have been purchased somewhere; and a set of capped white teeth so bright they were the first thing you noticed about the man. His black pinstripe Armani suit looked out of place in Kanab, even if he was here to attend a funeral.

They met at noon in the sheriff's office. After introductions, they settled down to business. Assuming a lawyer-like advocacy role, Stein began, "Perhaps, Ranger Books, you could take a moment and fill us in on the status of the investigation."

"I'm afraid I can't give you many specifics, but I can tell you that we now have a suspect and physical evidence linking this individual to the murder."

Greenbriar and Stein glanced at each other. Lillian asked, "What kind of evidence?"

"Sorry, can't get into that."

"Tell us, then, is an arrest imminent?" asked Stein.

"Probably."

"That's not exactly reassuring," said Stein.

"It wasn't meant to be," said Books.

Books handed Lillian a list of names of David's former colleagues. "Are any of these gentlemen going to be attending the memorial service?"

Greenbriar glanced at the list. "Yes. Three of them plan to be here—Simpson, Gladwell, and Stone."

"My assistant still hasn't been able to reach two of David's former colleagues," said Books. "We'd like to speak with Gladwell and Stone before they leave."

"In regard to what?" asked Stein.

"I told Lillian that someone claiming to be an old colleague of David's telephoned the EEWA office looking for him late Friday afternoon. We're wondering whether it was one of David's old friends or if it might have been the killer trying to determine his whereabouts."

"I see." Stein pondered that bit of information.

"Lillian, I need to ask a personal question," said Books. "Did you and David ever attempt to have children?"

"What does that have to do with anything?" asked Lillian.

"A fair question. I'm going to tell you something and ask that you both hold it in confidence. Agreed?"

They both nodded.

"Darby is pregnant and I need to know who the father is."

Lillian winced, obviously startled by this new information. "Well, it's not David, I can tell you that."

Now it was Books turn to be surprised. "What do you mean?"

"David was sterile. He couldn't have children."

"You're sure."

"Absolutely sure. I can refer you to the Berkeley fertility clinic where David and I dropped several thousand dollars exploring options and being tested."

For a moment nobody spoke and then Lillian asked, "Do you believe this issue might be connected to David's murder?"

"I'm not sure, but it's possible. I'd like the fertility clinic information when it's convenient."

"Okay. I'll get it for you before we leave this afternoon."

"The suspect you mentioned. Could he be the father?" asked Stein.

"Sorry, can't answer that one."

# Chapter Twenty-six

Books stared out his office window, sorting out this new and unexpected information regarding the paternity of Darby Greenbriar's child. If David wasn't the father, who was? Lance Clayburn? Probably. Had Darby deliberately lied to him about the identity of the father? Did she know about David's sterility? It was hard to imagine she didn't.

Was this another attempt to divert attention away from Lance Clayburn? Maybe Sutter had been right all along. Maybe they needn't have looked any further than Clayburn to bring David Greenbriar's killer to justice. Books had interrogated many murderers in his twelve years in Denver. Something about Lance Clayburn had left Books feeling decidedly uncertain about his guilt. The physical evidence, however, suggested something else entirely. Books knew that in Sutter's mind this new revelation would only serve to confirm any suspicion about Clayburn's guilt.

Books was also concerned about leaks to the press, to local political hacks, and even to people involved with groups like the Citizens for a Free West, people who might have had a hand in the murder. It didn't take a genius to figure out that either Sheriff Sutter or Brian Call was leaking information.

Books hatched a plan. He dialed Brian Call's number.

"This is Call."

"Hey, Brian, I just picked up an important piece of information. I haven't verified it yet, so keep it to yourself."

"No problem."

"David Greenbriar isn't the father of Darby's baby."

"Interesting. How'd you find that out?"

"His ex, Lillian Greenbriar, told me. David was sterile."

"That means it's gotta be Clayburn's kid," said Call.

"That's exactly what I think." Books had set the hook. Now, would Call take the bait?

"What else do you need me to do?" asked Call.

"Two things. Steve Gladwell and Brad Stone are in town as part of the Berkeley contingent. Get yourself over to the memorial service and find out whether either of them called David last Friday evening."

"Okay. What else?"

"I want you to call the St. George Police Department. I'm sure they'd have a polygraph operator."

"They do."

"Clayburn has volunteered to take a poly, and I don't want to give him time to reconsider. Schedule him as soon as possible, tomorrow preferably."

"Will do. I'll let you know about the poly. Are you going to be at the service today?"

"Yeah. I want to see who shows up and who stays home. I also need catch up with Barry Struthers. It's time to find out what he has to say about David's murder."

After he got off the phone, Books headed to the sheriff's office. When he walked in, Charley Sutter was sitting at his desk signing a stack of purchase requisitions.

"Morning, Charley. Are you planning to attend Greenbriar's memorial service this afternoon?"

Sutter looked up. "Wasn't planning to. Why? Should I?"

"Not necessarily. What did you find out at Escobars?"

"Exactly what you said I would. I spoke with the owners, Toby and Viola Gabaldon. They said Clayburn came in sometime late Sunday afternoon, three-thirty, maybe four o'clock."

Without looking up from his paperwork, Sutter added, "Doesn't change anything, J.D. He still had time to commit the murder."

"Maybe so." Books got up to leave.

"See you at the meeting tomorrow morning."

Books stopped at the office door. "What meeting?"

"Oh, maybe I forgot to tell you. We've got an appointment with Virgil Bell at 11:00 a.m. in his office. We need to bring him up to speed on the investigation."

That meant only one thing. Sutter planned to press for criminal charges against Lance Clayburn.

"I'll be there."

Books arrived at Blanchard's Mortuary shortly after the memorial service had begun. There was standing room only. He stood near the chapel's entrance, next to Brian Call, where he had an unobstructed view of the room. As he scanned the chapel, Books saw Lance Clayburn sitting with Celia Foxworthy directly behind Darby Greenbriar. Although he had never met the man, Books was looking for Barry Struthers. Call pointed to a couple seated several rows behind Lillian Greenbriar and the Berkeley entourage.

Struthers was a transplanted Californian who had earned a bundle as a Silicon Valley software engineer, so much in fact that he'd been able to retire at fifty. Initially, he and his wife had relocated to St. George, but he quickly became disillusioned with the uncontrolled real estate development and the burgeoning population. Within a year, they had settled in Kanab where Barry had immersed himself in a variety of environmental causes, including membership in the EEWA.

The graveside ceremony following the memorial service was mercifully brief. The triple digit temperature was tempered by an afternoon breeze. Black cumulus clouds to the northwest threatened an imminent thunderstorm.

At the conclusion of the service, Books introduced himself to Barry Struthers. He wasn't expecting a warm greeting, and Struthers didn't offer one. He was polite but wary. Books had learned quickly that wearing a federal badge wasn't endearing to locals, regardless of which side of the environmental chasm they were on. Struthers agreed to meet him for an interview at a nearby local restaurant.

The distant crack of thunder rolled over the Grand Staircase as a persistent light rain turned red clay soil into a sticky mud. Books found Struthers seated in a corner booth at the Subway restaurant drinking a soda and munching on a package of Sun Chips.

"Thanks for meeting with me," said Books.

"No problem. I'm surprised I didn't hear from you sooner."

"And why is that?"

"It's no secret that David and I didn't see eye-to-eye when it came to running the organization."

"So I heard."

Struthers blew his nose and replaced the Kleenex in his pants pocket. "You and everybody else, it seems. So, what would you like to know, Mr. Books?"

"In a nutshell, whether you had anything to do with David's murder?"

Struthers arched his eyebrows. "That's what I like, a guy who doesn't mince words or waste time. I don't either."

"Good. So tell me what you and David disagreed so vehemently about."

"First of all, I wouldn't characterize our disagreements as vehement. We didn't always see eye-to-eye when it came to the operational activities of the EEWA, but we shared common ground when it came to identifying the threats."

"I'm confused," said Books. "By threats, are you referring to the environmental issues confronting the EEWA and other Green groups?"

"Yes."

"And what are those threats?"

Struthers held up a hand and counted them off: "Livestock grazing, road expansion, mining and logging, and off-road vehicle use."

"You mentioned you and David disagreed when it came to operational activities. Would you explain that for me?"

Barry Struthers pursed his lips. "David was content to attack environmental threats through public information campaigns, lobbying elected officials, that sort of thing. While those activities are important, I also believe in what I like to call, 'constructive confrontation.'"

Books had a pretty good idea what that meant, but he asked the question anyway. "Interesting choice of words, constructive confrontation. What exactly are you talking about?"

"For the sake of clarification, let's use road expansion as an example. I have no problem leading members into the field and physically disrupting illegal road expansion activity. David never thought that was appropriate. He wasn't interested in rolling up his sleeves and getting his hands dirty."

Books moved on. "Several sources have told me that you and David not only engaged in shouting matches but that you had to be physically separated at a recent EEWA function. What can you tell me about that?"

"It's true, and I'm embarrassed about it. It shouldn't have happened. I regret it, and David did as well. As far as the verbal spats are concerned, no big deal. We had those with some frequency, and I'm sure, we would have continued to have them."

"Did you have anything to do with David's death?"

"Absolutely not. I wasn't even in town the weekend he was killed."

"Where were you?"

"A skeet shooting competition in Boise, Idaho. We left Friday morning. I competed Saturday and Sunday. We drove back to Kanab on Monday. We heard about David's death in a phone message left at the house by Cathy Carpenter Monday afternoon."

"You mentioned 'we.'"

"Oh, sorry. That's my wife, Alice."

"The woman seated with you at the memorial service?"

"That's right. She had to get back to work. Alice handles the bookkeeping at the Parry Lodge."

Books nodded. "Do you have any theories about who might have killed David?"

"It's hard to say, but probably one of the local nutcase ranchers, or maybe a professional outfitter. They all hated him."

"What makes you think his killer might be a professional outfitter?"

"Only that most of the outfitters spend much of their time in the wilderness, and a lot of them are right-wing crazies."

"Do you think he was stalked and then killed?"

"I doubt it. When the dust settles, I'll bet you'll learn that it was an opportunity killing. Somebody saw him out there by himself and figured, why not?"

Struthers sighed. "But, what difference does it really make. Dead is dead, right?"

"Suppose so," replied Books.

Books remained at the Subway after Barry Struthers left. He hadn't eaten anything since breakfast. He ordered a turkey sandwich and downed a can of Arizona iced tea.

Books put little credence in Struther's assertion that Greenbriar's murder was a crime of opportunity. At the same time, he had no doubt that Struthers was exactly where he said he was the weekend of the murder. He would send Brian Call to interview Alice Struthers and pick up whatever documentation supported their presence in Idaho during the weekend.

In the meantime, Books needed to find Trees McClain and settle a few issues.

# Chapter Twenty-seven

By his own count, Peter Deluca had killed twenty-seven men. That number didn't include scores of Gooks he'd shot during two tours as an Army sniper in Nam back in '72 and '73. His had been a long career spanning more than thirty years. How ironic that the federal government provided the job training that led to a lucrative career as a mob enforcer.

After the call, Deluca quickly packed a small duffel bag with several days' clothes. A second case carried an assortment of firearms—tools of the trade, as he liked to think of them. He left his home in suburban Henderson and made the thirty-minute drive to McCarron International Airport. On the way, he dropped his female Cocker, Rosie III, at the local doggie day-care facility. It was actually a posh resort for pampered dogs. To Deluca's way of thinking, nothing was too good for Rosie. At the airport, he parked his Cadillac Seville in long-term parking and caught a shuttle to the Hertz lot.

He had rented an all-wheel drive Ford Explorer for the return trip to Kanab, a place he had hoped never to see again. Deluca much preferred the creature comforts of his Cadillac, but depending upon how it turned out, this job might require a four-wheel drive vehicle, something suitable for the wild terrain of the Grand Staircase Escalante National Monument.

The three-hour drive from Las Vegas gave Deluca ample time to think. In hindsight, he now regretted accepting this assignment. In more than thirty years of contract work, he had taken jobs outside the mob on only two occasions. Both of those contracts had been completed without serious complications. Now this one had come along, and with it came problems, serious ones.

He arrived in Kanab at five p.m., pulling into one of those dumpy AAA-rated motels on the north end of town. He registered using false identification, and, as always, he paid in cash. Deluca enjoyed the better things in life, including good food. He couldn't imagine anything approximating fine dining in Kanab. He asked the front desk clerk for recommendations, and he ended up at a so-so diner called the Kanab Creek Inn.

Back in the Explorer, Deluca considered his dilemma. He knew exactly what he would do with Ronnie Gadasky once he found him. The problem was finding the little shit. He decided on a reconnaissance mission, knowing that he had to be ready to strike whenever the opportunity presented itself. One chance might be all he got.

First, Deluca drove south through town. He found the old brick house and the double-wide mobile home that belonged to the old man, Ned Hunsaker. The mobile home was located about two hundred yards south and slightly west of the main house. Deluca noticed a ratty old pickup truck parked in a circular gravel driveway in front of the main house. It belonged to Ned Hunsaker. The mobile home looked deserted, but the federal cop, J.D. Books, rented it from Hunsaker. If it became necessary to go after Books, the smart play would be to go in after dark, take out the old man, and then deal with Books.

Next, Deluca headed east on State Highway 89 to a narrow dirt road with a sign that read, Gadasky Towing & Salvage. Fortunately, he still had daylight. In the dark, he would have missed the turnoff. He located a shallow turnout next to the highway that provided an unobstructed view of any traffic entering or exiting the property. From what he'd been told, Ronnie Gadasky lived with his father and one brother. The kid drove a red dirt bike that shouldn't be difficult to spot. Given his druthers, Deluca preferred to kill Ronnie away from home, and, if possible, avoid having to deal with other members of his family. He was, however, prepared to kill the boy at home even if it meant taking out the entire Gadasky clan.

Deluca removed a disposable cell phone from his shirt pocket and dialed the Gadasky home. Nobody answered. Fifteen minutes later he called again. Still no answer. He decided to go in and have a look around.

From his gun case, Deluca removed a compact .380 caliber Ruger automatic with a six-round magazine. It was a nice little piece, good for close range work. He attached a sound suppressor to the barrel and then shoved it into the waistband of his pants.

He parked the Explorer next to the highway and walked down a winding dirt road. Everything at the house was as described except for the three-legged dog that gave a couple of disinterested barks and then hobbled his direction from the covered front porch. She was a friendly old girl, nearly blind, he thought, looking only for a pat on the head. Still she might become a problem should he have to return at night to an occupied house. He saw no reason to worry about that now. If it became a problem later, he'd deal with it then.

In his professional life, Peter Deluca had chosen to keep things simple. He conducted business using a few basic rules. He refused to kill women or children. He accepted assignments only from known mob associates in the Chicago Outfit or people recommended by them. And he fastidiously avoided jobs that might involve killing animals, dogs in particular. He was convinced that dogs, unlike people, were God's only living creatures capable of providing unconditional love, courage, loyalty, and trust. And sadly, he thought, they often gave far more to people than they received in return.

Deluca knocked on the front door and waited. When nobody answered, he twisted the knob and stepped into the small living room. He stood perfectly still, listening for any sound that might reveal someone's presence. Convinced that he was alone, he moved quickly from room to room until he came to a door on the second floor with a hand-printed sign on it that read, "Ronnie's Room—Stay Out." He tried the door. It was locked. It took him all of thirty seconds to pick the lock.

It was a small bedroom that resembled a train wreck, clutter everywhere. Several pairs of boots had been tossed haphazardly on the floor. Clothes were scattered all over the room. The bed was unmade. The sheets hadn't been washed in months.

The closet contained a three drawer metal file cabinet. In the bottom drawer, Deluca found an old shoe box. Inside was a stack of color photographs wrapped in an old washcloth and held in place with rubber bands.

The pictures were of the same strikingly beautiful woman, probably in her late twenties or early thirties. She had long black hair and a dark complexion, a petite body, firm and toned yet not muscular. The woman was photographed inside and outside the house. In some, she was dressed, or partially so. In others, she was completely naked. Several of the nudes had been taken in a backyard hot tub.

To Deluca, a couple of things seemed clear. In none of the pictures was the woman photographed looking directly into the camera, and the woman's hair and clothing were different from picture to picture. That meant the photographs were taken over a period of time, not in a single session. And the young woman in the pictures had no idea she was being stalked.

Deluca studied the photos. Ronnie Gadasky had a dirty secret. The fucking little pervert was a peeping Tom, a stalker who at least had the good taste to single out a looker for a victim. Who was the woman and why had the kid selected her? At random? Someone he knew? Deluca kept one picture of the woman and a second of the front of her home. The rest he returned to the shoebox.

Twilight was slowly giving way to darkness when Deluca heard the sound of an approaching diesel engine. He peeked out the bedroom window in time to see a three-quarter-ton flatbed truck pull up in front with a rusted-out Jeep Wrangler strapped on top. An elderly man wearing a dirty ball cap started up the walkway toward the front door, stopping just long enough to give the old dog a scratch on the ears. Deluca removed the Ruger from the waistband of his pants and slipped out the back door. He moved quickly away from the house, crossing an open area and then a shallow depression covered with rock, sagebrush, and scattered juniper. His departure went unnoticed. His path brought him onto the state highway a couple of hundred yards from his SUV.

Driving back to town, Deluca thought about the young woman in the photographs. Assuming she lived in town, how difficult could it be to find her? Probably not very. Kanab was a small town, and he had a picture of her and the house she lived in. It was a pueblo-style ranch home, probably in an upscale area. How many could there be in a place like Kanab?

Maybe the hunt for Ronnie Gadasky had just gotten easier.

# Chapter Twenty-eight

After leaving the Subway, Books drove to Neil Eddins' ranch looking for Tommy McClain, but there was no sign of him or his 2002 GMC pickup. Books stopped at the small bunkhouse that served as McClain's home, located a quarter mile from the main compound.

When nobody answered his knock, Books opened the front door and walked in. No sign of McClain. The bunkhouse was empty. He decided to snoop around.

McClain seemed an unlikely candidate to win the seal of Good Housekeeping Award. The place was a dive. The only source of heat was a pot-bellied wood-burning stove that sat in the kitchen. There was enough dust on the furniture to write your last will and testament. An old bunk bed with an equally old pair of stained mattresses was pushed against one wall. A single bed with sheets and a tattered blanket rested against another. Books found nothing in the bed or under the mattress. When he lifted the pillow, he found himself staring at a .357 Smith & Wesson revolver with a six-inch barrel. Only a paranoid man slept with a handgun under his pillow, thought Books.

On the dining room table, he sifted through a stack of mail, junk and unpaid bills mostly, and newspaper clippings describing the murder. He rifled through a dresser drawer but found nothing useful. A six-foot high metal locker stood next to the bed. On the floor of the locker, Books found a stack of Captain Marvel comic books and an assortment of adult skin magazines.

McClain's reading interests didn't appear to include Hemingway or Shakespeare. As he stood to close the locker, the front door opened and Neil Eddins walked in.

"I assume you have a court order giving you permission to search these premises," said Eddins.

"You caught me red-handed, Neil."

"I figured as much. What do you want?"

"I'm looking for Trees."

"Well, you won't find him hiding in that locker you're rummaging through."

"I'm sure you're right about that."

Eddins shook his head. "You just can't let it go, can you, J.D?"

"Let go of what?"

"You know darn well what."

Books shrugged. "No, I can't, and yes, I do."

"I just don't get it. You quickly solved a complex murder case that our sheriff probably wouldn't have, the BLM has to be pleased with the job you've done, and this community owes you a huge debt of gratitude. Why isn't that enough? Accept the accolades, J.D., and move on. It's in everyone's best interest."

"You mean everyone except the guy who's about to be charged with a murder he likely didn't commit. What about him, Neil? Do we just flush him down the toilet in the interest of community harmony?"

"Don't be foolish. There's more than enough evidence linking Lance Clayburn to this crime. Even you can't explain the incriminating evidence, can you? Everybody sees that except you."

"I'm amazed how much the armchair quarterbacks seem to know about this case, but you're right, Neil, at the moment, I can't explain the physical evidence. I'm working on it, though. There's more to this case than the evidence. Some things don't add up."

Eddins stepped closer to Books. "You know, J.D., I can be the best friend you've got in this town or your worst enemy. Unfortunately, you seem hell-bent on the latter. I can turn the thermostat on you up so high that you'll be dancing on your tip-toes like a ballerina. I wish you'd reconsider your position."

"Sorry, Neil, I'm afraid I can't do that. Now where can I find Trees?"

Eddins sighed. "Have it your way. Trees and a couple of his friends have gone bow hunting. I don't expect him back until sometime Sunday."

"Where does he like to hunt?"

Eddins studied him for a moment before answering. "He mentioned heading up Johnson Canyon. My guess is that you'll find him camped somewhere along the Skutumpah Road."

Books headed for the bunkhouse door. "Thanks, Neil. I'll see if I can find him."

"Hey, J.D."

"Yeah,"

"Be careful what you wish for."

After leaving Eddins, Books drove to the Johnson Canyon Road and turned north into the Grand Staircase on the long-shot chance he might find McClain. He knew that he was running out of time and options. Tomorrow's meeting with D.A. Virgil Bell would likely result in murder charges against Lance Clayburn, something he now saw little chance of forestalling.

◇◇◇

Peter Deluca returned to Kanab. He checked three real estate offices before he found one with a car parked in front and the lights on. He walked in and was greeted by a young man dressed in jeans, a sport shirt, and cowboy boots. "Can I help you with something?" said the realtor, a friendly smile on his face.

"I hope so," said Deluca. "I was just passing through on vacation and fell in love with the area. It's beautiful country."

"Sure is," said the Realtor. "I'm Stan Utley, by the way. And you are...."

"Andrew Wiley," replied Deluca.

"Where are you from, Mr. Wiley?"

"Reno, Nevada."

"And you're interested in land to build on or perhaps a second home?" said Utley.

"A second home." Deluca removed the photograph he'd just taken from Gadasky's home and handed it to the realtor. "I really like pueblo-style homes. They fit so well into the local landscape. Where can I find houses like this one around here?"

Utley studied the picture and then said, "Southwest style homes are very popular in Kane County. You could build a house like this on almost any property you purchased so long as there are no restrictive covenants."

"But what about existing homes? Where can I find houses like this?"

Utley thought some more. "There aren't any housing developments that specialize in pueblo-style homes. But I'd say, if you looked around on the west side of town, across Kanab Creek, you'll find more of this style home than anywhere else. Just get on Kanab Creek Drive and it'll take you into the area I'm talking about. Would you like me to search the multiple listing data base for you and see what we can find?"

Deluca smiled. "Why don't you just give me your business card? I'd like to drive around on my own tomorrow and then I'll check back with you. Would that be okay?"

"Certainly." Utley handed Deluca his card.

Deluca's next stop was the Kanab library. He introduced himself to the librarian as a reporter for the Associated Press. He asked to read everything pertaining to the murder and anything related to J.D. Books. He told her that he'd been assigned to write a breakout piece on Books. Much of what he read, particularly about the murder, he already knew. But he learned a few things about J.D. Books he hadn't known.

Books was a local, born and raised in Kane County. His father, Bernard, was a retired federal government employee who still resided in Kanab. The librarian told him that Books had a sister, Maggie, who had married into a prominent ranch family. Before he left the library, Deluca borrowed a local telephone directory and jotted down addresses for Bernard Books and Bobby and Maggie Case. He might never need this information, but if he did, he wouldn't have time to go looking for it. In the past, whenever he'd needed leverage, nothing worked better than putting family members in harm's way.

Deluca stopped at a convenience store on Center Street where he purchased cigarettes. He asked the store clerk to recommend a good bar, not a touristy place, but one frequented by locals. The clerk suggested a joint called the Cattle Baron.

Deluca was a likeable man. When necessary, he could be charming, friendly, and easy to talk to. He spent the next two hours in the Cattle Baron nursing several beers, buying drinks for other customers, and soaking up as much information as he possibly could. It was almost midnight when he returned to the motel.

# Chapter Twenty-nine

Books followed Johnson Canyon Road north into the national monument. Sunset glowed against the towering Vermilion Cliffs as daylight gradually surrendered to night. The road climbed and traversed the terraced Grand Staircase through jagged rock formations, sagebrush, and junipers. A pinyon mouse darted across the road in front of the Yukon, racing for the shelter of a twisted stand of juniper trees.

Most roads in the monument were unpaved and primitive, requiring high clearance, four-wheel drive vehicles to get around. Several miles up the forty-six mile stretch, the paved road suddenly forked and became a graded dirt surface. At the fork, he bore to the right following the Skutumpah Road northeast.

The day's rain storm had him worried. Experienced monument travelers understood that wet conditions frequently made the upper portion of the road impassable. Wet clay had an annoying habit of adhering to tires, leaving unsuspecting travelers stranded. Books had no idea how far McClain might have ventured into the monument. Finding him at all would take a stroke of luck.

He had just come around a narrow, rocky curve in the road and begun a steady uphill climb when he heard the shot. He pulled the Yukon to the side of the road, doused the headlights, and turned the motor off. It was silent. He waited.

Several minutes passed before Books saw the oncoming head-lights top the rise directly in front of him. The vehicle, whatever it was, crept along slowly, the occupants apparently oblivious to his presence. As it came closer, he heard loud, raucous laughter. The vehicle stopped not more than one hundred yards from him. How could the bozos not have seen him?

Books saw a muzzle flash and heard the loud report of a rifle. More laughter. They were firing into the darkness at something or maybe nothing. The vehicle inched closer to the Yukon. Books started the engine and hit his bright lights. His lights illuminated the cab of the GMC pickup, and Books saw clearly the surprised faces of two men. The driver was Trees McClain, and the passenger was Derek Lebeau, the same jerkoff who'd lobbed the rock through the front window of his trailer several days prior. He pulled the Yukon alongside McClain's pickup.

"Evening, boys. What are you shootin' at?"

"Nothin' in particular," said McClain. His speech was slurred and the cab of their truck reeked of alcohol.

"Suppose I don't have to tell you boys, but hunting from a vehicle is illegal in Utah."

"We weren't huntin'," said McClain. "It's too dark to see anything."

"Really. Then what were you shooting at?"

McClain glanced at Lebeau for help. Lebeau said, "Varmints. We was just shooting at varmints."

"Varmints, huh. That sounds like hunting to me. Shut the engine off, Tommy, and let me have a look at your permits."

Books moved the Yukon a few feet further up the road and radioed dispatch. He gave them his location and asked for immediate backup. The dispatcher told him that an officer from the Utah State Fish & Game Department would be sent but was at least thirty minutes away.

He was on his own. He knew it, and so would McClain and Lebeau. He got out of the Yukon, crossed the dirt road, and came up alongside McClain's truck from the passenger side. He eased the nine-millimeter from its holster and held it low at his side. In some ways Lebeau made him more nervous than McClain. Somebody in that truck had a loaded rifle and who could tell what other weapons. Books looked into the cab and immediately saw a rifle with its barrel pointed toward the floor of the truck. An opened half-gallon bottle of Early Times rested on the seat between the two men. Most of the bottle was empty.

"Hand me the rifle, Mr. Lebeau, butt first."

Lebeau complied. The weapon was a Savage Arms .30-06.

"Did you enjoy the jug of Early Times? Let me see those hunting permits."

Books examined the permits and handed them back to Lebeau. "Everything seems to be in order except for one thing. This is the bow hunt, not a rifle hunt. Where are your bows?"

"In the bed of the truck mixed into our camp gear," slurred McClain. "Are you fixin to arrest us?"

"I haven't decided yet."

Books told McClain to remain in the truck and ordered Lebeau out. He holstered his weapon long enough to reach for his handcuffs. He slapped one cuff on Lebeau's wrist and attached the other to the outside door handle of the truck.

"Sit tight, Derek, I'll be back with you shortly."

"Don't leave me shackled like this, man, I gotta pee."

"You can hold it or piss your pants. It doesn't matter to me."

"You cocksucker."

Books ordered McClain out of the truck and walked him over to the Yukon. "Tommy, I don't have a lot of time. I need you to answer some questions about David Greenbriar's murder."

McClain grunted, "Huh, I don't have no fancy education, Books, but I do know one thing. I don't have to say nothin' to you. I don't have to tell you jack-shit."

"That's true, Tommy, but if you don't, I'm going to hook your truck and throw your sorry ass in jail, Lebeau along with you. Last chance. What's it going to be?"

"Fuck you, asshole," shouted McClain.

Books anticipated McClain's next move. The big man threw a wild, round-house left hook that Books ducked. He took one step back and then kicked McClain on the inside of his right knee. He heard something pop and McClain screamed in pain.

McClain's legs went out from under him and both men went to the ground in a tangled wrestling match. McClain reached a beefy hand for Books' holstered gun. Books rolled to his side and brought his elbow down hard on top of McClain's hand, breaking his grip on the weapon. Books rolled again until he had McClain face down in the dirt road. He placed his own knee in the center of McClain's back and used the leverage to force his hands behind his back, slapping on a second pair of cuffs.

When the incident was over, Books realized that he'd been lucky. It had taken all his strength to subdue one highly intoxicated man, operating on only one good leg. If he hadn't had Lebeau handcuffed to the pickup, he might have been overpowered, killed, and his body dumped in some remote part of the monument never to be found. As it was, he'd gotten out of the incident with a torn, dirty uniform and numerous bumps and bruises.

Books got home after midnight. An officer from state fish and game arrived shortly after the melée ended. McClain required treatment at the hospital for a possible torn ACL in his knee. He and Lebeau had been booked into the Kane County Jail with numerous charges pending. The pickup truck had been impounded, and Lebeau's .30-06 booked into evidence. Books planned to submit the rifle for a ballistics test on the outside chance that it had been used to kill David Greenbriar.

# Chapter Thirty

Early the next morning, Deluca stopped at the Ranch Inn and Café for breakfast. The motel clerk recommended it as a local favorite. He was taking a calculated risk. While he might pick up valuable information in a local diner, he might also be noticed. This was a small town, a place where strangers stood out like drugstore cowboys at a pro rodeo bull-riding event.

He ordered coffee and breakfast. As he waited, he kept one ear open to the conversation around him while he perused the local paper, a rag called the *Kane County Citizen*. The paper's lead story was devoted to the continuing murder investigation. Deluca read it with interest. On the back page, in the Police Blotter section, he discovered that a local woman, Rebecca Eddins, reported a prowler around her home earlier in the week. The short piece provided no address for Eddins.

Could the prowler have been Ronnie Gadasky, stalking the woman in the photos? He intended to find out.

◇◇◇

Books stopped at the local Gas 'N' Go for coffee and a copy of the *Kane County Citizen* on his way into the office. The lead story confirmed what Books had been afraid of—that Brian Call was leaking sensitive information about the investigation to the press. The front page headline read Murder Investigation Stalls—Widow of Victim Pregnant. Books scanned the article. It mentioned that an anonymous source told the newspaper that

Darby Greenbriar was pregnant and that her murdered husband, David, was not the father. The article went on to name Lance Clayburn as a suspect in the slaying and intimated that he and Darby were having an affair at the time of the murder.

Books hadn't been in his office long enough for his morning coffee to cool before he was summoned to Alexis Runyon's office. Charley Sutter was there holding a copy of the newspaper. He was angry. Runyon didn't look particularly happy either.

"Jesus, Books, why didn't you tell me?" asked Sutter.

"Tell you, what, Charley?"

Sutter waved the morning paper in his face. "Don't stonewall me, Books. Did you know?"

Books closed his eyes and nodded. "Yes."

"Why wasn't I told the minute you discovered that Darby Greenbriar was pregnant and her late husband wasn't the father? Kind of an important piece of information, don't you think? And that's just the beginning of the shitstorm I found waiting for me when I walked into the office this morning."

"Hold on, Charley, let me explain."

"Go ahead, and it better be good."

"I learned about the pregnancy yesterday from discussions with Darby and Lillian Greenbriar. It's true that I deliberately withheld it from you, but I did it for a reason. Somebody's been leaking information about our case from the beginning. And now I know that that somebody is Brian Call."

"I don't believe it," replied Sutter. "Call has my full confidence. He wouldn't do anything like that."

"Well, he did. The reason I know is that Brian was the only person I told about Darby's pregnancy and David's sterility. Apparently, he couldn't wait to drop that information on the asshole that runs the local paper. I knew the leaks had to be coming from you or Call. I just took a guess that it was Call and baited the trap."

Runyon, who had been listening attentively, said, "What do you think, Charley?"

He sighed. "Frankly, I find it hard to believe. Brian Call has given this community more than ten years of dedicated service. It doesn't make any sense."

"Charley," said Books. "How much do you really know about Brian Call?"

"I know he's done an excellent job in this department for over a decade. That's all I need to know."

Books frowned. "Did you check him out thoroughly with Las Vegas P.D. before you hired him?"

"What the hell are you intimating, Books?"

"That maybe you don't know Brian Call quite as well as you think. Now, did you check him out or not?"

Sutter thought about it before replying. "I don't recall. I'd have to go into his personnel file and take a look."

"Why don't you? Maybe it's time to contact Las Vegas P.D. and find out a little more about him."

"But what's the point?" said Sutter. "Suppose he is leaking information. What's he trying to do—sabotage the investigation?"

"I don't know, Charley. But it's a question we need answered."

"Maybe he's trying to ensure a certain outcome in the case," said Runyon.

"What do you mean?" asked Sutter.

"She's suggesting that Call may want to do everything in his power to see that Lance Clayburn takes the fall for Greenbriar's murder."

"That's nonsense," replied Sutter. "Call probably does believe Clayburn committed the murder. As a matter of fact, so do I, because that's where the evidence points."

"Unfortunately," said Runyon, "what's going on with Call might turn out to be the least of our problems. Neil Eddins has been making phone calls to some people in high places, and there's bound to be fallout."

"That's putting it mildly," said Sutter.

Books said, "What's he saying?"

"Try an illegal search for starters," said Sutter. "You know the kind I'm talking about, one where you enter someone's home without a warrant, and then get caught by the property owner. In this case, that would be Neil Eddins."

"You mean the bunkhouse where McClain lives," said Books.

"One and the same," said the sheriff. "What the hell were you doing out there?"

"Following leads, Charley. I was trying to find McClain so I could ask him about the threats he'd made against the Greenbriars."

"Nothing wrong with that. It's conducting a search of his home without a warrant and without permission that crosses the line, J.D. You might be able to get away with that in the big city, but this ain't the big city. That little stunt is going to end up in the newspaper, and it isn't going to make us look very good."

Sutter was right and Books knew it. "I was wrong to do that, and I apologize for any embarrassment I may have caused the BLM or the Kane County Sheriff's Office."

"Apology accepted," said the sheriff, "but that might not be enough to get us through this. I've been summoned to a three o'clock meeting this afternoon with the commissioners in a closed-door session, and I know what's on their agenda. They're going to ask me to remove you from the investigation."

"And what are you planning to tell them?"

"I hope I can tell them that Lance Clayburn is about to be arrested for the murder of David Greenbriar, and the case will be closed. You haven't forgotten our eleven o'clock meeting this morning with the prosecutor. If everything goes as expected, charges should be filed in the next day or two."

"I haven't forgotten."

"Good. And just so you know, J.D., Eddins is not only complaining about the alleged civil rights violation, but he intends to portray you publicly as some kind of loose cannon with an ugly temper. He'll cite as evidence your Denver history, as well as the two arrests you've made the past several days, both involving what he claims is the questionable use of force."

"That's bogus and you know it. I used reasonable force when I arrested Lebeau and McClain. If they hadn't decided to put up a fight, force wouldn't have been necessary."

"Hell, I know that J.D., but think how it looks," said Sutter.

After Sutter left, Books stayed in Runyon's office. For a while, nobody spoke. Then Runyon said, "You don't think Clayburn did it, do you?"

"Nope, but I can't prove it. And there is the physical evidence. It's impossible to explain away. What would you like me to do, Alexis?"

"It's your decision, J.D. If you want to pull out of this thing, I understand. On the other hand, it might be interesting to see what you can find out about Brian Call. And what about that kid, Ronnie Gadasky? I wonder what he has to say."

Books returned to his office and phoned Grant Weatherby in Las Vegas. He picked up immediately.

"I hate to keep pestering you, Grant, but I need some more help."

"Not a problem. I needed to call you anyway. What's up?"

"Can you access personnel records from your department?"

"Depends on the reason and who's asking."

Books told him about Brian Call's past employment as a corrections officer in the Las Vegas Metropolitan Detention Center.

"What kind of information do you want?" asked Weatherby.

"I'd like to know the conditions under which he left your department, and anything else that looks interesting."

"How long ago did he work for us?"

"I'm not sure, but I think it's been twelve or thirteen years at least."

"I'll see what I can find out and get back to you."

"Thanks. You said you had something else for me."

"I do. I talked to several people from the room service department at the Hard Rock, and nobody recalls seeing Lance Clayburn on Sunday."

Books sighed. "It was a long shot anyway."

"But that's not the end of the story," said Weatherby. "The casino security staff was kind enough to search the floor tapes beginning at 12:01 A.M. Sunday morning. At 9:12 A.M., they found your boy playing the dollar slots."

"How long was he in the casino?"

"The security cameras picked him up leaving the casino twenty minutes later."

Books thanked him and they disconnected. Ten minutes later, Weatherby called back.

"That was fast."

"Don't get too excited. I haven't got the information you requested, but I did learn one interesting thing. When I called personnel, I was told that any inquiry concerning Brian Call would have to be routed through the department's criminal intelligence division. I placed a call to a contact over there, but he hasn't gotten back to me yet."

"What do you make of that?"

"It tells me Call probably separated from the department involuntarily. It also tells me he probably hung around with some bad boys. The intelligence division spends a lot of time tracking associations among a broad range of unsavory characters—pimps, drug dealers, gamblers, and, of course, organized crime figures. I'll get back to you as soon as I have more."

# Chapter Thirty-one

Deluca finished his breakfast and then drove a short distance to a convenience store with a pay phone out front. He used the phone book and tried to find a listing for Rebecca Eddins. There wasn't one, but there was a listing for R. Eddins in Kanab. Deluca figured if she was single and living alone, she might opt for a nonpublished number or drop her first name and use an initial instead.

He jotted the phone number and address on a napkin he'd taken from the restaurant. He dialed the number and waited. After several rings the call transferred into voice mail. A pleasant, female voice said, "You have reached Rebecca Eddins, please leave a message. If you are calling about possible legal services, please call my law office at (435)649-7200."

Deluca hung up. He made a second call to the home of Ronnie Gadasky. "Is Ronnie there, please?"

"No, he ain't. Who's this?"

"My name is Elliott Sanders. I'm a reporter with the *Las Vegas Sun Times*. I'm here covering the Greenbriar murder, and I've been asked to do a story on Ronnie. Do you happen to know when he might return?"

"No, mister, I don't—can't imagine why you want to talk to Ronnie, anyway. He's dumber than a sack of horse poop."

"To whom am I speaking?"

"George, George Gadasky. I'm his brother."

"Okay, George," said Deluca. "Would you happen to know where I might find Ronnie?"

There was a lengthy pause. "Depends. How bad you wanna find him?"

"I'm very anxious to talk with him. If you could take me to him, George, I'll make it worth your time."

"How much?"

"How about a hundred bucks?"

"My time's worth more than that."

"Well, how much would you like?"

"Oh, I'd have to have at least two hundred."

"Consider it done. When can we leave?"

"Soon as I finish my chores. You wanna come out here?"

"No. Why don't I meet you someplace?"

"Okay. Do you know where the turnoff is to the old Paria movie set?"

Deluca almost choked. "Yes, I do. It's outside Kanab, off Highway 89, right?"

"That's it," said George. "Meet me there this afternoon at one o'clock."

"I'll be there."

◇◇◇

Books still had an hour until the eleven o'clock meeting with prosecuting attorney Virgil Bell, so he drove to the home of Ivan Gadasky, hoping Ronnie had returned since he last talked with the old man. Ivan wasn't there, but the three-legged lab was, and so was Ronnie's older brother, George."

"Hey, J.D., how ya been?"

"Good, George. How about you? It's been a long time."

"Damn straight. How about fifteen years."

His math wasn't very good, but close enough. "About right."

George invited him in. "What brings ya out this way, J.D.?"

"Maybe your dad didn't mention it, but I'm trying to find Ronnie."

"You and everybody else."

Books frowned. "What do you mean?"

"Oh, some reporter called lookin for him. The flakey little bastard's become a real celebrity."

"You mean that little weasel from the *Kane County Citizen*?"

"Mr. Christensen. No, it weren't him."

"Who was it?"

George scratched his chin. "Said his name was Elliott some-thin-or-other, Sanders, I think he said."

"Did he say who he worked for?"

"Yeah. He mentioned some newspaper in Las Vegas."

"The *Las Vegas Sun Times?*"

"I think that was it," said George.

"What did he want?"

"Said he wanted to interview Ronnie for some story he was doing about the murder."

"What did you tell him?"

George lied. "Told him I got no idea where he's at."

Books handed him a business card. "If you hear from Ronnie, I'd appreciate it if you'd tell him to call me. I really need to talk with him."

George looked at the business card and said, "I'll do it, J.D."

◇◇◇

Books arrived ten minutes late for the meeting with prosecutor Virgil Bell. His office was located in an old brick home on the north end of Kanab that had been remodeled into a law office. A receptionist escorted him to a small conference room in the rear of the house that at one time had been a bedroom.

Seated at the conference table were Charley Sutter, Brian Call, and a short, pudgy man in his early forties with a receding hairline, a bad comb-over, and pasty, yellow skin that made him look like he was suffering from jaundice. Sutter made the introduction. Books could only shake his head in frustration at Sutter's decision to allow Call to attend the meeting. Clearly, Call was the source of leaks to the press, and to anybody else interested in hearing the local gossip. If Call's motive was to bias the local jury pool should Lance Clayburn be brought to trial, he was doing a good job of it.

Virgil Bell had Greenbriar's file opened on the table in front of him. "Well, gentlemen, I've completed my review of the file, and I believe I'm ready to make a decision."

Glancing at Books, Bell continued. "I understand there is some disagreement about what course of action this office should take. Perhaps, Ranger Books, I could ask you to share your concerns about proceeding against the prime suspect in the case, Lance Clayburn."

"You mean the only suspect," said Sutter, a touch of sarcasm in his voice.

Books explained the timeline problem, but when pressed by Bell, he was forced to acknowledge the possibility that Clayburn could have returned to Kanab in time to have committed the murder.

When Books finished, Bell said, "Anything else?"

"Only that David Greenbriar was a lightning rod for controversy in this community. There were plenty of people who hated the man and everything he stood for."

"So, do you have any other suspects?" Bell asked.

Books had walked into that one leading with his chin. "Nobody that I can make a case against, at least not at the moment."

"The evidence seems more than convincing," said Bell. "You've got physical evidence—Mr. Clayburns fingerprints found at the crime scene. Then you have Clayburn calling the EEWA office trying to locate the victim on the Friday before the murder. The investigation further established that Greenbriar was killed with a .30-06 rifle, a weapon Clayburn owns, but now, conveniently, he can't seem to find. Then you uncovered an extramarital affair between Clayburn and Darby Greenbriar. When you put it all together, it makes a pretty compelling case for a murder charge."

Books couldn't deny it.

Sutter added. "Plus, we just learned that Darby is pregnant and that her late husband isn't the father."

Bell frowned. "Who is?"

"Good question," replied Sutter. "It'll probably turn out to be Lance Clayburn's kid, but at the moment, Darby insists that it's David's child."

For the first time, Call spoke. "Greenbriar's ex-wife, Lillian, maintains that David was shootin' blanks—says she's got medical documents that prove it."

"Have you verified that?" asked Bell.

"Not yet," said Sutter, "but we will."

Looking directly at Books, Bell had one last question. "What do you see as the weaknesses in the case, assuming it goes to trial?"

"I'm no lawyer, but if I were defending the case," said Books, "I'd hang my hat on reasonable doubt. We were able to place Clayburn in Las Vegas midmorning on Sunday. I'd argue that the likelihood of his returning to Kane County in time to commit this murder were slim to none. Don't forget, Clayburn had to get back to Kanab, but he also had the problem of how to find Greenbriar in the nearly two-million-acre Grand Staircase National Monument."

Bell shrugged. "Frankly, we've got enough evidence linking Clayburn to the crime that we should be able to overcome the lack of opportunity defense, if that's what they decide to try."

"You might be right," replied Books. Looking directly at Call, he said, "I wouldn't be the least bit surprised to see a defense motion seeking a change of venue."

"What makes you say that?" said Bell.

"Because somebody's been intentionally leaking information to anybody who'll listen. A good defense lawyer is going to want this trial moved to a different location, preferably to a large metropolitan area where there's at least a shot at getting an unbiased jury."

Call's face suddenly reddened and his body stiffened.

Bell yawned, looking somewhere between indifferent and bored. "If it happens, it happens. No sense worrying about it unless it does."

The meeting ended exactly the way Books figured it would. Bell would file a murder one charge against Clayburn with special circumstances. That would make him eligible for the death penalty if a jury convicted him of first-degree murder. Sheriff Sutter could make the arrest just as soon as a judge signed the warrant.

Books turned to Brian Call. "What about the polygraph exam for Clayburn?"

"The detective sergeant who handles lie detector tests for St. George P.D. has been on vacation," said Call. "I managed to get it scheduled for Monday morning at ten o'clock. That's his first day back."

"You probably ought to cancel the appointment. Once you arrest him, Clayburn'll be lawyered-up before you can blink. There won't be a poly once he's arrested."

"Has he agreed to take the test?" Bell asked.

"He did."

Bell turned to Sutter. "Your call, Charley. I don't care one way or the other, but Books has a point. Once you bust Clayburn, the poly is probably history."

"I'd feel better with Clayburn in jail," said Sutter. "We'll still make the poly available to him if he's willing to take it."

Bell turned to Sutter. "Then it's decided. Somebody needs to go to work on the affidavit. Once you've got a draft of the probable cause statement, bring it to me and I'll look it over before it goes to the judge. In the meantime, I'll have my paralegal prepare the charging documents. I'll file the paperwork first thing Monday morning in district court."

"Any problem if I schedule a news conference announcing the arrest?" asked Sutter. "That should get the press off my ass for a while."

"Not a problem," said Bell, "except I think it should be a joint press conference with both of us in attendance."

Sutter agreed.

# Chapter Thirty-two

Sutter and Brian Call went to work on the arrest warrant. Books realized that if he was lucky, he might have as much as twenty-fours hours before Lance Clayburn would be arrested. There was a lot to do and very little time.

Books returned to his office hoping he'd find a message from Grant Weatherby. He didn't. While he waited, he decided to examine David Greenbriar's day planner. Darby had given it to him days before, and he hadn't taken the time to go through it. He discovered that the planner contained a comprehensive record of the victim's activities from the beginning of the year until his August murder, and it did so in startling detail. Greenbriar had been a meticulous record-keeper.

Books noticed the amount of time Greenbriar spent in Salt Lake City during the state legislative session in January and February. He had testified in front of both house and senate committees on a variety of environmental bills.

Some days his appointment calendar was filled with meetings with state legislators from both sides of the aisle. He moved from legislator to legislator in fifteen- to thirty-minute intervals. There was also a detailed record of numerous lunches and dinners in which it appeared Greenbriar was schmoozing state legislators over one environmental issue or another.

At first, nothing seemed to jump off the pages. Then he noticed that one name appeared repeatedly. The man's name was Randall Orton. Who was Orton and what was his relationship with Greenbriar? A telephone call to a public information office at the state capitol revealed that Orton was a former state senator turned lobbyist. He lived an hour north of Kanab in the small town of Panguitch. Books was given a phone number and told that Orton Associates operated from an office in Randall Orton's home.

Books called Charley Sutter. "Yeah, J.D."

"How's that warrant coming?"

"Slow but steady. It'd go a lot quicker if you were here writing it."

"I'll drop around in a little while and take a look at it. That okay?"

"Sure. What's up?"

"What do you know about a guy named Randall Orton?"

Sutter paused. "I'm surprised you haven't heard of him, J.D. The Ortons are an old cattle-ranching family from southern Utah. Randy served two terms in the state senate and then figured out that there were a lot of available perks working as a lobbyist. The day his second term ended, he became a registered lobbyist."

"Who does he typically represent?"

Sutter chuckled. "Anybody with a fat bank account. Just kidding. I don't have any specifics, but I'm pretty sure he's represented mining and timber interests as well as the Utah Cattleman's Association. What makes you ask?"

"His name has come up in the Greenbriar case."

"In what way?"

"I'm not exactly sure, but I'll tell you as soon as I find out. All I know now is that Orton's name appears repeatedly in Greenbriar's planner. There wasn't a month between January and the time of his murder when the two weren't in touch by phone or face-to-face, sometimes both."

"Give him a call. I'm sure he'll tell you," said Sutter.

"Exactly what I was thinking."

Books had to give some credit to Charley Sutter. If the sheriff was worried about him continuing to chase leads, he wasn't saying anything about it. Books dialed Orton's number, and a pleasant sounding woman, probably his wife, answered the phone. A minute later, Orton picked up. Books introduced himself and explained his role in the Greenbriar murder investigation.

Orton spoke in a slow, deliberate fashion, carefully enunciating each syllable of every word. "I recognize your name from the newspaper and television coverage of the story. It's a terrible crime, a real tragedy. I'm so sorry for his family. I actually met Mrs. Greenbriar once or twice. I hope you apprehend whoever is responsible."

"Thank you, Mr. Orton. We're doing our best. I wonder if you could tell me the nature of your relationship with David. The reason I ask is that your name appears frequently in his planner in the months leading up to his death."

Orton took a moment to carefully measure what he was about to say. "In my lobbying practice, I am frequently retained to represent a diverse group of clients whose primary interest is in economic development—specifically companies in industries that will provide economic growth and jobs, particularly in rural parts of Utah."

"Are those companies mostly from the mining and timber industries?"

"Yes. Those as well as farm and ranching interests," replied Orton.

"Would it be a safe bet," said Books, "that you typically do not carry the banner for environmental groups like the Southern Utah Wilderness Alliance (SUWA) or David Greenbriar's organization, the EEWA?"

"Yes. That would be a safe bet, Mr. Books," he chuckled.

"Then why all the contact with Greenbriar in the months preceding his death?"

"In this instance, I had been hired by a Las Vegas public relations firm to try to negotiate a reasonable solution with the EEWA and SUWA to the road expansion problem in southern Utah wilderness areas."

"You mean you were trying to get those organizations to stop engaging in activities that might hamper the road expansion plans of your clients—activities like filing law suits."

"Precisely," said Orton. "We were hoping that we might reach some reasonable compromise that would facilitate economic growth and job creation in southern Utah."

"And I take it they weren't buying."

"That's right. There wasn't an ounce of compromise in SUWA or the EEWA, I'm sorry to say."

"I'll need the name of the Las Vegas PR company that hired you."

"Certainly. That would be Valley Public Relations and Marketing, LLC. The individual you need to speak with is Candace Fleming. She runs the place."

After the call, Books sat at his desk. Why would a Las Vegas PR firm retain a Utah hired gun to lobby environmental groups to promote economic development in Utah? It didn't make sense.

Books went on-line to the Nevada state government's official web site. With a handful of key strokes, he found himself on the home page of the Nevada Department of Business Regulation and Licensing. He plugged in the business name Orton had given him. Valley Public Relations and Marketing, LLC, listed three corporate officers: President, Candace Fleming, Vice President, Stephanie Lloyd, and Treasurer, Anthony Oliver. Books Googled all three and came up empty. Next, he entered each name into the National Crime Information Center (NCIC) system and again got nothing.

Books leaned back in his chair, planted his feet on the desk, and sipped the last cold swallows of his morning coffee. He decided to ask Grant Weatherby to run the business and its corporate officers through Las Vegas P.D.'s Criminal Intelligence Division and see what they could tell him.

Books' telephone rang. He glanced down at the number and realized it was Weatherby returning his call. Maybe now he'd get some answers.

# Chapter Thirty-three

A few minutes before one o'clock, Deluca turned off State Highway 89 onto a dirt road that led to the old west Paria movie set. He backed the Explorer into a shallow turnout that gave him a clear view of anyone traveling the dirt road or along Highway 89. He didn't particularly like sitting in plain view where any cop who just happened by might stop and begin asking questions. He loaded a clip into the silenced .22 caliber Taurus and replaced it behind his back in the waste band of his khaki pants. It was nearly one-thirty before George Gadasky turned off the highway in a rusted-out, canary yellow Ford pickup and pulled up next to Deluca's Explorer.

Deluca extended a hand out the window, "Elliott Sanders, *Las Vegas Sun Times*. Pleasure to meet you, Mr. Gadasky, George isn't it?"

Gadasky shook hands. "That's right. You got some green for me, Mr. Sanders."

"Right here." Deluca handed across two crisp hundred-dollar bills.

Gadasky smiled as he shoved the bills into his shirt pocket. "You want to ride with me?"

"No, I'll follow along behind you. No sense in you having to haul me back here when we're done."

"Suit yourself."

"How far are we going, anyway?"

"It's a ways, most of it through rough country. Think that shiny new Explorer of yours can make it?" Gadasky grinned.

"I'm sure of it. How sure are you that Ronnie will be at this place you're taking me to?"

"No way to know for sure where that crazy brother of mine might be. I just know this is a place he likes to go to when he wants to be by his self."

"I'll follow you. Let's get going." Deluca had no desire to sit around making small talk with Gadasky in a location where somebody might notice, nor was he interested in leaving his fingerprints all over Gadasky's truck.

Deluca followed Gadasky south along Highway 89 headed toward Lake Powell and the town of Big Water. They passed the BLM Paria contact station and then abruptly turned north on to a graded dirt track called Cottonwood Canyon Road. They followed the rutted, bumpy road for more than an hour, crawling through places requiring a high-clearance vehicle to pass. The road crossed dry creek beds that might become impassable in rain storms because of flash floods.

The landscape was dotted with juniper pine, cottonwood, and sage brush. As they climbed higher, two things struck Deluca. One was the stunning variety of colors on the surrounding hills. They changed from a drab gray to gold, similar to the color of honey. In other places, the hills were a shade of reddish-orange, almost the color of fire. The other was the sheer enormity of this land and the overwhelming sense of isolation that he felt driving through it.

One thing was certain: if you got lost out here, nobody would find your body for a hundred years, if then. Scavengers would eat your flesh, and your bones would be left to bleach in the hot desert sun.

Eventually the road forked. Gadasky turned right. He drove past a road sign that said 'Grosvenor Arch.' The road snaked almost another mile before emptying into a small parking lot. The lot was empty. Both men got out.

Deluca said, "It doesn't look like anybody's around. What's that brother of yours drive anyway?"

"It don't mean nothin just cuz the lot's empty. Ronnie most times rides a dirt bike. He wouldn't park it here. Come with me."

Gadasky led the way down a single-track dirt trail that meandered past several scattered picnic tables. A short distance later, the trail opened into a brush covered area large enough to build a camp fire and spread a sleeping bag. Gadasky squatted next to a fire pit and held his hands above the ashes.

"Still warm," he said. "I'll bet Ronnie spent the night here and cleared out sometime this morning."

"When Ronnie comes out here, is this the only place he camps?" said Deluca, trying to keep the anger from his voice.

"It's the only place I know about. I camped here with him one time."

"Where else does he hide out?"

Gadasky shrugged. "No idea. That boy moves like the wind when he's up here. He could be anyplace."

Gadasky stood and kicked more dirt on to the still warm ashes. "Well, let's head back to the trucks."

The kid felt genuinely disappointed. Little did he know that that was about the last thing in the world he would ever feel.

"What's over here?" Deluca walked out on to a sandstone outcropping.

Gadasky followed. "Ain't nothin' out here 'cept fucking hot desert."

The two men stood next to each other. Deluca pointed toward the horizon at nothing in particular. "What is that?"

Gadasky cocked his head straining to see what Deluca was pointing toward. His last words were, "What you lookin' at?"

In one fluid motion, Deluca brought the twenty-two up until it was almost touching the flesh behind Gadasky's left ear. He squeezed off one round into Gadasky's head as he muttered, "This Bud's for you." The kid's head twitched once, and then he dropped to the ground without a sound.

He liked nothing better than working with the .22 caliber at close range. It made a small entry wound and no exit wound.

The bullet just rattled around inside the head. No fuss, no muss, and best of all, no mess afterward.

Deluca quickly scanned the area looking for any sign of unwanted visitors. He was alone. He bent quickly over the body and plucked his two hundred dollars from Gadasky's shirt pocket. He lifted Gadasky by the shoulders and dragged him to the edge of a shallow ravine. The cliff dropped about twenty feet into what looked like a narrow slot canyon. He laid the body on its side and then used his boot to roll it over the edge, watching as George Gadasky tumbled out of sight.

Deluca returned to the Explorer and started back to town. He left Gadasky's old truck in the parking lot. Even when somebody found it, the authorities wouldn't suspect foul play, at least not for awhile. The ensuing search would eventually uncover the body, but not before Deluca had finished his business in Kanab and returned to Las Vegas.

# Chapter Thirty-four

The phone rang. Books planted his size-twelve boots on the floor. The last remnants of his morning coffee spilled down the front of his shirt. He cursed to himself as he lifted the receiver.

"Morning, Grant."

"Hey, J.D. Ready for the rundown on Brian Call?"

Books grabbed a pen and a legal pad. "You bet. Fire away."

"First thing you should know is there's nothing in the record that indicates the Kane County Sheriff's Office ever contacted our department for a reference check on the guy."

"No surprise there."

"Call was employed as a corrections officer in our jail for nearly four years. His performance appraisals were actually pretty good. He'd risen to the rank of corporal and was about to test for sergeant when some things finally caught up with him."

"Hold on for a second, I'm taking notes. Okay. What kind of things?"

"Hang on. I'm getting to that. The department gave him the option of resigning or being suspended from duty, pending the outcome of an IA investigation. Call opted to bail. Shortly after that, he dropped off our radar screen. Nobody in intell had heard anything about him in years, at least not until I started asking questions."

"What got him canned?"

"A couple of things. Right after his promotion to corporal, he showed up in surveillance photographs in the company of several Las Vegas organized crime associates. At first, our intell people didn't know who the hell he was. Somebody picked up a license plate number, and we got him identified. Imagine the surprise when we realized he was one of our own."

"Why didn't you fire him right away? In a lot of departments, the associations alone would have gotten him shit-canned."

"Couldn't agree with you more," said Weatherby. "My guess is that some genius up the chain got the bright idea to put him under surveillance and just keep an eye on him for a while."

"So what happened?"

"Several weeks later, he was spotted in the company of a local hooker who had just been released from jail. She was on felony probation for credit card forgery. Consorting with a known felon and somebody still under correctional supervision is a big no, no. That's when the department finally confronted him."

"Given what you've described, I don't understand all the secrecy over his personnel file," said Books. "It seems like a run-of-the-mill dirty cop kind of case, unless of course, there's more."

"As a matter of fact, there is. We've got a family here in the valley by the name of Calenti. The patriarch is an old man named Victor Calenti. Ever heard of him?"

"Nope."

"Anyway, as a kid, Victor grew up dirt-poor working in the Pennsylvania coal mines. Then his family moved west to Chicago. Over time, Victor grew pretty tight with leaders in the Chicago Outfit—Sam Giancana, Tony Accardo, and the Fischetti brothers. When Calenti moved to Las Vegas in the early 1970s, he leased space in an industrial park and opened a company called Nevada Mining & Manufacturing. We suspected that that the Outfit was laundering money through Calenti's mining company, although we were never able to prove it."

"You think they were skimming casino revenue, then washing it through the mining company? Tax-free income with everything neat and tidy."

"Exactly," said Weatherby. "The Chicago Outfit made a fortune running the Stardust."

"So, what does Nevada Mining & Manufacturing do, exactly?"

"They manufacture mining products, drilling equipment mostly. The old man also bought up the controlling interest in a coal mine in some Godforsaken place in Wyoming, and then another one near Price, Utah. Supposedly, the company also buys up mineral rights on land they believe might have future mining potential."

"I still don't see what this has to do with Brian Call," said Books.

"Here's the connection. The old man is out of the picture now. The business is run by his two sons, Vic Junior and younger brother, Michael. Michael's had his dirty little hands in a high-end call girl operation in Vegas for years. That aside, he's also has an expensive coke problem. He's been in and out of court and jail numerous times on a variety of beefs. Our intell people checked the duty rosters at the jail. It seems that every time Michael became a guest in our facility, Brian Call was assigned to the same cell block. Intell suspects that Call illegally provided some creature comforts for Calenti to make his time pass a little easier. Those creature comforts probably included contraband—specifically drugs and cash. Most of the intelligence information was pieced together after Call resigned."

"What about the hooker? Any connection to Calenti?"

"Not that we could prove. She denied it, but a snitch, working off a drug beef for one of our vice detectives, claimed she was in Michael's stable of ladies. Intell believes the services of the call girl were pay-back for whatever Call did for Calenti while he was locked up."

Books then explained what he'd learned in his conversation with former Utah legislator turned lobbyist, Randall Orton. Weatherby had never heard of Valley Public Relations and Marketing, nor was he familiar with any of its corporate officers.

When he got off the phone, Books sat wondering whether he was chasing another dead-end lead. It was small consolation to discover that Brian Call had once been a corrupt cop in Las Vegas who had been forced out of the department, only to have been subsequently hired by Charley Sutter without so much as a reference check.

He wasn't exactly sure what he was looking for, but Books returned to the web site of the Nevada Department of Business Regulation and Licensing. He plugged in the name of the mining company and brought up the names of the corporate officers as well as a list of the corporation's board of directors.

The only board member name he recognized, besides that of its chairman, Victor Calenti, Sr., was that of Randall Orton of Panguitch, Utah. The lobbyist had failed to mention his cozy relationship with the company during their recent phone conversation. The names of the corporate officers coincided with the information Weatherby had given him. Victor Calenti, Jr., President, Michael Calenti, Vice President, Maria Calenti, Secretary, and Anthony Oliver, Treasurer.

He stared at the list. At first, nothing registered with him as unusual or suspicious. Then it struck him. One name among the corporate officers, Anthony Oliver, seemed vaguely familiar. At first Books couldn't put a finger on it. Then it came to him. From the murder book, he grabbed the list of officers from Valley Public Relations and Marketing. Anthony Oliver was listed as the Treasurer on the corporate documents of both Valley Public Relations and Nevada Mining & Manufacturing. Books figured the PR firm had to be a subsidiary of the mining company.

In a fuzzy sort of way, the whole thing began to make sense. He'd discovered a connection between a shady mining company in Las Vegas and a dirty cop in Kane County. But what did it mean? He wasn't sure. A good place to start might be with Ned Hunsaker. The old man might have some ideas.

In the meantime, he had another priority. Why had Darby Greenbriar deliberately lied about who the father of her child was? If it was done to protect Lance Clayburn, the move had backfired. If anything, the lie made Clayburn look all the more guilty and probably gave Charley Sutter reason to believe she might be involved in the murder herself.

Books grabbed the keys to the Yukon. It was time to pay an unannounced visit to Darby Greenbriar. And it was time for him to stop playing Mr. Nice Guy.

# Chapter Thirty-five

Books headed straight to the EEWA. The office was locked. He drove north several miles out of Kanab and turned onto a private dirt road that served several homes, including Darby Greenbriar's. There were several vehicles parked in the driveway with out-of-state license plates—probably friends and relatives who came to town for the funeral service. Books parked in a gravel area next to David's Suburban. As he approached the house, he was greeted by a large German shepherd. The dog eyed him suspiciously but didn't bark. Books wondered if the animal was a trained guard dog, purchased by the Greenbriars to provide home security. If it was, Fido wasn't doing much of a job.

A distinguished-looking older woman, her black hair streaked with gray, answered the front door. The woman looked remarkably like Darby. She introduced herself as Darby's mother. Moments later, Darby appeared at the front door. She looked surprised to see Books.

"Darby, we need to talk. Sorry about not calling you ahead of time, but it can't wait."

She invited him in, introduced him to a knot of people in the living room, most of whom had either a beer or a glass of wine in hand. Darby led Books down a narrow hallway into a spacious office. One wall contained built-in book shelves filled from end-to-end with a striking variety of books. It definitely looked like the home of an academic, or maybe two.

"I don't see why this couldn't wait until next week," she said, her voice and demeanor taking an icy tone.

"Oh, it can wait, so long as you don't mind if Lance spends the weekend in jail."

"You're about to arrest Lance?" She was indignant.

"I'm not, but Charley Sutter is. How does a murder one charge with special circumstances sound? That means the state plans to seek the death penalty. And it's happening, in part, because you've been lying to us."

She started to interrupt, but Books cut her off. "No. Do me a favor this once. Will you just shut up and listen? If you think that lying to us about who the father of your baby is will help Lance, think again. It makes him look even guiltier, plus it's got the sheriff and the DA wondering whether you and Lance conspired to murder David."

"I don't understand."

"Of course you do. How long did you think it would take us to learn that David couldn't have children? I've got a file sitting in my office filled with interesting clinical reports from a fertility clinic in Berkeley. David was sterile and you knew it."

Darby drew both arms across her chest. She bent forward and began to cry.

"Look Darby, just tell me the truth. It can't be that difficult. Haven't you read the local rag? People already know that you and Lance were having an affair. You finally admitted that to me. And I took you at your word that David was the father of your baby. And now I know he isn't. I assume the father is Lance. For crissake, tell me the truth and stop lying about it. It isn't doing anybody any good. Is Lance Clayburn the father of your child?"

She continued to cry. "No, he isn't," she managed to say.

Books couldn't believe what he'd just heard. "Excuse me. Then who is?"

She was rocking up and down as she spoke, avoiding eye contact. "If I tell you who the father is, will you hold it in confidence?"

"No, Darby, I can't do that. If Lance isn't the father, then frankly, it makes him look less guilty. For all I know, the real father of your child might be David's killer. Have you thought about that possibility?"

She shook her head, wiping away the tears with her fingers. "No, he isn't."

Books sighed. "Darby. Who is the father of your baby?"

For the first time, she looked directly into Books' eyes. "The baby's father is Neil Eddins."

Books' face registered stunned disbelief and shock. All he managed to get out was, "You and Neil Eddins. I don't believe it. Have you told him about the pregnancy?"

"Yes. He's begging me not to tell his wife. He says she'll divorce him and take him to the cleaners financially."

"Well, maybe she should. I know this is an indelicate question to ask, but it needs to be asked anyway. Since you've been having affairs with two different men, how do you know for sure which one is the father?"

"Because I know the baby's due date. I also know when I last had relations with Neil and Lance. Until this past weekend, Lance and I hadn't been together in more than six weeks."

Books nodded. "What does Neil want you to do?"

"Get an abortion—he wants me to abort the child—says he'll cover all the expenses."

"What did you tell him?"

"I told him I wouldn't abort the child. I can't do that."

"Absent an abortion, what's Neil want you to do?"

"He says he'll pay my medical bills and provide financial support for the child so long as he's never identified as the father."

"Gee, that's kind of him. Have you agreed to do that?"

"I told him I'd think about it."

"Tell me something, Darby. Are you in love with Neil Eddins?"

"No, I'm not. I'm in love with Lance."

Books didn't ask her why. He didn't want or need to know.

After Darby regained her composure, Books asked if she had ever heard of Nevada Mining & Manufacturing or Valley Public Relations and Marketing. She hadn't. She had also never heard of Victor or Michael Calenti.

"What's this about, anyway?"

Books ignored her question. "Are you familiar with a man named Randall Orton?"

She paused. "I think he's a lobbyist David introduced to me one time."

"Where did you meet him and what can you tell me about him?"

"I met him once at a restaurant in downtown Salt Lake City. It was during this year's legislative session, late January I think. As I recall, Mr. Orton was attempting to convince David that the EEWA should assume a more conciliatory approach on the issue of road expansion in wilderness areas in southern Utah."

"And why would the EEWA want to do that?"

"The EEWA won't support increased roads in wilderness areas. Mr. Orton tried to make the case for local control—that many of these roads existed long before the federal government and the Congress began carving up the southwest into large tracts of protected land. He also pointed to the high unemployment rate in rural Utah and that new roads would lead to increased employment and prosperity for everybody."

"And was David buying?"

"No. David was convinced that more roads would permanently destroy sensitive eco systems and that whatever economic development resulted wouldn't be worth the price."

"And Orton accepted that?"

"He wasn't happy about it. But what choice did he have?"

"None really, I suppose."

The edge had returned to her voice. "Why are you asking me these questions? Do you think this has something to do with David's murder?"

"I don't know. I'm trying to figure that out."

"Well, let me know if you do. I can tell you one thing. You're making a big mistake by arresting Lance."

"Try telling it to the sheriff. I'm afraid it's not my call."

Back in the Yukon, Books received a message from dispatch. The sheriff wanted to see him as soon as possible, and Books knew why. The two men met in Sutter's office.

"I just got back from the DA's office. We wanted you to take a look at our affidavit and see if you think anything's missing." He reached across the desk and handed Books the paperwork.

Books read the PC statement and passed it back. "I think you got it all."

"Pretty damned convincing, isn't it?" said Sutter.

"Yes, it is."

"But you're still not sure, are you?"

"No, Charley, I'm not."

Books then laid out what he'd learned about Nevada Mining & Manufacturing, Valley Public Relations and Marketing, and the connections to Chief Deputy Brian Call and lobbyist Randy Orton. When he finished, Sutter leaned back in his office chair and planted his boots on the desk. He folded his hands across his distended belly.

"So what's it all mean, J.D.?"

"I'm not sure."

"Well, if you're not, nobody else will be either. Frankly, I don't see what it has to do with the murder of David Greenbriar, or the possible involvement of Lance Clayburn in his death."

Sutter might be right. Still, Books had one card left to play. And now was the time to play it. "Charley, you would agree, in part, that the case against Clayburn is strengthened by his affair with Darby, and the fact that she's pregnant with his child."

"Most definitely."

"So what would you think if I told you that the father of Darby's baby isn't Lance Clayburn?"

"Oh, come on, J.D.," said Sutter. "What the hell are you talking about? We know that her dead husband isn't the father."

"Yes, we do." Books said.

Sutter was starting to look concerned. "Cut the theatrics— who is it then, for crissake?"

"The father is Neil Eddins."

Sutter's feet came off the desk and he leaned forward staring hard at Books. His contorted face made him look like a guy suffering from a bad case of gas.

"Who told you that?"

"Darby did. I was just with her."

"Horseshit. I don't believe it."

"Well, I do. And if you could have seen her making that painful confession, you would too. She was in agony. This lady has had her hands full. She wants whoever is responsible for killing her husband brought to justice, and at the same time, she's managed to convince herself that the two men she's been having affairs with had nothing to do with it. Go figure."

"Has she confronted Neil?"

"Yup. He wants her to have an abortion and keep it all hush-hush."

Sutter wasn't dumb. He had to be considering what it might mean to him politically if Darby was telling the truth. What if it became public knowledge that one of the most revered and powerful members of the community had had an affair with a well known environmentalist whose husband had just been murdered? Not a pretty picture.

"If the press hears about this," said Sutter, "assuming she's telling the truth, the shit's going to hit the fan. But even if it is the truth, it still doesn't mean that Clayburn didn't kill Greenbriar."

"That's true," said Books, "but it sure weakens the case and opens the door for an astute defense attorney to point an accusing finger in the direction of Neil Eddins. The defense is probably going to argue that somebody besides Lance Clayburn had a motive to commit murder."

"Shit," muttered Sutter. "What a clusterfuck."

"Yes, it is, Charley. It might explain some of the pressure Neil has put on us to get on with prosecuting Lance. He figures if we stop digging and Lance takes the fall, this whole thing might go away. And nobody ever finds out that he fathered Darby's baby."

"It's possible, I suppose. What do you think we should do?"

"Hold off on the warrant. We need to confront Neil with this information. And I'd like a little more time to explore Call's connection to these folks at Nevada Mining & Manufacturing."

"Jesus, Books, you don't simply confront somebody like Neil Eddins. This could ruin him, and he isn't going to take it without putting up a fight. As it is, I've got the commissioners up my ass. I met with them earlier today. I all but promised we'd have this thing wrapped up in the next day or two."

"Then let's give it a couple of more days. Don't get the warrant tonight. Wait until Monday morning. If we haven't put a wrap on it by then, by all means, go get your warrant. Clayburn isn't going anywhere."

Sutter thought about that before he answered. "Okay, you've got until Monday morning, J.D. But if you don't get it resolved, I'll be in Judge McIntyre's courtroom at eight o'clock Monday morning. Agreed?"

Books nodded.

Books needed Charley Sutter's help with something else. He wanted to see the telephone records from Call's home number as well as his cell phone, and he didn't have a contact at the phone company in Salt Lake City to access those records. Sutter, however, did.

"How far back do you want to go?"

"Three months ought to be enough," said Books.

"His home phone records are going to take some time to get. I can't even make the request until Monday morning," said Sutter. "But his cell phone, that's a different story. The county provides and pays for his cell phone. Those records are kept in the administrative services office in the county courthouse. We can get those right away."

"Let's do it then."

Books was surprised Sutter hadn't balked at the request. Until now, Sutter had been defensive anytime anything had come up regarding his chief deputy. Perhaps now he had begun to rethink that proposition.

By the time their meeting ended, the DA's office was closed. Sutter and Books drove to the home of district attorney Virgil Bell. They brought Bell up to speed on the latest developments and got his approval to place everything on hold until Monday.

Before they parted, Books and Sutter agreed to meet early Saturday morning and pay a visit to Neil Eddins. Sutter wasn't happy about the idea, but he didn't see an alternative that made any sense.

Books stopped at the town market and selected a bouquet of fresh cut flowers for his mother's grave. On the way home, he stopped at the cemetery. The flowers he had left the previous week had been replaced with fresh ones. If his sister, Maggie, wasn't caring for the grave, who was? Bernie? He didn't think so. Ned Hunsaker? That made more sense. He wanted to talk to the old man anyway, so he made a mental note to ask him about the grave site.

# Chapter Thirty-six

It was late evening by the time Deluca made it back to Kanab. He parked the Explorer in the Cattle Baron parking lot and went inside. He ordered a pitcher of draft beer and took a seat in a rear booth facing the front door.

For the next hour, Deluca munched pretzels and downed several glasses of beer. He was a big man, and the beer did little to take the edge off. Rarely prone to melancholy, Deluca began to ponder how his life had ended up as it had.

As a teenager in Chicago, he'd been a rebellious kid who'd stretched to the max whatever boundaries his widowed father had set for him. He was in and out of trouble with the police, and by sixteen, over the objections of his father, had quit high school. Deluca was certain his father, although outwardly angry, was relieved he no longer had to pay the hefty tuition to send him to St. Benedict's Catholic High School. During the ensuing months, his encounters with the police intensified. Finally, with a nudge from his father, he enlisted for three years in the army. The Vietnam War was hot, and Deluca thought it sounded like an exciting adventure.

They sent him to Ford Ord, California, for basic training. After basic, he was assigned to Advanced Infantry Training at Fort Bragg, North Carolina. At Bragg, he was selected for specialized training that would alter the course of his life in ways he never would have imagined. Deluca was asked whether he was interested in attending sniper school. He liked the idea. During weeks of intensive training, it became clear to his army superiors that he was a young man with a unique skill set. He became highly proficient at his new job.

By the fall of 1973, he was back on the streets of Chicago with little to show for his two tours in Nam with the exception of a string of ribbons and a large number of confirmed enemy kills.

His father had put him to work in the family floral business, but that didn't last long. He soon reconnected with some of his former cronies from the old neighborhood. An acquaintance introduced him to an area loan shark who had direct ties to the Chicago Outfit. Deluca became an enforcer for the loan shark. In time, he developed a reputation as reliable, efficient, and ruthless. Eventually, the employer asked him to eliminate a witness who was about to testify before a federal grand jury against the loan sharking operation. The hit came off without a hitch, and Deluca suddenly found himself with a new and prosperous career.

Over the next thirty years, he had killed more than two dozen men. The police had questioned him in a handful of the murders, but he'd never been charged. He attributed his success to meticulous planning and endless patience. He never moved against a mark until he was ready—until he knew his intended victims' every move and habit. Because of his army training, Deluca preferred to kill from long range using one of several rifles from his small arsenal. But he prided himself on his versatility. He had killed at close range using small caliber firearms, and he had also strangled a few targets.

In his personal life, Deluca chose to live simply and without extravagance. He had a long string of girlfriends, but he never married. He considered it incompatible with his career. When his father died, he inherited the old house in which he was raised. He kept it until he moved to Las Vegas five years ago. The home he purchased was a modest one located in an established middle class neighborhood in suburban Henderson. The fenced back yard was large enough to accommodate a greenhouse, where he nurtured his roses, and the cocker spaniels who had become his children. There had been three such dogs, Rosie I, Rosie II, and Rosie III.

His out-of-town business trips had become increasingly hard, not only for Rosie but for himself as well. His physical skills had diminished despite a serious weight-training and aerobics program. Retirement from the life seemed like the best option. In the sunset of his years, Deluca longed only for the simple pleasures—a life filled with service to his church, to his beloved Rosie, and to his flowers.

◇◇◇

Deluca left the bar and crossed Kanab Creek to the west side of town. He drove the poorly lit streets until he found the home of Rebecca Eddins. He retrieved the pictures he'd taken from Ronnie Gadasky's bedroom. This was it, no doubt about it. The million-dollar question was whether the little perv would make an appearance, given his newfound celebrity status and the fact that every cop on the planet was looking for him. There was no way to know. He drove up and down several adjacent streets hoping he might spot the kid's red dirt bike. He didn't.

Deluca reached for his cell and dialed the Gadasky home. A man answered. "Hello."

"Is Ronnie there, please?"

"No, he isn't. Who's this?"

He disconnected.

Deluca felt discouraged and frustrated. At some point, the kid had to surface. The question was when and where? He couldn't be in two places at once. Given the circumstances, he concluded that his best bet was to plant himself outside the Gadasky home and hope for the best. He was certain of one thing: by morning, the authorities would begin mounting a search for George Gadasky. They would find his truck without too much difficulty, but it would probably take longer to locate the body.

Deluca returned to his motel room just long enough to change into his camouflage fatigues, select his weapons, and pick out a pair of night vision goggles. He returned to the Gadasky home and parked in a concealed location near the spot he'd parked the previous evening.

Since he couldn't see the home clearly from the highway, Deluca left the Explorer for a brief reconnaissance of the property. His original plan had been to catch the kid away from home, but time had become a factor. Deluca figured by Monday morning he needed to be out of Kanab and back in Vegas, so he hoped to find Ronnie's dirt bike parked at the house. If it was there, he would break in, kill the kid, and anybody else in the house.

He looked around the property for several minutes, checking the area near the house as well as a couple of out-buildings close by. Deluca cursed under his breath. Nothing. No sign of the little shit. He backtracked to the Explorer and settled in for what he suspected might be a long wait.

# Chapter Thirty-seven

It was almost dark when Books arrived home. Seeing the lights on inside Ned's place, he parked by the trailer and walked the short distance to the house. The screen door was locked, but the front door stood wide open. He could hear the sound of a television set, the volume cranked way up. Maybe the old man had lost some hearing. His mother had gotten like that late in her life. He'd walk into a room and realize that a conversation was impossible until he got the volume on the television turned down.

Books knocked on the screen door but got no answer. He rapped again, this time louder. Still no answer. He rapped a third time and shouted, "Hello, Ned, anybody home?"

After a moment, the old man stumbled to the front door. His eyes were glassy and he reeked of booze. He gave J.D. a weak smile. "Come on in, J.D. Can I get you something?"

Books stared at him. "I guess I'll have whatever you're having, Ned."

The old man looked away dropping his gaze to the floor. "Guess I kinda fell off the wagon."

"I guess you kinda did. Are you all right?"

Hunsaker shrugged, motioning Books to follow him into the kitchen. He grabbed a beer from the refrigerator, twisted the cap off, and handed it to Books. Books followed him into the living room. Both men sat, neither speaking for more than a minute.

Finally, Hunsaker broke the silence. "I hope you won't mention this to my daughter and son-in-law. It'll just get them all upset."

"I'm sure it would. I won't say anything to anybody, Ned."

The old man nodded. "Thanks."

"That doesn't mean that I approve or that I'm not concerned about you. Is anything wrong?"

Tears welled up in his eyes and spilled down the craggy face, deeply lined by sun, wind, and the passage of time. "I don't really know. Sometimes, I just feel an overwhelming sense of sadness."

Books waited.

Hunsaker paused as though carefully gauging what he was about to say. "I guess I never imagined that my life would end up like this."

"Afraid I don't understand, Ned. You're a well liked and well respected man in this community. You always have been."

"Thanks, but that's not what I meant. What I meant was that the two women I loved most in my life died before me. It shouldn't have been like that. I'm older. I should have gone first."

Books considered that. "Maybe so. It's just not something we get to choose."

The two men fell silent for a time. The women Ned referred to were his late wife Winnie and Books' mother, Maggie. Obviously, he had never fully understood the strength of the bond between his mother and Ned.

"I think I just figured something out, Ned. Since I got back in town last week, I've been to mom's grave twice. Somebody's been caring for the grave site. I assumed it was Maggie but she denied it. It sure didn't seem like anything Bernie would do, so that leaves you. Are you the one who's been tidying up and leaving the fresh flowers?"

Hunsaker nodded. "I go to visit both graves twice a week. They're not buried very far apart—don't know if you knew that."

"I didn't. And thanks for doing it."

"You're welcome, J.D."

"Forgive me for being so blunt, Ned, but were you in love with my mother?"

The two men stared at each other for a moment. "Yes, I was. I've loved only two women in my life. I had the good fortune of being married to my wife for thirty-seven years. Your mother was the other."

"I guess I should tell you something, Ned. Right before mother died, in fact, it was the last time I saw her, she told me how much you meant to her. I think she was closer to you than almost anyone else in her life. She told me how blessed she felt, blessed, those were her words, at getting to work at your side all those years in the library. She said it more than made up for some of the shortcomings that existed in her marriage to Bernie. And I'd like to thank you for that. It was a special gift."

"I wouldn't have had it any other way."

◇◇◇

Books asked Hunsaker what he knew about lobbyist, Randall Orton, Valley Public Relations and Marketing, and Nevada Mining & Manufacturing. He'd never heard of the two Las Vegas companies, but Books got an earful about Orton, none of it complimentary.

"Cowboy Randy Orton, that's what we used to call him. His family runs a spread this side of Panguitch, some hogs, cattle mostly. He served two terms in the Utah State Senate and then realized there was a hell of a lot more money to be made using his legislative contacts as a registered lobbyist. Greedy little bastard, if you ask me."

"Tell me about his politics." said Books.

"He's pretty much your stereotypical Utah conservative. Soft-spoken, affable, but don't let that fool you. He'd slip the blade between your ribs without a second thought. When he served in the legislature, he belonged to a group of rural Utah Republicans who called themselves the Cowboy Caucus. Most of them are so far right politically they'd make members of the John Birch Society look like left-wing liberals. That said, they exert a fair amount of influence in the legislature."

"Was he willing to work with elements in the conservation movement?"

Hunsaker shook his head. "Not as far as I could tell. Orton always struck me as a guy who appreciated the land only for what he could take from it. When he looks out over the Vermilion Cliffs, he's not thinking what a beautiful place this is to preserve for future generations. He's thinking about how the land can be used for a logging or mining operation or how many head of cattle a rancher could run per acre."

Books explained to Hunsaker the relationship between Orton and the Nevada Mining & Manufacturing Company. The old man listened patiently before making what would later turn out to be a telling observation.

"J.D., you mentioned this Nevada mining company operates coal mines in Wyoming and Utah. Maybe they were planning to establish a coal mining operation down here and needed the help of somebody like Orton to get it done."

"Possible, I guess, but where would they set up shop down here?"

Hunsaker paused, giving the question some thought. "I know where I'd do it if I was them. I'd do it on the Kaiparowits Plateau."

"Why?

"Because the coal reserves on the plateau are enormous. Given the energy crunch we're facing in this country and the push for clean burning coal technology, the potential for economic growth and new jobs might make it a downright attractive proposition."

Books decided that a follow-up contact with Randall Orton would be a good idea. As a member of the corporate board of directors for Nevada Mining & Manufacturing, Orton had to know more about the operation of the company than he had let on in their previous conversation.

Books stayed with Ned long enough to fix both of them scrambled eggs, sausage, toast, and coffee for dinner. When he returned to his trailer, he found a voice message from Ivan Gadasky asking him to call as soon as possible. Gadasky didn't explain the reason for the call but he sounded upset.

"Thank you for returning my call, Mr. Books," said Gadasky.

"Sure. Is everything all right?"

"I'm not sure. When I returned home this afternoon, I found a note from my son, George. It said he'd gone off into the monument with some newspaper reporter looking for Ronnie. Said he'd be back before dark."

"And you haven't seen or heard from him?"

"Not a word."

Books glanced at his watch. It was nearly midnight. "Here's what I think we should do. I'll call county dispatch and have them send an officer to your house to take a missing persons report. Hang onto the note. The deputy will want to see it. In the meantime, I'll notify Charley Sutter."

"Will they mount an immediate search?" said Gadasky.

"I'm sure he'll want to get county search and rescue involved. They'll set up a command post and probably begin to search at first light, assuming George hasn't surfaced by then. You probably don't know this, but I stopped at your place this morning and talked with George. He mentioned receiving a phone call from a news reporter who wanted to interview Ronnie. He didn't say anything to me about actually going with the reporter to look for Ronnie."

"Did he tell you the name of this reporter?" Gadasky said.

"I asked him who it was. He told me the guy's name was Elliott Sanders and he worked for the *Las Vegas Sun Times*. We can check that out very easily. Do you have any idea where George might have taken him?"

"One time I overheard Ronnie and George talking about places Ronnie liked to go when he headed off into the monument. Ronnie mentioned the Cockscomb."

"That could be important information, Mr. Gadasky. I don't have to tell you how large and how remote the monument is. Be sure you share that information with the deputy. Sit tight until we can get a deputy to your house." Books disconnected.

Books knew the area pretty well around the Cockscomb. It was located on the Cottonwood Canyon Road, a remote forty-mile stretch of the Grand Staircase Escalante National Monument that passed Grosvenor Arch and eventually connected up with Kodachrome Basin State Park. The land was so inhospitable in the summer that if you broke down or got lost, you might not make it back alive.

Books got Charley Sutter out of bed and let him contact dispatch. In the meantime, Books went through directory assistance and found a phone number for the *Las Vegas Sun Times*. It was a busy Saturday night in the city that never sleeps, so finding a live body in the newsroom was easy. The problem was that nobody at the paper had ever heard of a reporter named Elliott Sanders, nor did they have anyone in Kanab covering the Greenbriar murder.

# Chapter Thirty-eight

Deluca sat in the Ford Explorer trying to resist fatigue and remain alert. It was past midnight, and traffic passing on the highway had become less and less frequent. He'd brought snacks and a small thermos of coffee. The caffeine helped, but the coffee worked its way through his system so fast that he'd had to get out of the vehicle twice to relieve himself. Each time he had to wait for a minute, allowing his eyes to adjust to the darkness. The sliver of moon provided little natural light. It was so black that it gave him the creeps. Hadn't these people ever heard of street lights?

There had been no activity around the Gadasky home in the nearly four hours he'd been watching. He was parked close enough to the property turnoff so that he could easily see anybody coming or going. At the same time, he was far enough off the highway to remain invisible to passing cars.

An approaching vehicle popped into view above the starlit horizon from the west, its high beams illuminating the highway in front of it. As it neared the turnoff to the Gadasky property, the driver slowed and turned on the truck's right blinker. The overhead rack of lights confirmed what Deluca already suspected. The insignia on the door of the SUV read Kane County Sheriff. Somebody at the home, probably the elder Gadasky, had begun to worry about the whereabouts of George and had called the police.

Deluca was disappointed. He had hoped to buy a little more time. The authorities wouldn't begin to search in earnest until daylight. He still had time but probably less than he originally thought. He waited until the cruiser was out of sight and then eased the Explorer on to the highway pointed back toward Kanab. He hid the guns and night vision goggles, not wanting to explain to some sheriff's deputy what he was doing in the middle of the night dressed in camouflage fatigues. It was best to let things cool off for a while. He would return later.

Deluca drove the streets around the home of Rebecca Eddins hoping to spot Ronnie or his dirt bike. Nothing. He headed back to the motel for a few hours of much needed sleep.

◇◇◇

Books met Sutter early Sunday morning at the sheriff's office. Sutter had placed Brian Call in charge of the search and rescue effort to locate George Gadasky. That was fine with Books. Keeping Call on a short leash until all of this got sorted out seemed like a good idea. Coordinating the search for Gadasky should keep him occupied for a while.

Call had established a mobile command center at the mouth of Johnson Canyon. At the urging of the boy's father, Ivan Gadasky, two teams of volunteers had agreed to simultaneously search the remote Cottonwood Canyon Road as well as Johnson Canyon. A small single-engine Cessna was preparing to join the search from the North Rim of the Grand Canyon.

Sutter listened intently while Books explained a possible theory for the murder of David Greenbriar. When he finished, the sheriff didn't say anything for a minute while he poured himself a cup of coffee, sat down at his desk, and began dunking a chocolate cake donut into his coffee.

"Want a cup, J.D.?"

"Had some already this morning, thanks anyway."

"Probably a wise choice," said Sutter. "It's yesterday's brew."

"Looks like used motor oil."

"Tastes like it, too."

"Don't see how you drink that stuff."

Sutter shrugged. "This theory of yours, you aren't saying you think Randy Orton had something to do with Greenbriar's murder."

"I don't think so, but I'll bet he knows some things about the future plans of Nevada Mining & Manufacturing. As a member of the board of directors, how could he not?"

"Could be. I don't see how your theory explains the physical evidence linking Clayburn to the killing."

"It doesn't."

"So…."

"So, I'm working on it and I may have an idea."

"I'm listening," said Sutter.

Books explained the mystery of the nonexistent *Las Vegas Sun Times* newspaper reporter. By the time he finished, Sutter was listening intently.

"Let me be sure I understand this," said Sutter. "George Gadasky told you this morning that he'd received a phone call from a guy who claimed to be a reporter with a Las Vegas newspaper who was trying to find Ronnie for an interview."

Books nodded. "The guy said his name was Elliott Sanders and claimed he worked for the *Las Vegas Sun Times*."

"And you called the newspaper, and somebody told you they don't have a reporter named Elliott Sanders."

"Yup."

"Maybe George got the name wrong. He's not the brightest bulb in the box, you know."

"Possible, I suppose, but the guy I spoke with at the newspaper claimed they didn't have anybody up here covering the story."

"Seems kind of strange. What do you make of it?"

"Hard to know, Charlie, but one thing's for sure. We've got ourselves a mystery man poking around the community asking a lot of questions."

Neither man spoke for a time, each absorbed in his own thoughts.

"You don't suppose, J.D., that George's disappearance might involve foul play."

"That thought has occurred to me. What if this guy is our killer?"

"That's quite a stretch, don't you think? Like I said before, the evidence still points to Clayburn."

Sutter was right and Books knew it. Maybe Books' instincts about Clayburn had been wrong all along. Maybe Sutter was right and Clayburn was the killer. What if Clayburn was somehow connected to Nevada Mining & Manufacturing? But how? And even if he was, why would he agree to commit a murder? For money? It didn't seem very likely. He already had plenty of that. For love? He couldn't rule it out, but again, it didn't seem likely. And if he had killed for love, he certainly didn't need the mining company for that.

Neil Eddins had agreed to meet them in the restaurant of the Parry Lodge at ten AM. Sutter called him the night before to set the meeting. Eddins acted wary—as though he knew what might be coming. And who knows? Maybe Darby had tipped him off. It was certainly plausible. She had lied before, and Books didn't trust her.

For several decades beginning in the early 1930s, the Parry Lodge served as the headquarters for Hollywood movie moguls who were drawn to Kanab because of the area's rugged beauty. Hundreds of television shows and movies, many of the them westerns, were filmed in and around Kanab. The Lodge played host to such film luminaries as John Wayne, Clint Eastwood, Glen Ford, Ava Gardner, and Charlton Heston as well as members of the Rat Pack. Many of the hotel's eighty-nine rooms were named for the Hollywood stars who stayed in them during film shoots.

On the drive to the Parry Lodge, Sutter was quiet and looked genuinely uncomfortable. He had to be contemplating his future as the Kane County Sheriff, if indeed he had a future. Crossing a man like Neil Eddins would make his chances for re-election tenuous at best.

As Books parked the Yukon, Sutter said, "Let me take the lead with Neil."

"Suits me. Are you sure that's a good idea? It might be easier to let me do the heavy lifting."

"Appreciate the offer but this is something I need to do."

When they entered the restaurant, Eddins had already taken a seat in a far corner of the place, well out of earshot of any restaurant employees. He was drinking coffee and looked about as miserable as Sutter. The initial small talk was polite, but the tension in the room was palpable. Eddins had given Books a curt nod but otherwise hadn't spoken to him. He directed his conversation to Sutter. That suited Books just fine.

Finally, after an indefatigable period of small talk, they settled down to business. It was Eddins who began. "This is clearly no social call, Charley, so tell me why we're here."

Sutter cleared his throat. "There's no easy way to ask you this, so I'm just going to come out with it. Darby Greenbriar has told us she's pregnant. She also told us you're the father."

"That's a preposterous allegation, Charley. I'm disappointed in you. You of all people should know that the EEWA would do anything to destroy my reputation in this community. Divide and conquer, that's what they're all about."

"But, Neil," said Sutter, "she says she was having an affair with you, became pregnant, and that the two of you have discussed what to do about it. She even went so far as to say that you suggested she get an abortion and that you'd cover all expenses."

"That's utter nonsense, and I categorically deny it. His voice had taken on a quiet but edgy tone. "If the child isn't David's, then it must belong to Lance Clayburn. That's who she was having an affair with, and everybody in town knows it."

Books had to give Eddins credit. If the allegation had caught him completely unaware, his body language certainly wasn't giving him away.

"Just so we're clear, Neil. You're telling us that you are not presently having an affair with Darby Greenbriar and that you've never had an intimate relationship with her. Therefore, you can't possibly be the father of her child. Is that correct?"

Eddins raised his eyebrows and heaved a sigh of mock exasperation. "For crissake, Charley, do I have to get a color crayon and draw you a picture? That's exactly what I'm telling you. This is nothing more than a vicious, unsubstantiated rumor, and I promise you this, if any of this rubbish finds its way to my family or gets leaked to the news media, I'll file a lawsuit against you so fast it'll make your head swim. Am I making myself clear?"

"Perfectly," said the sheriff.

"Now, is there anything else? Because if there isn't, I'm a busy man and I've got things to do today."

Sutter glanced at Books, uncertainty written across his face. Eddins started to rise when Books spoke up. "Yeah, there is something else, Neil. You need to account for your whereabouts last Sunday."

Eddins returned to his chair. "Why, you pompous little shit. How dare you accuse me of murder?"

"We're not accusing you of anything" said Books, "but you have become a person of interest in our case. And the things that got you here were an extramarital affair, a pregnancy, and now a murder. You don't have to answer our questions, but if you don't, I'll be forced to start asking all kinds of unpleasant questions all over town. And if the word does get out, and it will, you'll have only yourself to blame."

"This is absolutely outrageous," said Eddins, his voice rising into one of controlled fury. He stood up again, placing his hands palms down on the table leaning closer to Books and Sutter. "You'll be hearing from my lawyer before your breakfast has a chance to digest."

"Neil, shut up and sit down for a minute," said Sutter.

Eddins sat, his facial expression conveying shock at Sutter's tone and choice of words. Telling arguably the most powerful man in Kane County to sit down and shut up took guts. It also bordered on political suicide. Books was certain that this kind of insult was something Eddins was not used to, nor was he the kind of man to simply forgive and forget.

And Sutter wasn't finished yet. "I'm disappointed in you, Neil. We've been friends for a long time, or so I thought. Right now, I don't have time for this malarkey. You need to answer our questions and answer them truthfully. And if I find out you lied to us about your relationship with Darby Greenbriar or anything else, I promise you that I'll do everything in my power to see that you're charged with obstruction of justice. Am I making myself clear?"

Eddins nodded slowly, glaring at Sutter, his eyes tiny slits. He was clearly struggling to maintain his composure. "All right," he finally said. "I spent Sunday morning at church with members of my family. We got home shortly after noon. I remained at home the rest of the day working in my office. Around four o'clock the wife and I drove to Becky's home for a family dinner. My son, Alex, and his wife attended as did Boyd and his family. We went home around eight-thirty. Satisfied?"

"That's all we wanted you to tell us," said Books.

Sutter added. "Anything else you want to tell us about your relationship with Darby Greenbriar?"

Eddins glanced at Sutter, then at Books, and then back again at Sutter before answering. "What if, say, just for the sake of argument that I did have a brief fling with Darby Greenbriar. If I were to admit that to you, would you promise to hold that information in confidence?"

"We would have absolutely no reason to release that kind of information to anyone," said Sutter, "unless we discover that you're somehow involved in David's murder, and then all bets are off. But you also need to understand that I don't control the press. If they dig long enough and deep enough, who knows what they'll come up with? It's a crap shoot. That's all I can say."

Eddins considered that momentarily and then proceeded to confirm what Books and Sutter already suspected. He admitted having an affair with Darby that had lasted for most of the past year. Initially, their paths had crossed at contentious land use functions and county commission meetings. They had become increasingly friendly when they served together on a planning committee for Kanab's annual Western Legends Festival. There was instant chemistry between them. Their intimate trysts had occurred away from the small town of Kanab in St. George, Page, and, on occasion, Las Vegas.

Eddins vehemently denied any involvement in David's murder. He insisted that neither he nor Darby had ever discussed leaving their respective spouses. From his perspective, the relationship with Darby was a dalliance, a fling, that both realized had no long-term future.

By the time Eddins had finished describing his relationship with Darby Greenbriar, Books was ready to jump across the table and pound his smug face into pulp. At least Books understood his own anger, or thought he did anyway. Eddins' behavior mirrored what his soon-to-be ex-wife had done to him and what his father had repeatedly done to his mother throughout their marriage. The light-hearted rationale was all too common: What's so bad about a harmless little bout of sport fucking? After all, boys will be boys. It's only an innocent fling, no commitment required, no harm, no foul. Books had heard it all before.

And when they left Eddins sitting alone at that restaurant table, the only feeling Books had for him was utter contempt.

# Chapter Thirty-nine

Books and Sutter returned to the Yukon. "Well, what do you make of that little tête-à-tête?" asked Sutter.

"A brief fling, it wasn't," said Books, "but I don't think he's our trigger man."

"Me, neither. His alibi'll check out, wait and see. That doesn't mean he didn't pay somebody else to kill Greenbriar."

"Possible, I guess, but I doubt it. No, Charley, I think we're going to find the answer to this puzzle lies with Brian Call and his friends in Las Vegas. I can smell it."

"I don't know whether to hope you're right or hope you're wrong."

◇◇◇

They had barely cleared the Parry Lodge when Books received a call from dispatch. The dispatcher relayed a message from Brian Call asking Charley Sutter to call him immediately.

Sutter reached for his cell, punched in Call's number, and then hit the speaker button so Books could listen in. "Let's hope he's calling in with some good news on George Gadasky."

Call answered on the first ring.

"Got your message, Brian. What's up?"

"It's nothin good, I can tell you that. I'm at Grosvenor Arch. The boys found George Gadasky's old pickup parked here about seven this morning."

"Any sign of George?"

"Not at first, not until Laray Bingham showed up with one of his coon hounds."

"And."

"It took that old hound about ten minutes to find the body." His voice broke.

"Get a hold of yourself, Brian. Tell me what happened?"

"Somebody shot the dumb-ass kid in the head, that's what happened."

"Ah, Jesus," said Sutter. He glanced at Books shaking his head. "Where did you find him?"

"His body had either fallen or been pushed into a shallow ravine a couple of hundred yards from the parking lot."

"And the murder weapon?"

"We're searching for it now, but so far nothing."

"What about brass?" said Books.

"None," said Call.

"What kind of weapon?" asked Sutter.

"Not sure, but it looks like some kind of small caliber handgun. There's a small entry wound behind his left ear. No exit wound that I could see."

"Sounds like a .22 or maybe a .25 caliber," Books whispered.

Sutter nodded. "Sit tight, Brian, and secure the scene. We'll notify the medical examiner's office and get a CSI unit rolling right away. I'll be along shortly unless I decide to send Books."

Sutter used his cell and called the dispatch center. He told them to call for a CSI team and to notify the ME. "This one's going to be a logistical nightmare," said Sutter.

"Afraid so," replied Books. "That crime scene is out in the middle of bum-fuck, and I'd say you'll be lucky to get support people to him inside five hours. And that's assuming they don't get lost trying to find the place."

"I don't want to risk that. I'll have somebody guide them from Kanab."

When they arrived at the sheriff's office, Books said, "We'd better sit down in your office and see if we can start to make sense out of this. Besides, I think we need a plan."

Sutter heaved a sigh. "I think we do."

◇◇◇

Deluca got up early. He wiped the room down as thoroughly as possible and checked out of the motel. He drove ten miles north of Kanab to the small town of Mt. Carmel. He rented a room for one night at a Best Western motel using a different set of false identification. As always, he paid with cash.

His decision to change motels was purely a precaution. He'd survived for nearly three decades by carefully planning each and every move. He'd learned to live by what he called the two C's rule: Caution and common sense. Kanab was a small town, and while he didn't think he had done anything to arouse suspicion, he saw no reason to take a chance. Once the body of George Gadasky was discovered, the cops would invariably start taking a careful look at anyone in town who wasn't a local.

Deluca carefully unpacked his things. He placed his under-wear, socks, and pajamas inside one of the dressers. Then he neatly laid out his toiletries on the bathroom counter. He hung his remaining clothes in the small closet. He was a fanatic about neatness, a habit he'd developed in the military.

After he finished, he laid his two-hundred twenty pound frame on the queen-size bed and dialed the Las Vegas phone number of the pet spa caring for his beloved Rosie. The answer-ing attendant informed him that Rosie had eaten breakfast, gone on a play date with several other like-minded canines, and was now sequestered in a quiet room where she was receiving a massage. Deluca thanked the pleasant sounding attendant and disconnected. He smiled to himself thinking that Rosie was receiving such cushy treatment she might have second thoughts about wanting to come home.

Deluca gathered his things and prepared to return to Kanab. No camouflage fatigues today. He dressed to look as much like a tourist as possible. His ability to blend into a place was directly proportional to its size, and Kanab was a damned small place.

Deluca had begun to get that uneasy feeling that things were not going as expected. He was running out of time and ideas for finding Ronnie Gadasky. Every hour he spent in Kanab increased his risk of discovery. Never in his career had Deluca failed to fulfill a contract, but, for the first time, he was forced to consider just such a plan. He wouldn't exercise that option until he'd played his final cards.

Deluca parked the Explorer in front of the Ranch Inn & Café, and took a seat at the counter. He ordered a short stack of pancakes, sausage, and coffee. He figured this was as good a place as any to pick up on the local gossip. He hoped he might hear whatever scuttlebutt was going around about the whereabouts of Ronnie Gadasky. He was confident that it was too soon for any information to have surfaced about the missing and dearly departed George Gadasky. As it turned out, he was wrong about that.

Deluca guessed the man behind the counter was about his age. He had a ruddy complexion, thinning gray hair, and a droopy mustache. He also had information he was readily sharing with two men seated across the counter from him. Like everything else at this stage of his life, Deluca had lost some hearing. He strained to hear the conversation but managed to catch only bits and pieces. From what he gathered, George Gadasky had been reported missing, and the locals had mounted a search. He didn't hear anything about a body being discovered. Deluca decided to take a chance and enter the conversation.

"Pardon me for interrupting," he said, "but I've been visiting the area for the last week and keep hearing stories about somebody being killed, and some kid who saw it all, and now he's disappeared. Is that what you're talking about?"

Rusty Steed looked at Deluca and shook his head. "No, it's not the kid who supposedly witnessed the crime. He's still missing. It's the witness' brother who's gone missing."

"What happened to him?" said Deluca.

"Details are a little sketchy, but evidently he went looking for his brother in the monument and never came back."

"That's a shame," said Deluca, shaking his head.

"Sure is."

For a moment, nobody spoke. Then Deluca said, "Did this kid actually see the murder?"

"Apparently," said the stranger seated on the stool next to him. "If he didn't, I can't imagine why the cops would be spending all this time trying to find him."

"That makes sense," said Deluca, "but maybe the youngster doesn't want to get involved. You know how kids are these days."

"Maybe so," said Steed. "Hard to say. He's a strange boy, anyway."

You don't know the half of it, thought Deluca.

"Seems like I heard they haven't caught the killer yet," said Deluca.

Rusty Steed stared at Deluca for a minute before answering. The stare didn't go unnoticed. "Not yet, but the police got their eyes fixed on somebody."

"That must be the young fellow who had his picture in the paper," said Deluca. "I think his name was Lance......something-or-other."

"That's right," said Steed. "Lance Clayburn. You seem to have a real interest in this case, mister. I'm Rusty Steed, by the way. I own this place. What's your name, anyway?"

Deluca reached across the counter and shook Steed's hand. "Pleasure to meet you, Rusty. My name's Curry, Del Curry."

"Nice to meet you, too. You said you were vacationing here. Where are you from?"

Deluca reached for his wallet. "Chicago."

"You're a long way from home. What brings you to these parts?"

Deluca was becoming annoyed. Rusty Steed was a nosy old fart. Perhaps his questions had made the old man suspicious. "Visiting the national parks, mostly. My sister and brother-in-law live in Salt Lake City. I'll stop and see them, then fly home from Salt Lake."

Steed nodded.

Deluca was pushing his luck but decided to try one more tack. "Sometimes people on the run hide out with friends or family—even turn themselves into a lawyer. I wonder if the police have considered that possibility."

Steed glanced at him again but didn't answer. The stranger seated next to him did. "Never knowed Ronnie to have any friends—boy's always been a loner. Family wouldn't hide him out, neither. Don't know nothin' about no lawyer though."

Steed had overheard the exchange. "Ronnie's got himself a lawyer, but I imagine if he contacted her, she'd turn him in."

Rebecca Eddins, thought Deluca.

Deluca finished his breakfast and left cash on the counter to pay the bill. Rusty Steed had disappeared. He got into the Explorer and drove down the street to a pay phone at the local supermarket.

Rusty Steed stood in the lobby of the Ranch Inn & Café and watched as Deluca left the restaurant and drove away in a late model Ford Explorer.

# Chapter Forty

At the sheriff's office, Books and Sutter hammered out the semblance of a plan. Sutter would respond to Grosvenor Arch to assist Brian Call at the murder scene. He would also stop at the Gadasky home and deliver the tragic news of George's murder to the boy's father. That would free Books to sort through the complex web of lies and deceit surrounding the death of David Greenbriar.

Books found himself with a new and growing sense of respect for Charley Sutter. He respected the way the sheriff had handled Neal Eddins at the Parry Lodge. That, along with his decision to deliver the worst possible news to Ivan Gadasky, reflected strength and courage. Books had delivered more than his fair share of death notifications to family members when he worked robbery/homicide in Denver. It never got easier.

Books drove to BLM headquarters. Since it was Sunday, the parking lot was mostly empty. Alexis Runyon's Toyota Highlander was parked behind the building. That was good. He had something he needed to ask her.

Runyon was busy in front of her computer when Books tapped on her office door. She glanced up, her reading glasses perched on the end of her nose. "Come in, J.D. Just trying to catch up on my email. Give me another second and I'll be done."

When she finished, Runyon leaned back in her office chair, munching on a piece of dried fruit. "Any news?"

"Yeah, there is, and I'm sorry to say, it's not good."

Her smile gave way to a look of concern. "What's happened?"

Books told her about the discovery of George Gadasky body at Grosvenor Arch and about the unknown subject who had passed himself off as a Las Vegas newspaper reporter trying to locate Ronnie Gadasky for an interview.

"You think this person took George into the monument and then killed him?"

"It looks that way, but it's too soon to know for sure," said Books.

"But why would he do that?"

"Good question. I think whoever did this wasn't about to leave a witness behind who might identify him later. And George probably thought he knew where to find Ronnie."

"And when George couldn't, the guy killed him?"

"It's possible."

"Jesus," said Runyon. "Charley must be beside himself right about now."

"You might be surprised. He's actually holding up pretty well." Books told her about the paternity issue and the subsequent encounter with Neil Eddins.

Runyon's jaw dropped with this revelation. "You're kidding me. This thing's turning into flippin' soap opera. I appreciate your keeping me informed."

"No problem."

"With a second murder, I wouldn't be surprised if a team of agents showed up from the regional BLM office in Salt Lake City."

"Maybe the FBI, too," said Books.

"Has word of George's murder gotten around town?"

"Not yet, but it won't take long. It's not exactly the kind of thing you can sit on for any length of time," said Books. "Since you're here, I need your help with something else."

"Name it."

"How difficult would it be to find out who holds mining rights in the Grand Staircase?"

"Any place in particular?"

"The Kaiparowits Plateau."

"Let's take a look." She slid back in front of her computer. Several key strokes later, Books had his answer.

"How about a company called Nevada Mining & Manufacturing," said Runyon.

◇◇◇

Deluca left the Ranch Inn & Café feeling uneasy. He had pressed too hard for information, and the old man, Rusty Steed, had become suspicious. That was obvious. But what the hell was he supposed to do. This was no time to be cautious. He had to find that kid and fast.

He drove across Kanab Creek past the home of Rebecca Eddins. Nothing. No lights on in the house. No vehicle parked out front. Deluca returned to town and drove past Eddins' law office. Hallelujah. There was an SUV parked in the lot and the lights inside the office were on. The place actually looked like it was open for business. Odd for a Sunday, he thought. He slowly circled the block looking for Ronnie Gadasky's dirt bike. He couldn't find it, but that didn't mean the kid wasn't in the law office. The bike could have been stashed anywhere.

Deluca found a pay phone in the lobby of a motel that provided a modicum of privacy and a refuge from the noisy sounds of the street. He dialed Eddins' law office number and waited. Moments later, a pleasant sounding woman answered, "Law office. This is Becky Eddins. How can I help you?"

"Good afternoon, Ms. Eddins. My name is Elliott Sanders and I'm a newspaper reporter from the *Las Vegas Sun Times*. I'm in town covering the murder investigation of the local environmental activist, David Greenbriar."

"And what does that have to do with me, Mr. Sanders?"

"A fair question. My paper would like to interview a young man whose name has surfaced in the case as a possible witness. His name is Ronnie Gadasky."

"I still don't see what that has to do with me." Eddins' voice had a new steely edge.

Snippy little bitch, thought Deluca.

"I was just getting to that," said Deluca. "Our own investigation led us to you. It seems that you have acted as Mr. Gadasky's attorney in the past. The paper would like to interview Ronnie, and we were hoping you might know how to contact him. And of course, the paper would be happy to compensate you for your time."

"Two points, Mr.…I'm sorry, what was your name again?"

"Sanders, Elliott Sanders."

"Two points Mr. Sanders. First, I haven't heard from Ronnie Gadasky, and I have no reason to believe that I'm going to. Second, if I did hear from Ronnie, I would encourage him to surrender to the police. I would not sit him down with you or anybody else from the news media."

"I understand," said Deluca. "I'm sorry to have bothered you."

"It's no bother Mr. Sanders, but tell me something. Isn't this a bit unusual? I mean a newspaper reporter trying to interview a material witness in a murder case even before the police have an opportunity to talk with him."

"Maybe so, but this is an extremely competitive business we're in, Ms. Eddins. My newspaper is simply trying to land the big story ahead of our competitors."

"I'm sorry I can't help you, Mr. Sanders. Best of luck to you."

"Thanks." Deluca disconnected.

When he got back into the Explorer, Deluca glanced at his cell phone on the seat next to him. The message light was blinking. He listened to a brief message, deleted it, and then returned the call.

"This is Michael."

"You called."

"We have another problem."

"Tell somebody else. I've got enough of my own."

"You need to hear about this one."

"Why?"

"It came from our local contact in Kane County. He's threatening to expose us if we don't back off right now—seems the little rat bastard freaked out when he heard about your recent, how shall I say it, 'encounter' with one of the locals."

Deluca paused. "Actually, he might be giving you pretty good advice." He explained the difficulty he was having trying to find Ronnie Gadasky. "Maybe it's time to cut our losses and get out while we still can."

"This doesn't sound like the man who never failed to fulfill a contract," said Calenti. "It sounds more like a man who's gotten too old and too soft around the middle to get the job done. Perhaps you ought to consider retirement on some Florida beach where you can sip Pina Coladas, look at pussy, and dream about the good old days."

"Listen to me you snotty little cokehead. I was taking care of business when you were still running around in diapers, so don't talk to me about not getting the job done. I warned you from the beginning that this job was ill-conceived, but you didn't want to listen, did you, you little faggot?"

Michael Calenti was shocked. Nobody talked to him like this, particularly not some cranky, aging, two-bit gangster like Deluca. Yet there was something cold and sinister about the old man. Assuming a conciliatory tone was prudent, at least for the time being.

"Look, I was only trying to light a little fire under you, that's all," said Calenti. "Don't take everything so personal."

"Is that right, Michael? Isn't it a shame that neither you nor Vic Jr. have got the business savvy or balls your old man had? If you did, we wouldn't be in this mess."

Calenti didn't take the bait. "I'm just telling you that if this guy goes off on us like he's threatened to, we could all end up in a world of hurt."

"It's not my problem, Michael. This guy doesn't know me. I don't know him. I've never seen him or spoken to him. Besides, I don't kill cops—too much heat. He's your problem, Michael. You fix it."

"I don't think you're listening, Mr. Deluca. If these murders end up on our doorstep, we're not going down alone. Don't you understand? You'll end up being the one with a needle in your arm."

"You'd rat me out. Is that it, Michael? Is that what you're telling me?"

Michael cleared his throat. "All I can tell you is a man's gotta do what a man's gotta do."

"Okay, Michael. Give me all the particulars and I'll fix your problem. But let me tell you something. If these loose ends aren't resolved within twenty-four hours, I'm out of here. And then whatever happens happens. Understand?"

Calenti didn't answer.

"Do you understand?"

"I understand."

After the call, Michael Calenti leaned low over the marble coffee table and snorted a line of cocaine. He walked outside his high-rise condo onto an expansive deck that overlooked the Las Vegas strip from thirty floors above. Through a cocaine induced fog, he reflected on what Deluca had just said. The two-bit thug had threatened him and he didn't like it. He didn't like it because it scared him, and nobody threatened Michael Calenti and got away with it.

# Chapter Forty-one

Books left BLM headquarters and drove the short distance to the Ranch Inn & Café. He had almost an hour to kill before meeting Roberta Weekly, a supervisor in the Kane County Administrative Services Department. Sutter had arranged for her to meet him to pick up Brian Call's monthly cell phone records.

Books scanned the restaurant as he took his customary seat at the counter. Trees McClain was seated in a corner booth with a guy Books didn't know. If McClain saw him enter the restaurant, he didn't acknowledge it.

Rusty Steed walked over and dropped a menu in front of him. "Get you something to drink, J.D.?"

"Iced tea."

Steed nodded and shuffled off.

When he returned with the iced tea, Steed said, "Any word on George Gadasky?"

Books nodded. "Bad news, I'm afraid, Rusty. Search and Rescue found his body early this morning near Grosvenor Arch. He'd been shot in the head."

"What?" Steed was obviously shocked.

"Looks like somebody killed him at close range with a small caliber handgun."

"Jesus, J.D. What's going on in this town?"

"Wish I knew, Rusty. There is something you can do to help, though.

"Name it."

"You're in a place that gets a lot of traffic. I'd appreciate a call if you see or hear anything or anyone who seems unusual or suspicious,"

"Funny you should mention that. There was a fella in here not more than two hours ago. He seemed unusually interested in any information about the Gadasky brothers."

"Had you ever seen him before?"

"Nope."

"Did he claim to be a newspaper reporter from Las Vegas?"

"No, said he was a tourist here visiting the parks. He was driving a white Ford Explorer with Nevada plates."

"How do you know that?"

"Watched him drive away."

Books left the restaurant with a description of the inquisitive stranger as well as the SUV he was driving. Could this be the same man who was hunting Ronnie Gadasky and who had killed his brother, George? It was a long shot, but definitely worth looking into.

◇◇◇

Books hadn't seen Roberta Weekly since he'd left Kanab more than a dozen years ago. She had been a teacher's aide at Kanab Elementary when Books was in the fourth grade, patiently tutoring him in an attempt to bring his below-average reading skills up to grade level.

She and Books chatted amicably, mostly about family, while she manually searched through a large, shoulder-high filing cabinet. She removed a thick file folder.

"How far back would like me to go?"

"How far back do your records go?"

"We archive records annually, so I should have everything since January 1of this year."

"In that case, I'll take everything you've got."

Weekly disappeared with the file and returned minutes later with copies of Brian Call's cell phone records for 2009. "Sorry,

J.D., I don't have the August statements yet, but this is everything else." She didn't ask why he wanted the records and he didn't offer an explanation.

Books thanked her and left. Minutes later, he was back in his office perusing the records for Las Vegas calls. He moved sequentially, month by month, starting with January. He found nothing from January through April. He was beginning to believe he was chasing his own tail; however, when he reached mid-May, Las Vegas numbers began to appear. At first, they were infrequent, but as he moved through the June and July statements the frequency increased. Some were sent calls and others were calls he'd received. In the end, Books came away with four different Las Vegas numbers. He needed to find out who they belonged to.

He dialed the first number. It was no longer in service. The second number was answered by a pleasant sounding female who said, "Arcadia Outcall Massage. How may I help you?" Books hung up. The third number was a recorded message, "You have reached the offices of Nevada Mining & Manufacturing. We are currently closed. Our office hours are..." The fourth number, the one with the most sent and received calls also went into voicemail. The message said, "This is Michael. Please leave a message." Again, Books disconnected.

Could Michael be Michael Calenti from Nevada Mining and Manufacturing? Was Arcadia Outcall Massage part of the prostitution enterprise allegedly run by Calenti? Books wondered. The information from the Las Vegas numbers added to his suspicion that Call was mixed up with some shady and possibly dangerous people—people who would have the motive and means to have killed David Greenbriar.

Books called Charley Sutter with the news about Brian Call as well as the information he had received from Rusty Steed. Sutter and Call were still at Grosvenor Arch where a CSI team and the medical examiner were combing the crime scene.

"I'm so disappointed to hear that I can hardly stand it," said Sutter. "It makes me sick to my stomach to think somebody on my own staff, somebody in a position of trust, would involve himself in something like this. I still want to believe you're wrong, Books, but it's getting harder and harder to do that. What do you wanna do next?"

"A couple of things. We need to sit down with Call right away and challenge him the same way we did Neil Eddins. If Call is mixed up in a murder-for-hire scheme, we've got to find out what's going on and right away. If I'm right, we've got a killer loose in this community who won't hesitate to kill again."

"All right," said Sutter. "See if you can get hold of Virgil Bell. I'd like to have him involved in Call's interrogation."

"I'll do it. Also, I'll see if we can do the interview at the DA's office. We need to get Call out of his comfort zone."

"That makes sense. What's the second thing?"

"I'll get a BOLO out on the Ford Explorer Rusty Steed told me about. And I think if anybody spots it, they should follow, but not initiate a stop without backup. Whoever this is, I don't think he'd hesitate to kill a lone officer in a traffic stop."

"Right," said Sutter. "Tell the dispatch supervisor to be sure to notify the Highway Patrol, state Game & Fish, and the National Park Service. I don't want anyone caught unaware."

"Will do."

The BOLO went out for a white late-model Ford Explorer with Nevada license plates. Books enlisted the help of the Kanab City police to search every restaurant and motel parking lot in town. If the killer was someone from out of the area, as Books suspected, he had to be staying someplace. Books was to be notified immediately if the vehicle was discovered.

Books dialed Grant Weatherby's cell number in Las Vegas. He told Weatherby about George Gadasky's murder and the apparent connection between Brian Call and Nevada Mining & Manufacturing.

"Well, this has been an interesting case from the start, and it gets more interesting all the time. That said, how can we help you from this end?"

"I need a couple of things, Grant."

"You're about to ruin the rest of my Sunday, aren't you?"

"Probably. Would you see what you can find out about a company called Arcadia Outcall Massage? Brian Call dialed their number several times in recent months. Could that business be part of Michael Calenti's prostitution operation?"

"We'll find out. What else?"

"I'd like you to check a phone number for me," said Books. "When I dialed the number, somebody named Michael had recorded the greeting. I'd like to know whether the Michael on the recording is actually Michael Calenti."

"I can do that, and it shouldn't take long. Give me the number."

◇◇◇

Books called District Attorney Virgil Bell at home. Bell was astounded when Books told him about the murder of George Gadasky and the possible involvement of Brian Call in a murder for hire scheme.

Bell sounded worried. "This puts things in a whole different perspective. You realize you're going to be walking a tightrope when you interrogate Call."

"Why's that?"

"In a nutshell, I don't see any proof that Brian Call has committed a crime. Yeah, he apparently has associations from his Las Vegas days with some criminal types. And yes, those same criminal associates hold mineral rights in the Kaiparowits Plateau. Could be a coincidence though, couldn't it?"

"Possible, I guess," replied Books, "but it doesn't seem likely."

"Based on what you said, you don't have any evidence directly linking this Las Vegas Corporation to the murder of David Greenbriar or George Gadasky. The evidence against Lance Clayburn still remains uncontroverted."

Bell was right. "We at least have the makings of a circumstantial case, don't you think?"

"Yeah, but you're still gonna need more to sustain any kind of prosecution. You either need Brian Call's help, or you need to catch the mysterious character you think killed George Gadasky. Without that, you don't have much."

Bell agreed to participate in the interrogation of Brian Call. Books promised to call him as soon as Sutter and Call returned to Kanab.

# Chapter Forty-two

After his phone call to Rebecca Eddins, Deluca returned to his motel room in Mt. Carmel. He was surprised that searchers had discovered George Gadasky's body so quickly. He needed the extra time, and now he didn't have it. News of the second murder would heighten community anxiety and put everybody on high alert—especially the cops. He needed to lay low until after dark.

Deluca sat at a small table next to the bed studying the information Calenti had given him about the local contact, Brian Call. He had Call's home address and cell phone number. It sounded like the stupid-assed cop had gotten himself mixed up with Victor and Michael Calenti without having any idea just how ruthless they could be. Then he made the mistake of threatening to expose the entire operation because Deluca had found it necessary to eliminate George Gadasky.

Deluca considered Call, like Gadasky, little more than collateral damage, with one major exception—Call was a police officer, and killing cops, even deserving ones, always brought unrelenting heat from other cops. These cases always remained perpetually active, never going into cold-case files like other unsolved homicides. Only once in his thirty-year career had Deluca killed a police officer, and he'd sworn to himself never to do it again.

Deluca carefully considered what story he could concoct that would convince Brian Call that a face-to-face meeting was imperative. He decided to schedule the meeting in the city park at 11:00 p.m. The park was isolated and poorly lit. By eleven o'clock, it would be completely dark and likely empty.

Deluca dialed Call's cell number. It rang several times and then kicked into voicemail. He waited ten minutes and dialed again.

This time he answered on the first ring. "Call."

"Deputy Call. This is Arthur Tate. I work for Victor and Michael Calenti."

"Hold on," said Call. The line was so full of static that it was hard to hear anything. Deluca figured he must still be out in the middle of bumfuck where searchers had discovered George Gadasky's body.

Call came back on the line. "Listen, Mr. Tate, or whoever the hell you are, what the fuck do you think you're doing? This wasn't part of the deal. You think you can just come in here and kill anydamnbody you please? Well, you can't. It doesn't work like that around here."

Call sounded like he was whispering. With that and the static on the line, Deluca could barely hear him. "Listen to me carefully, Brian. I think we may have come up with a way out of this mess that doesn't involve harming Ronnie Gadasky," he lied, "but we can't discuss it on the phone. For this plan to work, I may need your help with something. We need to meet."

"Look, asshole, we don't need to meet. You just need to get your sorry ass out of town, and right now."

"Sorry, but I'm afraid I can't do that until this situation gets resolved. I suppose I don't need to remind you that if this mess blows up in our faces, you're going down right along with everybody else. So it's very important that we all keep our cool until we get over this little bump in the road."

"That's what you call this, a little bump in the road!"

"Hey, friend, I'm just doin' my job same as you. All I can tell you is we need to hang together a little longer, and then we can put this nasty business behind us. And if that's not enough, I've got a little present for you, courtesy of Michael. He sent it up this afternoon."

That piqued Call's interest. "Yeah, what is it?"

"An envelope full of cash and a plastic sandwich baggie stuffed with what Michael tells me is your favorite recreational drug, OxyContin. Michael wanted me to convey his apologies, and he hopes you'll accept this small token of his appreciation for the extra trouble."

The promise of cash and drugs seemed to tip the balance with Call in favor of the face-to-face rendezvous. They agreed to meet in the city park at eleven o'clock on the tennis courts.

After the call, Deluca settled on the bed for an afternoon nap. The night ahead promised to be a long one. As for Brian Call, Deluca remained wary. A junkie cop with addictions to hookers, money, and pills hardly inspired confidence.

With luck, he would end it all tonight.

◇◇◇

Books was about five miles north of town when he received the call from dispatch. He was on his way to check the mom-and-pop motels in a string of small towns between Kanab and Panguitch. Unless he was chasing his tail, and he might be, the missing Ford Explorer had to be hidden somewhere nearby and with it, a possible double murderer. The dispatcher told him to meet a Kanab City police officer at the Angel Canyon Motel on the north end of town. The officer had discovered information about the missing Explorer.

When Books arrived, he spotted the marked cruiser parked under the portico next to the motel office. A Kanab patrol sergeant stood next to the cruiser talking to a young man who appeared to be no more than nineteen or twenty. Books introduced himself to Sergeant Dave Curry. Curry, in turn, introduced Books to the young man standing next to him. Jimmy Johnson was a Brigham Young University college student who had returned home for the summer recess to help his parents run the motel.

"J.D., Jimmy here says he had a guest for the past couple of nights who was driving a white Ford Explorer," said Curry.

"Really. Was it a new rig?"

Johnson shrugged his shoulders. "Yeah, I'd say it was pretty new, '08 or '09 model."

"Did you happen to get the license plate number?"

"Sure did." Johnson handed Books a slip of paper with a Nevada license plate number written on it.

Books turned to the sergeant. "Dave, could you run me a registration check on this plate number and get out a new BOLO?"

"Sure." Curry took the slip of paper from Books and climbed into his patrol car.

Books turned back to Johnson. "The room this guy was staying in. Has it been cleaned?"

"Yeah, sorry about that. We didn't know……"

"That's okay. Can you describe this guy for me, Jimmy?"

"Yeah, he was an old guy, maybe late 50s. I remember him cuz he had a really bad pock-marked face. His hair was almost white and slicked back on the sides. It looked shiny like he'd used too much hair gel."

"What about his height, weight, and race?"

"He was a white guy, tall, maybe six-three or four, probably… I don't know, two-ten, two-twenty. He was a big guy really, in pretty good shape too, especially for an old fella."

"Anything else you can remember about him—tattoos, scars, anything like that?"

Johnson shook his head, "Naw, not that I remember."

"When did he check out?"

"Early this morning. I'd just come on shift."

"Did he mention anything to you about where he was from or what he was doing here?"

Again, Johnson shook his head. "No. He was friendly enough but he didn't mention any of that kind of stuff."

"Did he fill out a room registration card?"

"Yeah, he did. Want me to get it for you."

"Please. What name did he register under, do you recall?"

"Tate. Arnold or Arthur Tate, something like that," said Johnson.

Books followed him into the lobby of the motel. Johnson walked behind the front desk and began to manually search a small metal box holding alphabetized registration cards.

"Let me stop you right there. Did Mr. Tate actually handle the card?"

"Sure did. I handed it to him. He filled it out, signed it, and gave it back."

"Did anybody besides you handle the card?"

Johnson paused. "I don't think so, but I can't be sure. I checked him in the other evening when he arrived, and I checked him out this morning."

"Hold on a minute and don't touch the registration card." Books walked outside and approached the squad car.

Curry handed Books a Post-it note with the registration information. "The Explorer is a 2009 registered to Avis Rent-a-Car at the Las Vegas International Airport. It was rented to some guy named Arthur Tate. He produced a Nevada driver's license with an address at an apartment complex in North Las Vegas."

"Interesting. That's the same name he used to register here at the motel."

Books handed Curry a slip of paper. "Here's the physical description Jimmy gave me of the subject driving the Explorer."

"Great. I'll pass this information along to dispatch and we'll get a new BOLO out to the troops. You think the guy's split?"

"Either that or he's taken up residence somewhere else."

"Well, we'll keep looking for him,"

Books thanked him and Curry left.

Books had an idea that might finally reveal the suspect's identity. He would ask a fingerprint examiner to process the registration card for latents. If prints were found, they would be submitted to IAFIS, the FBI's Integrated Automated Fingerprint Identification System. If the suspect had a criminal history or had ever served in the military, his fingerprints should be in the system. Best of all, the entire process could be completed in just a few hours.

◇◇◇

Books placed the guest registration card in a plastic evidence bag, careful not to contaminate the document with his own prints. Jimmy Johnson accompanied him to the sheriff's office where a set of his fingerprints were taken for comparison purposes.

On the drive back to the motel, Books received a phone call from the sheriff. Sutter told him that he and Call were on their way back to Kanab. George Gadasky's body had been turned over to the medical examiner, and everyone had cleared the crime scene.

Books informed Sutter about what had occurred at the Angel Canyon Motel. Books arranged to meet the fingerprint examiner from the CSI unit at the sheriff's office where he would turn over the registration card for processing.

The logistics of getting Brian Call to the DA's office without arousing his suspicion had turned out to be easy. As they prepared to leave Grosvenor Arch, Sutter told him they were expected at the DA's office for a conference with Virgil Bell. Sutter told him Bell wanted to discuss the murder of George Gadasky and its impact on the case against Lance Clayburn.

The interrogation was set.

# Chapter Forty-three

Word about George Gadasky's murder had spread around Kanab faster than a wildfire through dry sagebrush on a windy day. People were afraid. Several folks stopped Books to ask questions. He didn't know the answer to some and wouldn't answer others.

Books waited at the sheriff's office until Sutter, Call, and the members of the CSI unit arrived. He turned over Jimmy Johnson's fingerprints and the guest registration card to the latent fingerprint examiner who agreed to process it immediately. She promised to run any latents that didn't belong to Jimmy Johnson through IAFIS.

Books ran into Rebecca Eddins in the parking lot on his way to the meeting with Virgil Bell.

"Just the man I was looking for," said Eddins.

"Sorry, Becky, but I'm kind of in a rush. Can this wait until later?"

"I don't think so, J.D. I just heard what happened to George Gadasky. Awful! What I need to tell you is that I received a call late this morning from a guy who claimed to be a reporter from the *Law Vegas Sun Times*. He said he wanted to arrange an exclusive interview with Ronnie Gadasky."

"What name did he use?"

"Elliott Sanders."

Books took her arm. "I think it would be best if you got your little boy and headed over to your dad's place for a day or two."

"How come?"

"I think you just spoke with the guy who killed George. He used the name Elliott Sanders and claimed to be a reporter with the *Sun Times*. How did he get your name?"

"He claimed his paper discovered I'd represented Ronnie in a couple of cases and figured I'd know how to get hold of him."

"What did you tell him?"

"I told him that I hadn't heard from Ronnie and had no idea how to find him."

"How did he take that?"

"He was businesslike, polite, and well spoken."

"Any accent or was there anything unusual about his voice?"

"I didn't detect any accent or regional dialects. He definitely didn't sound like a young guy. His voice sounded older, more mature."

"You handled that well, Becky. Don't stay at home for a night or two."

"That's not necessary. I can take care of myself and my family."

"No, you can't. Listen to me. This guy has already killed two people and he won't hesitate to kill again. Why take the risk? You've got someplace else you can go. Now go get your son and get the hell out of there until it's safe."

She shook her head. "I won't do that. Nobody drives me out of my home."

"Pardon me, Becky, but that's just stupid female pride talking—and it's a damned bad idea besides."

She was adamant, so Books went to Plan B.

Books tried to reach Ned Hunsaker. The old man didn't answer his cell phone. He had probably left the thing inside that Velveeta box in the glove compartment of his truck. Books left him a message on his home phone explaining the situation Becky Eddins was in, and her stubborn refusal to leave home.

◇◇◇

Sutter and Call arrived at Virgil Bell's office ahead of Books. When Books got there, he found a somber-looking group gathered around a small conference table in Bell's office. The tension in the room was palpable. Call looked decidedly uncomfortable, as if he sensed something he wasn't going to like. It got worse when Books placed a small voice-activated tape recorder on the table.

"What's that for?" asked Call.

"So that we'll have an accurate record of everything that's said," Sutter piped up. "And for the record, Brian, I want you to understand that I consider this an internal personnel investigation as well as a possible criminal matter. I've asked Ranger Books to conduct the interview."

Virgil Bell sat with a legal pad in front of him and a pen in his hand. He stared at Call without speaking, his face expressionless.

Call's eyes darted around the room like a trapped animal's. "I don't get it."

"Sure you do, Brian," said Books.

Call became belligerent. "What the hell is this all about, anyway?"

"Regrettably, Brian, we have reason to believe that you're mixed up with some bad characters out of Las Vegas," said Books. "Before we can go any further, I'll need to advise you of your constitutional rights under Miranda." Books walked him carefully through the Miranda warnings.

Call looked frightened but defiantly stood his ground. "I know my rights and I don't have any goddamned thing to hide. I'll answer your questions, and I don't need a lawyer to do it." He'd just violated the first rule of the career criminal—when challenged by the police skip the bluff and bravado. Keep your mouth shut.

"We appreciate that," said Books. "What can you tell us about a Las Vegas company called Nevada Mining & Manufacturing?"

"What's that got to do with anything? That's ancient history."

"We'll be the judge of that. Tell us about your ancient history with the company."

"I didn't say I had any history with Nevada…whatever you called them."

"So you're telling us that you've never heard of Nevada Mining & Manufacturing. Is that correct?"

"I didn't say that."

"Then what are you saying?"

"I'm saying I knew the people who ran that company from the old days when I lived in Vegas. I haven't had any contact with them for years."

"Those people you're referring to…that would be Michael and Victor Calenti. Is that correct?"

"Yeah."

"And in those old days, you were employed as a corrections officer in the Las Vegas County Metropolitan Jail. Is that right?"

"That's right."

"How did you meet the Calentis?"

"I didn't know Victor. I knew Michael because he had legal problems. He had some minor scrapes with the law and ended up serving jail time."

"So you met Michael in your official capacity as a law enforcement officer."

"Yeah, so what?"

"The *so what* is that you were subsequently canned by the police department because they caught you consorting with a hooker who happened to be under correctional supervision—probation, I think—and because you were suspected of bringing contraband into the jail for Michael Calenti."

"Pure conjecture. It was never proven."

"If it wasn't true, why didn't you stick around and fight for your job?"

Call's face reddened and he struggled to hold his temper. "Because they'd made up their minds. I wouldn't have gotten a fair hearing, so I decided it was time to move on."

"A minute ago you said you haven't had any contact with the Calentis in years. Was that the truth, Brian?"

Call hesitated, wondering if Books was bluffing or really knew something. He hedged his bet. "I can't say definitively that I've never had any contact with the Calentis since I moved here."

"How frequent have the contacts been?"

"I don't know, on and off, not very often, though."

"Tell us why you would continue to have contacts with a family everybody knows has organized crime connections."

"That was just a rumor. I never believed it."

"For sake of argument, let's say you continued to have intermittent contacts with the Calentis after you moved here and after you got back into law enforcement. What kind of business could you possibly have with them?"

"Social, mostly. One time when I was working as an outfitter, Michael called and asked if I would guide him and some friends on a deer hunt."

"And did you?"

"Naw, the trip fell through."

"How recently have you had contact with Nevada Mining & Manufacturing or the Calenti brothers?"

"Not for months."

Books removed Call's cell phone records from a file folder on the table in front of him. "These are your cell phone records for 2009. We don't have your home phone records, but we'll have them shortly. You've been lying to us, and we know it."

"Bullshit."

"Okay. Let's look at the calls." Books slid a highlighted copy of the records in front of Brian Call. "During the past several months, you've made numerous calls, more than two dozen, to two different Las Vegas numbers. One is the main number to the company and the other is Michael Calenti's cell phone. And you have almost as many calls from him. How do you explain that?"

"This is ridiculous. I don't have to answer any more of your questions, and I'm not going to."

Sheriff Sutter said, "Listen up, Brian. As an officer in this department, you are obligated to cooperate with any internal investigation and truthfully answer our questions. If you don't, I can fire your ass, and I will."

Call looked confused and upset. He was on the edge, unsure of what to do or say. Beads of sweat dotted his forehead.

Books saw an opportunity to break him. "Look, Brian, let me tell you what I think is going on. We've got a killer loose in this community—a killer who I believe murdered George Gadasky and David Greenbriar. I think this guy's probably a pro, a contract killer dispatched by the Calentis. I think you're involved, and I think you've gotten in way over your head."

Call interrupted. "That's bullshit. We caught the killer. It's Lance Clayburn, and we've got the evidence to prove it. He killed Greenbriar, and he probably killed George, too."

"He didn't kill George, I'm sure of that."

Call sneered. "Yeah. How can you be so sure?"

"Because Lance called me two nights ago from New Hampshire. The kid got scared and ran home to his family. He wasn't around to kill George Gadasky."

That news nearly brought Charley Sutter out of his chair, but he didn't say anything. Virgil Bell raised his eyebrows, but, like Sutter, kept quiet.

"Let me tell you something, Brian, I've been thinking about the physical evidence implicating Clayburn in Greenbriar's murder. You know what? I think somebody planted that evidence so it would look like Greenbriar was killed by Darby's jealous boyfriend. It actually made a lot of sense. And if you happened to be the guy who provided that evidence, it would explain the frequent calls between you and Michael Calenti."

"You're crazy. You can't prove any of it. It's all speculation. Besides, why would the Calentis want to kill Greenbriar?"

"So they could remove a serious obstacle to road expansion in the Grand Staircase. They couldn't buy David Greenbriar, so they had him killed."

The sweat poured off Call's forehead. "Why would the Calentis care about that?"

"Because David and the Escalante Environmental Wilderness Alliance opposed Nevada Mining & Manufacturing's plan to mine coal in the monument. The coal deposits are there. The company owns the mineral rights to what's under the ground. All they need is new roads to make it cost effective to get their product to market. There's a lot at stake—economic development, new jobs, and enormous profits for the Calentis."

"For Godsakes, man, if there's some reasonable explanation for all these calls to the Calentis, please tell us what it is," implored Sutter.

Call stared at the floor, unblinking, like he had entered into a catatonic state.

"Come on, Brian. We're wasting time," said Books. "You need to tell us what's going on before this guy kills somebody else. And he will kill again. We have to assume he's still looking for Ronnie Gadasky—that he killed George because he either couldn't or wouldn't lead him to Ronnie."

"Suppose, just suppose I do know something," said Call. "What's in it for me if I agree to cooperate?"

Books looked from Sutter to Virgil Bell. "Gentlemen….."

"It's the DA's call," said Sutter.

"All right," said Bell. "If you come clean, and I mean completely clean right now, I promise you that I'll take the death penalty and life in prison off the table. You turn state's evidence, testify against these guys, if necessary, you'll do some time, but you'll get out of prison with some good years still in front of you."

"You'll guarantee it—put it in writing?"

"I'll do it tonight, but only if you cooperate fully and tell us the complete truth. If I find out later you lied about anything, the deal's off the table. Understood?"

Call took a deep breath. "All right. What do you want to know?"

# Chapter Forty-four

The most pressing need was to find the killer before he killed again. Everything else had to take a back seat to that. "Tell us, Brian, who is this guy, and how did you meet him?" asked Books.

"That's just it. I've never met him. I've never even seen him. Everything I did went through Michael or Victor; Michael mostly."

"Any idea how we're going to find him, then?" asked Books.

Call glanced at his watch. "Yeah. I'm supposed to meet him in about three hours."

Books and Sutter glanced at each other. "Tell us about that. When and where are you supposed to meet?"

"This is what happened. This morning at the crime scene I get this call from a guy who introduces himself as Arthur Tate. He apologizes for killing George and claims he's got a plan that will make it so he doesn't need to go after Ronnie. Problem is, he needs my help to do it, or so he says."

"What does he want you to do?"

"He wouldn't discuss it over the phone—said we needed to meet face-to-face, tonight at eleven o'clock at the city park."

"Why the city park?" asked Sutter.

"How should I know—probably because it offers privacy and little chance that anybody would see us."

Books considered that. Arthur Tate and Elliot Sanders had to be one and the same. But why would he agree to meet Brian

Call when he had gone to some lengths to avoid just such a meeting? Books wasn't sure. What he was sure of was the invitation created an opportunity to bring this guy down, if Call was willing to help.

"How about you help us nab this guy tonight?" said Books. "We'll wire you up, stake out the park, and catch this bastard before he can hurt anybody else."

Virgil Bell chimed in. "At some point, Brian, you're going to end up standing in front of a judge pleading for leniency. I can help you only so far. If you do this for us, it'll show the court you cooperated and did your part to stop this monster."

Call mulled over the implications of their request. "This could be downright dangerous, couldn't it?"

"Absolutely," said Books.

"All right. I've gone this far, I might as well go all the way. Let's do it."

Books looked at his watch. At a few minutes after eight, they had less than three hours to mobilize personnel, create a plan, and get everyone in position. If Books was right, this guy was a pro, and a pro would be cautious, leaving nothing to chance. He would probably scout the area well ahead of the scheduled meeting time. If anything looked out of place, he'd be a no-show.

Books and Bell continued to question Call. Sutter left the interrogation to begin mobilizing equipment and personnel.

"Explain to us how incriminating evidence implicating Lance Clayburn managed to end up at the crime scene," said Books.

Call sighed. "It was actually the easiest part of the whole deal. One night a few months ago, I drove past Clayburn's house the night before garbage pickup. His garbage can was out on the street, and I picked up a couple of bags. I took them back to my place, sorted through them until I found what I needed."

"What did you do with the evidence then?"

"I drove it to Las Vegas and gave it to Michael Calenti."

"And when was that?"

"I can't remember—about two months ago, I'd guess."

"Where did you meet?"

"Michael's condo."

"And what did Michael do with the evidence?"

"I don't know for sure. I assume he passed it along to the guy you're looking for."

"So you had nothing to do with planting the evidence at the crime scene. Is that correct?"

"That's right."

"What about Clayburn's hunting rifle. Did you steal it?"

"I did."

"Tell us about that."

"I broke in and stole it out of his house. I knew he had a .30-06 and figured if it disappeared, he'd look even more guilty."

"What did you do with the rifle after you stole it?"

"I got rid of it at the county landfill."

"When was that?"

"I can't remember dates, man—six, seven weeks ago, maybe."

Books shook his head and sighed. "Why did you get mixed up in this, Brian—afraid I just don't get it?"

"I can't tell you how many times I've asked myself that very question since Greenbriar was killed. I guess I really don't know—habit, I suppose. I'd been doing favors for the Calentis for years. Michael would set me up with some of his girls from time to time, and I got some money, not a lot, but some."

"What about the Calentis? Besides the roads issue, what, if anything, were they trying to accomplish?"

"The Calentis figured that eliminating Greenbriar would have a quieting effect on the environmental movement all over the West. There's a lot at stake."

"Like what?" Bell asked.

"Not only was Greenbriar causing problems with road expansion, he was also pressing various Congressional committees to raise grazing fees, which would cripple the livestock business. The Calenits didn't care about that, but they damned sure cared about Greenbriar's recommendation that companies like Nevada Mining & Manufacturing start paying royalty fees for mining on federal lands. Victor told me once that if Greenbriar got his way, companies like his could end up paying an 8% royalty plus the true costs of land reclamation. He figured it would cost the company millions."

◇◇◇

After the interrogation, Books and Bell escorted Call to the Kanab Police Department. Call was fitted with a wire enabling officers parked in a nondescript surveillance van near Kanab City Park to monitor his conversation with the suspected killer.

Sutter had managed to assemble a ten-person rag-tag team of sheriff's deputies, city police officers, and two members of the CSI unit from St. George who had just spent the day processing the crime scene at Grosvenor Arch to take part in the sting. Sutter also dispatched two members to prepare a sketch of the park and select the best positions around its perimeter to place officers. Everyone would assemble in the police department's training room at nine-thirty and be in place an hour before the scheduled rendezvous.

Books caught up with the sheriff in the police department's lunch room where Sutter was scarfing down a Hostess Twinkee and a can of diet Pepsi. "That shit'll kill you, Charley."

"Tastes good, though," he said, around a mouthful of Twinkee.

"Anything from the fingerprint examiner?" asked Books.

"Good news. After dusting the card, she found several identifiable latents. When she eliminated Jimmy's from the mix, she was left with a partial index finger and a thumb print. All we're waiting on now is a response from IAFIS."

"Boy, I hope we get an IAFIS hit. It sure would be nice to know who we're up against out there tonight."

"Sure would. How'd it go with Call?"

"Once he made the decision to cooperate, he never wavered. He gave us everything he knows."

"That's what we needed," said Sutter. "I've known the man for a lot of years, and I think he's wracked with guilt over this thing, particularly George's murder."

"Well, he ought to be. He was up to his eyeballs in it."

"Better late than never, I guess," replied the sheriff.

The two went over the logistics of the night's operation. Getting everyone in position an hour ahead of time was essential. "I think we're dealing with a pretty savvy killer. This guy knows what he's doing. I think he's smart and doesn't make mistakes. He'll sniff around out there early to see if anything looks out of the ordinary."

"You're probably right," said Sutter. "I'm damned uneasy about sending Call into that park after dark. We won't be able to see a thing once he goes in."

"The wire has to serve as both our eyes and ears. And don't forget, he'll be wearing a vest."

"That's true, J.D., but we don't have much experience with this high tech equipment—almost no call for it out here. I'll bet we've only had that stuff out of the box once or twice in five years."

"First time for everything, Charley. Here's a thought. If Call is wired up and ready to go, send him home and have the surveillance van follow him and park nearby. It's a good way to test the equipment. Assuming everything's working fine, have the van take up its position near the park. Brian can follow from his house right before eleven. This guy may have decided to follow Brian from his house to the park. That way he gets a chance to see if everything looks okay."

Sutter liked that idea. He huddled with Call and the two officers assigned to drive the surveillance van and operate the monitoring equipment before he sent them out the door. It was almost nine-thirty. Officers began to gather in the training room for the briefing and to receive their respective assignments.

As Books and Call were about to start, the fingerprint examiner hurried into the training room. "We've got a match. We've got him identified."

Books and Sutter stared at a grainy black and white photograph of a much younger Peter Deluca. "He's got a criminal history, and he also served in the U.S. Army."

Neither man spoke as they read the biographical information in the report. Finally, Books said, "A lot younger, but this looks like our boy, Charley. Mr. Deluca matches the description Jimmy Johnson gave us of the guest from the motel."

"Sure seems to."

Books continued. "He's a white, male, age.....let's see, I'd make him fifty-eight years old, six feet-four inches, two-hundred-fifteen pounds. He's got three misdemeanor arrests in Chicago in the late sixties. Arrested again in Chicago, 1994, suspicion of murder, charges dismissed—insufficient evidence. That's it on the criminal history.

"Enlisted U.S. Army, 1969, honorably discharged as a sergeant in 1973, after serving three years. This guy was an army sniper and served two tours in 'Nam. Can't say I like that. It looks like he spent much of the next twenty-five years working as muscle for the Chicago Outfit. He moved to Las Vegas four, maybe five years ago."

"Geez," said Sutter. "He's gettin a little long in the tooth for this kind of work, don't you think?"

"You'd think."

◇◇◇

Sutter conducted the briefing. The information on Deluca was disseminated to everyone. Officers were assigned to work in pairs. Each team was assigned a geographical area around the perimeter of the park. When he was finished, Sutter turned to Books. "Can you think of anything else, J.D.?"

"Just a word of caution. The park's closed, so we don't anticipate civilians being out there. But you can never be sure. If it becomes necessary to shoot, be damned certain you've got a target. And for crissake sake, don't be shooting at each other. If we end up on the move, it's possible that we could catch each other in a cross fire. Be careful and know what you're shooting at."

The briefing ended at 9:45. Eight officers, excluding Books, took up positions around Kanab City Park.

# Chapter Forty-five

Deluca slept until early evening, knowing the approaching darkness would provide him with a much-needed veil of anonymity. He planned to be on the move by nine o'clock.

Regardless of tonight's outcome, Deluca would return to Vegas by early morning in time for a steak and eggs breakfast at DiJulio's, followed by a trip to Pampered Pooches to collect his beloved Rosie. She would be paw-stomping mad because he had left town without her. He, in turn, would become the victim of an elaborate dog extortion scam in which Rosie would demand increased attention, more treats, and longer walks at the local dog park. Then there was the green house and the delicate roses that required tender nurturing and constant vigilance.

Deluca spent the evening packing and preparing his weapons. Unsure exactly what he would need, he selected a .308 caliber Remington Model 700 rifle with a night vision scope and a silenced .22 caliber Colt for close range work. He cleaned both weapons, leaving a residue of gun oil on each.

Deluca ate a late meal at a diner within walking distance of the motel. Afterward, he went back to his room, loaded the Explorer, and returned to Kanab. When he reached the north end of town, he turned off Center Street and meandered along side streets rather than the main thoroughfare, coming out on State Highway 89 next to the cemetery.

It was a little after nine o'clock when he turned off the highway into the shallow turnout near Ronnie Gadasky's home. He pulled the Colt from under a nylon windbreaker on the front passenger seat, got out of the Explorer, and jogged down the dirt driveway until the home came into view. He could hardly believe his good fortune. After all this time and effort, there it was: the red Kawasaki dirt bike parked right in front of the house.

He crept along the driveway, staying in the shadows as much as possible. Out here in the middle of bumfuck, the full moon made him feel like he was moving under flood lights. In Vegas, a city known for its overstated glitzy neon, a full moon went largely unnoticed. As he neared the house, Deluca was on high alert for the three-legged lab. He tapped a zippered pocket of the windbreaker to make certain he hadn't forgotten the dog treats. An old army sergeant from his Vietnam days had regularly reminded his subordinates that lack of prior planning always made for piss-poor performance. Deluca had never forgotten the advice.

The dog was nowhere in sight. The lights were on all over the main level of the house, and the blinds were open. On the second floor, the light in Ronnie's bedroom was turned on but the blind was closed. Deluca crept to a side window with a view into the living room. He saw the kid's father sitting on the couch with a pillow in his lap and an open bottle of Smirnoff vodka on the coffee table in front of him. The old man looked like he was asleep or passed out. Ronnie wasn't there. He was probably upstairs in his bedroom. That meant Deluca would have to go inside, something he didn't relish.

He moved to the back of the house, nearly tripping over a shovel lying in his path. The back door was unlocked. Deluca stepped inside and closed the door. He waited for several seconds, listening for any sound, but heard nothing. He tiptoed through the kitchen to a stairwell that led to the second floor. The old man hadn't moved. His head was tipped forward, his chin touching his chest.

As Deluca started up the stairs, Ivan Gadasky looked up and spoke. "I thought you might come. He's not here. You killed

George, but you won't kill my youngest, my Ronnie. In fact, your killing days are over."

Deluca frowned and walked slowly into the living room. His eyes never left Gadasky. The room stunk of BO and vomit. The old man had thrown up on the pillow in his lap. "Look old man, I'm sorry about your son, but business is business. I came for Ronnie. Where is he?"

A faint smile played at the corners of Gadasky's mouth. His bloodshot eyes filled with tears—the tears of a grieving man. "He's somewhere safe, someplace an evil man like you can't hurt him."

Deluca smiled back. Before he could say anything else, Gadasky's right hand came out from under the pillow brandishing a gun. The old man squeezed off two wild shots. One of them struck Deluca's upper left arm. Deluca spun to one side and fired twice. Both shots entered Ivan Gadasky's chest. His third shot, carefully aimed, struck Gadasky in the forehead right between the eyes. The old man let out one long breath and then his head rolled to the side where it rested against the back of the couch. His vacant eyes stared at nothing.

Deluca cursed but managed to choke back the pain long enough to race upstairs and kick down Ronnie's bedroom door. The kid wasn't there. The old man had set him up. Shit!

He found a linen closet in the hallway where he grabbed a hand towel and a wash cloth. He soaked the wound in warm water as he surveyed the damage. He'd been lucky. The bullet had struck the soft, fleshy part of his upper arm and exited out the back. The wound bled freely, but it wasn't life-threatening. Using the towel as a compress, he hurried back to the SUV for a first aid kit he carried as a precaution but had never had to use. He cleaned the wound as best he could, using an antiseptic liquid that burned like a bitch and made his eyes water. He wrapped the arm with a sterile pad and taped it using narrow strips of adhesive.

Back in Vegas there was someone, who, for the right price, would treat the wound without asking questions. In the meantime, he would change the dressing as needed and continue to apply the antiseptic. Deluca had always kept a supply of prescription pain killers in the first aid kit, but he opted instead for a handful of Tylenol. He had to keep his mind clear.

◇◇◇

Deluca turned off the highway a couple of miles east of Kanab onto an unmarked, unlit dirt road. Scattered sagebrush and juniper pine dotted the moonlit landscape. The road led into a sparsely populated, ramshackle neighborhood of modest single-family houses, mobile homes, and even some trailers. Brian Call lived here, and Deluca had come like the Grim Reaper to pay his last respects.

It was nearly ten-thirty. Call might not even be at home, but if he was, why wait to see if the deputy had set a trap for him in town? He negotiated a couple of turns before he parked the Explorer and shut off the engine. He looked around, momentarily confused, unsure whether he was in the right place. The terrain looked vastly different in daylight from the stark, shadowed night scene.

Deluca reloaded the .22 and got out of the truck. Only the occasional sound of a barking dog or the volume from a television set interrupted the eerie silence of the night. He started up the dirt road, moving as fast as he could. The pain from the gunshot wound reverberated up and down the length of his arm. His breathing grew labored as the dirt road climbed steadily higher toward a black mesa that blotted out the starlit sky. He began to perspire and stopped to catch his breath when he felt light-headed. Christ, he was getting too old for this. He continued for another fifty meters until the road crested and then flattened out.

Call's double-wide mobile home sat on a shallow circular driveway next to the road. His 4 x 4 Dodge pickup, with the Kane County Sheriff's Department logo emblazed on the side, was parked in front. The lights in the home were on, so Call had not yet headed into town for their eleven o'clock meet.

The front door stood open. Deluca pulled the .22 as he climbed two wooden steps and reached for the screen door. He pulled gently. The screen door was locked. Deluca gave it one hard yank, nearly ripping off its hinges, and burst into the small living room.

Call emerged from a room down the hallway. As Deluca raised the pistol to fire, Call abruptly turned and ran for a back bedroom. For a middle-aged fat man, Call was far more deft on his feet than Deluca would have imagined. He fired one shot as Call dove into the bedroom out of sight. The shot struck Call in the upper back and the man yelped in pain. As Deluca ran down the hallway in pursuit, he heard the sound of breaking glass. He peeked around the corner into the bedroom just as Call dove headfirst through the window, grunting as he landed on the ground. Deluca reached the window in time to fire twice more at the retreating figure, unsure whether either shot found its mark. He jumped out the window feet first and followed Call into the darkness. A short distance from the back of the home, he stood perfectly still and listened. The only thing Deluca heard was the sound of his own ragged breathing. The further he moved away from ambient light provided by the house, the darker it became. Soon he became disoriented. The exertion of the chase gave him a serious case of nausea.

He decided not to waste any more time. He retreated to the Explorer as quickly as his weakened condition allowed. Blood from the bullet wound soaked through the bandage and ran down his arm.

Deluca cursed himself for not using a larger caliber weapon with more stopping power. The twenty-two had failed to do the job, and Call had escaped. The best he could hope for now was that Call would crawl away into the dense brush and die from his wound.

The gig was over. Deluca was going to have to run, but not before he made one last stop in town.

◇◇◇

Books had a bad feeling about the stakeout, but he wasn't sure why. Perhaps Sutter's anxiety had become his own. Everybody was in position. Hand-held radios had been issued to each officer. The surveillance van had taken up a position about one-half block east of the city park. They seemed to have the bases covered. Sutter had suggested that Books remain mobile on the perimeter of the park since everyone else would be on foot. Books agreed and dropped the Yukon at home, picking up his personal vehicle, an F-150 truck.

Books glanced at his watch. It was five minutes until eleven. Where was Call? He couldn't afford to arrive late for this party. Deluca was elusive, and it wouldn't take much to spook him.

In the next instant, everything changed.

The radio crackled and an obviously distraught Brian Call screamed into the mike. "Dispatch, dispatch, this is Call. I've been shot—request medical assistance and backup."

The dispatcher remained calm. "Your 10/20, Deputy Call?"

"My house. Get somebody to my fucking house now. Christ, I'm bleeding all over the place."

Police and ambulance were sent immediately. Officers at the stakeout broke for their vehicles, two civilian SUVs stashed nearby. When Books heard the radio traffic, he punched the accelerator and sped toward Call's home. If Books got lucky, he might intercept Deluca. The white Explorer shouldn't be difficult to spot, assuming Deluca hadn't changed vehicles.

The dispatcher tried to get additional information from Call. "Try to remain calm, Brian. Can you tell us what happened?"

"The suspect showed up on my door step and started shooting."

"Is the suspect still on scene?"

"Negative. I think he's gone."

"Did you observe a suspect vehicle?"

"Negative. I think he came on foot, but I'm not sure."

"Where did you last observe him?"

"In my goddamned living room," shouted Call.

Books raced out State Highway 89, hoping he'd be able to spot the turnoff into Call's neighborhood. The ambulance siren wailed some distance behind him. Oncoming traffic was light. The surveillance van closed quickly behind him. Books slowed and waved it around, allowing the van to lead him to Call's home.

They traveled another quarter-mile before the van turned north onto a dirt road. Books followed. Seconds later they topped a small hill and Call's sheriff's vehicle came into view.

They found him lying on his stomach on the floor of the living room, conscious, in pain, and losing a lot of blood. A small entry wound in the upper left part of his back bled freely. It looked to Books like a wound from a small caliber gun, a twenty-two, or maybe a twenty-five.

While the other deputies went to work on Call, Books began a circular search of the grounds, using the home as center point. He could hear the sound of approaching emergency vehicles, their sirens screaming in the night. Within minutes, Call's property was crawling with police.

Books continued his search until he became convinced Deluca was long gone. Where would he have gone? If Deluca was as smart as he seemed, he'd resist the temptation to run. Instead, he would find a place to hide until things cooled down. But what if he had used the attack on Call as a diversion? It seemed like every cop in the county had converged on Call's home. What if Peter Deluca had another agenda?

Books could think of only one possibility. He jumped into his truck and headed back into town.

# Chapter Forty-six

Deluca heard the sound of sirens as he crossed Kanab Creek. He was disappointed. The sound meant only one thing: Brian Call was still alive, and the cavalry was riding to the rescue. He'd hit him once for sure, and maybe twice.

Ivan Gadasky had mentioned sending Ronnie someplace where he'd be safe. To Deluca, that meant Ronnie was already in police custody or he'd taken refuge at the home of his lawyer, Rebecca Eddins. That's where he was going. If he got lucky, he might still complete the job and get out of town with his reputation intact. If the drive-by gave no indication that Ronnie was inside, he would leave immediately and never set foot in this cowboy town again.

Deluca was unsure what Ronnie Gadasky might be driving. The dirt bike was back at the house. He drove slowly down the dimly lit street past Rebecca Eddins' fake adobe home. Parked in the driveway was old man Gadasky's rusted-out hulk of a pickup. He couldn't believe his luck. Finally, he'd found the little pervert. What would Eddins think if she knew that her erstwhile client was a peeping Tom who'd stalked her and filmed some of her most intimate moments?

He needed to move quickly to get this over with and be on his way. While he had no reason to believe the Eddins woman would be particularly dangerous, he wasn't about to take any unnecessary chances. Everybody in this neck of the woods owned guns. He'd been duped once tonight, and he wouldn't let it happen again.

He parked down the street. From his gun case, Deluca removed a nine-millimeter Glock, loaded it with a nine-bullet clip, released the safety, and walked toward the house.

On his way into town, Books radioed Charley Sutter. "Where the hell did you disappear too?" asked Sutter.

"On my way to check something out in town. I need you to get somebody out to Ivan Gadasky's place right away."

"Why?"

"It's just a hunch, but what if our suspect decides to make one more try at Ronnie Gadasky. He might show up at the Gadasky home."

"Doesn't seem too likely, but I'll send a couple of officers out there to check it out. Where are you gonna be?"

"I'm on my way to Rebecca Eddins home."

"How come?"

"Same reason you're sending officers to Gadasky's home." Books disconnected.

Books was almost at the house when her 911 call came into dispatch. It was just what he'd feared. Rebecca Eddins had called the sheriff's department claiming that someone was outside her home, trying windows and doors. Books knew exactly who the intruder was and hoped Eddins did as well.

He doused his headlights as he turned down Eddins' street. He drove slowly past her house, spotting Ivan Gadasky's truck in the driveway. The white Ford Explorer was parked several houses down the street. He parked and got out of the pickup, careful not to announce his presence by slamming the truck door.

Drawing his BLM-issued .357-magnum Smith & Wesson revolver, Books quickly disabled the Explorer, and then hurried on to the house.

As he looked through the front windows of the house, Deluca sensed that the place was empty. Maybe Eddins had done the smart thing, taken her son and Ronnie Gadasky and headed straight to the police. The dark exterior windows deflected glare and heat from the sun. It was difficult, even from up close, to see much inside.

First, Deluca tried a window to a corner office. It wouldn't budge. He stayed close to the house, moving along the front, until he came to a portico leading to a double set of Spanish-style front doors. He tried those—locked. Across the portico, he passed under a window with opaque glass, probably a bathroom. It, too, was locked. Deluca left the cover of the darkened portico passing in front of a triple-car garage. From the corner of the garage, he moved westward toward the back of the home. A lava rock path surrounded by desert shrubs and decorative bark led to a stucco wall shaded by a large juniper tree. Deluca jumped and pulled himself up and over the wall. His feet landed in a small patch of cacti in the back yard.

He stopped and listened. At first, the only thing he heard was the shrill, chirping sound of the resident crickets. Then he heard a television set. Maybe they were home. Maybe she was feeding the little perv milk and cookies. Maybe she felt safe, or maybe she felt like he used to feel—invincible. He didn't feel invincible any longer. Every instinct in his body told him something was wrong and he should get out while he still had the chance. But he didn't. For once, pride and stubbornness to fulfill the contract overcame good judgment.

Deluca started across the back of the house, staying low and hugging the wall. He stopped again and listened. He heard the unmistakable sound of the TV, canned laughter, a sitcom, maybe. He could see lights on inside. Then he heard the woman's voice.

"Can I get you anything else to eat?"

"No," came a faint reply. It was the Eddins woman and the kid. It had to be.

Deluca considered whether to attempt a shot from the outside through a window, or try a frontal assault—go right in after them. Then he saw the open sliding glass door leading into the kitchen. Decision made. A frontal assault it would be.

He removed the Glock from its holster, clicked the safety into the off position, and chambered a round. He stood, took a deep breath, and rushed the door.

◇◇◇

From behind a large landscape rock near the edge of the property, Books scanned horizontally across the front of the sprawling home looking for any sign of movement. Nothing.

He moved quickly toward the corner of the house, his gun extended in front of him moving back and forth along an imaginary firing line. From the garage, Books started for the rear of the house. A five-foot-high stucco wall stood in his path. He jumped over it and dropped into the backyard before continuing to the rear corner of the house. He peeked around the corner in time to see Deluca kick down a flimsy screen door leading into the house. Books stepped around the corner in a combat crouch and yelled at Deluca to drop his weapon. Deluca spun and fired three quick shots as Books dove to the ground. Deluca's speed had surprised him. He felt an intense burning sensation in his left leg and realized that at least one of Deluca's shots had found its mark. Lying on his right side, Books gripped the Smith & Wesson with both hands and returned fire. He didn't stop shooting until the gun was empty.

◇◇◇

Deluca stood to his full six feet three inches and gaped at the growing red stain across the front of his white Polo shirt. The bullet had entered his abdomen just above the belt line. Until tonight, he'd never been shot. Now he'd been shot twice. He had always wondered what it might feel like. Rather than pain, Deluca's belly felt numb. Nauseated and lightheaded, he staggered toward the prone figure of the uniformed cop. The man's face was a mask of sweat and pain as he continued squeezing the trigger of the empty handgun. Deluca noticed the dark stain spreading on the cop's trouser leg. He was losing a lot of blood. The men stared at each other for an instant. Something passed between them, mutual respect, maybe, certainly not fear.

"Out of ammo, huh," said Deluca. He raised the Glock and pointed it at Books' head.

Books stared back at him but said nothing.

"I'm not," said a voice from behind him.

As Deluca turned, he heard a deafening explosion and saw a bright muzzle flash as Ned Hunsaker fired the 12-gauge Remington shotgun. The shot caught him in the neck and face. The force of the blast knocked him to the ground. The Glock skittered away along the brick patio floor.

The last conscious thought Peter Deluca had was about Rosie. What would happen to her? Who would care for his beloved Rosie? He tried to speak, to form the words, but he couldn't. Then everything faded to black.

◇◇◇

Books would remember little of the next twenty-four hours as he drifted in and out of consciousness. He remembered pressure on the wound and words of encouragement from Becky Eddins and Ned Hunsaker. He recalled being jostled into the waiting ambulance, someone at the hospital cutting away his trousers, and bright overhead lights as he rolled into the operating room.

# Chapter Forty-seven

## Afterword

September brought relief from the intense summer heat. The tourist season was winding down, autumn was around the corner, and the deer hunt was in full swing. It had been nearly three weeks since the showdown at Becky Eddins' home. The gunshot wound Books had sustained, courtesy of Peter "the Rose" Deluca, was on the mend. In retrospect, he'd been lucky. The bullet hadn't shattered bone nor had it struck a major artery. He had endured a low grade infection in the leg, but ten days of antibiotics had cured it. The leg chronically ached, so he was forced temporarily to use a cane to get around.

Becky Eddins and Ned Hunsaker became self-appointed managers of his rehabilitation program. They'd hovered like mother hens since his release from the hospital and elevated the art of well-intentioned nagging to a whole new level. Even his father, Bernie, had lent a hand.

After the autopsy, the Utah Medical Examiner's Office released the body of Peter Deluca. Despite a concerted effort, nobody had been able to locate family, and consequently nobody claimed the body. His remains were eventually returned to Las Vegas, where he was buried in a pauper's grave in a city-owned cemetery.

Books still hadn't been cleared to resume work in the field, but in the last days, inactivity and sheer boredom drove him to BLM headquarters, where he pestered Alexis Runyon for something to do. She obliged by assigning him mundane clerical jobs that kept him busy and out of her office.

On this night, Books left headquarters late. He stopped at the town market and purchased two bouquets of fresh flowers. One was for Becky Eddins, who had invited him to dinner, and the other was for his mother's grave. He parked the Yukon near the cemetery office and hobbled, cane in hand, the short distance to the grave. He laid the flowers across his mother's headstone and sat down on the lawn next to her. He stayed for a while. When he glanced up, Ned Hunsaker was striding toward him.

"Evening, Ned."

"J.D."

"I'll bet I know what brought you here."

Hunsaker grunted, "Same as you. I figured it was time to tidy up around the graves."

"Yup."

Neither man spoke for a time. Books broke the silence. "Something on your mind, Ned?"

"Sure is. I've been meaning to talk with you when it felt like the time was right."

"Well, I guess that makes two of us because I've got something to say to you, too."

"You do?" said Ned, looking puzzled.

"Yeah. I never thanked you for saving my life. If you hadn't been on guard duty at Becky's that night, I'd have been toast. So thanks for saving my life."

"You don't need to thank me, J.D. If you hadn't called and given me the heads up, Becky and I wouldn't have had the opportunity to set up the welcoming committee for Mr. Deluca." Hunsaker cleared his throat. "Besides, you didn't think I'd let anything happen to my own son, do you?"

For a moment, Books thought he hadn't heard Hunsaker correctly. Then he looked the old man in the eyes, and he knew. "I'm your son."

Hunsaker looked away into the distance. Tears filled his eyes. "Before you say anything, please hear me out."

Books didn't know what to think or say. "Okay," he mumbled.

"Look, I don't really know how to explain this, so I'm just gonna say it. Thirty-three years ago, your mother and I had a brief affair. Lord, I hate that word 'affair.' It sounds so cheap. Anyway, it didn't last long, at least the physical part didn't. But nine months later, you came along. I want you to know that I loved your mother until the day she died. And I'm still in love with her."

Books interrupted. "What about Bernie? Did he know?"

"No. Bernie never knew, and your mother and I agreed we'd never tell him or anyone else. And that's a promise we kept all these years. It was only on your mother's deathbed that she gave me permission to tell you. In the end, she left it up to me."

"But Ned, if you loved each other, why didn't you get divorced and marry? People would have understood."

"No, son, they wouldn't have, not in a small Mormon town like this one. We considered it, but never very seriously. Your mother was married. I was married with a daughter by then. It became a secret we carried for thirty-three years."

"What made you decide to tell me this now?"

"Selfish reasons, mostly. Having you back in Kanab and near me, I just couldn't bear to keep the secret any longer. I think your mother would have wanted you to know. And in the end, I think you deserved to know. Truth is, there was a risk in telling you the truth. I probably would have told you sooner except I was scared—scared you might hate me and your mother. I know how your own marriage ended, and I know how you feel about your father's indiscretions."

Books was stunned. He didn't know how to take this revelation, how he should feel knowing his mother and Ned had kept this secret from him his entire life. It meant that his sister, Maggie, was really his half-sister, and that Ned's daughter was his half-sister as well. And what about the man who'd raised him all these years never knowing he was really someone else's son? Maybe for Bernie there was poetic justice in all this, thought Books. The philandering father who had raised a son for thirty-three years, never knowing the boy wasn't his own. Should Books tell him now, after all this time? Probably not.

◇◇◇

The U.S. Attorney's Office for the State of Utah convened a federal grand jury in St. George. In recent days, the grand jury had unsealed indictments against Victor Calenti Jr. and Michael Calenti. The brothers had been charged with three counts of conspiracy to commit first-degree murder in the deaths of David Greenbriar as well as Ivan and George Gadasky. They were also charged with two counts of conspiracy to commit attempted first-degree murder in the shootings of Books and Brian Call.

Call was recovering from his own gunshot wound in the medical unit of the Washington County Jail in St. George, where he was being held without bail. As far as Books knew, the final details of his plea deal with the prosecutor still had not been worked out. He was widely expected to be the star witness in the Calenti brothers' trial.

At the behest of federal prosecutors, the assets of Nevada Mining & Manufacturing had been temporarily frozen. Rumor had it that the feds planned to bring additional charges using federal racketeering statutes. The brothers were being held without bail in the Las Vegas Metropolitan Detention Center awaiting extradition to Utah.

◇◇◇

In Kanab, little was being said publicly about the fate of Neil Eddins, but the gossip mongers were out in force. The local newspaper, citing unnamed sources close to the investigation, revealed Darby Greenbriar's pregnancy and named Neil Eddins as the father. Like most religions, the Mormon Church took a dim view of marital infidelity, so his future in the Church was uncertain at best. And despite his impending fatherhood, Eddins' wife of more than thirty years remained stoically at his side. From what Books had heard, Darby had decided to have the baby and raise it herself. Only time would tell how that would play out.

Nobody had seen or heard from Lance Clayburn since his abrupt departure several weeks earlier. As far as anybody knew, he was still back east in New England visiting family. Maybe he'd decided that spending his life surrounded by the cloak of family wealth and privilege wasn't such a bad idea after all.

Sometimes tragedy lurks at the confluence of fate and plain bad luck. One week after the burial of Ivan and George Gadasky, a neighbor stopped by the Gadasky home to look in on Ronnie. When he couldn't find him in the house, the neighbor walked over to the barn. He found Ronnie hanging from a crossbeam, a step stool overturned under his feet. The town gathered for yet another funeral. This time, however, there was a collective sense of something, guilt or shame perhaps—a sense that this time the community had failed to watch over the life of a shattered boy whose family had been destroyed in a calculated act of violence.

◇◇◇

Books stood lost in thought under the shaded portico at Becky Eddins' home, beer in hand, grilling steaks. They were alone. Her son was spending the night with Grandma and Grandpa Eddins. Becky was watching Books from the picnic table over a glass of Shiraz.

"Are you feeling all right, cowboy?"

"Sorry. I'm fine. I guess I just drifted off someplace there for a minute."

"Maybe you ought to sit down and take a load off. I grill a mean steak."

Books lifted his beer in salute. "I'll bet you do, but I feel fine, really I do, and I've got two medium rare steaks coming right up."

"Penny for your thoughts. What were you thinking about, anyway?"

"A little melancholy, I guess. I've been home for more than a month and look at what's happened. We've had three people murdered, a fourth committed suicide, the Gadasky and Greenbriar families destroyed, and one dead contract killer left on our hands. By comparison, it makes the mean streets of Denver look tame."

Books steered clear of the startling admission earlier that evening from Ned Hunsaker.

"None of that was your fault, J.D. The community was lucky to have you here to help sort it out. I don't know where we'd have been without you. Charley Sutter would never have figured it out. Lance Clayburn would have been arrested and prosecuted for a crime he didn't commit. Brian Call wouldn't have been arrested, and the Calenti brothers would have gotten away with murder and then some."

"I suppose that's true, but think about where things stand today. After everything that's happened, this community is still deeply divided over land management issues. The Green organizations hate the locals, the locals hate the environmentalists, and both sides dislike and distrust the federal government—one big happy family, wouldn't you say?"

"There's truth in that, J.D., but I don't think the picture is as negative as you paint it. There are examples of cooperation—of both sides showing a willingness to sit down at the table and talk. At least that's a start."

Becky was right about that and Books knew it. So on this night, Books would happily settle for the company of a beautiful woman, a cold beer, and a good steak. The rest of it could wait.

# Author's Note

This book is a work of fiction. Names, characters, places, and incidents are either the product of the author's imagination or are used fictitiously.

The above disclaimer aside, many of the environmental issues raised in the story are very real and extremely contentious throughout the West. Perhaps a few statistics are in order. The federal government owns more than 650 million acres across the U.S. Approximately 90% of that land lies in a dozen or so western states, including my home state of Utah. In Utah, the federal government owns 70% of the land. In neighboring Nevada, it's about 76%.

In the early 1970s, a movement that started in Nevada quickly spread throughout many western states. This organized resistance to federal public land use policies became known as the Sagebrush Rebellion. The Sagebrush Rebellion's goal was to wrestle control of public lands away from the federal government and place it in the hands of state and local government. Supporters of the Sagebrush Rebellion have argued that federal lands rightfully belong to the states and that states, not the federal government, can more effectively manage these lands.

During the past thirty years, the Sagebrush Rebellion has lost momentum but has never completely gone away. The principal reason for the failure of the Sagebrush Rebellion was the inability of the movement's proponents to sustain the legal argument that federal public lands truly belong to the states. Thus, public lands have remained under the federal government's control through oversight by federal agencies such as the Bureau of Land Management.

Unfortunately the rancorous debate continues. Its intensity is still as strong as it was 30 years ago. As we go to press, I am reminded of the similarities between the ongoing public land use debate and the virulent diatribe surrounding the discussion of health care reform in America.

With the Sagebrush Rebellion as backdrop, I chose to create a fictitious character named John David (J.D.) Books. As the protagonist in the story, J.D. is employed as a Law Enforcement Ranger in the Bureau of Land Management (BLM), a branch of the Department of the Interior. The BLM has jurisdiction over more than 260 million acres of public land located primarily in the aforementioned dozen western states.

In telling this story, I attempted to keep my personal views outside the framework of the plot and story. I wanted to allow the characters to express their own opinions and points of view through the use of dialogue. Ultimately, you, as readers, will decide how well I accomplished that.

Michael Norman
Salt Lake City
October, 2009

To receive a free catalog of Poisoned Pen Press titles, please contact us in one of the following ways:

Phone: 1-800-421-3976
Facsimile: 1-480-949-1707
Email: info@poisonedpenpress.com
Website: www.poisonedpenpress.com

Poisoned Pen Press
6962 E. First Ave. Ste. 103
Scottsdale, AZ 85251